Claire's Song

Claire's Song

Nancy,
They say three's a charm.
Hope you all enjoy #3: Claire's Song.
Best,
Sunny
11/3/2014

The Storyteller
and the
Healer

SUNNY ALEXANDER

My beloved spoke and said unto me,
"Arise, my darling,
my fair one, come away.
See! The winter is past;
the rains are over and gone.
Flowers appear on the earth;
the season of singing has come..."

—The Song of Songs, The Old Testament

PROLOGUE

Canfield, California, 2011

A year had passed since Kathleen Moore, MD, and Claire Hollander were reunited through a romantic dance, a Superdoc cape, and a Sherlock Holmes disguise.

They continued to live happily in the halcyon town of Canfield, sharing their lives in a two-story Victorian Queen Anne home. They focused on keeping their relationship fresh by finding unique places and ways to make love and to communicate honestly using the active listening technique.

Kathleen had rediscovered her sense of humor, learned to dance, and perhaps most challenging of all, to—almost always—accept the not-so-subtle quirks of the love of her life, Claire.

Claire recently became convinced that Canfield House was haunted and insisted upon wearing her Sherlock Holmes deerstalker cap while presenting newfound evidence to their closest of friends: Robert and Gayle Sutherland, Sam and Helen Hughes, and Linc Hathaway. Ever the storyteller, Claire had gathered everyone in the darkened solarium, lit only by the flames coming from the fireplace and a few flickering candles.

1

Claire presented her ghostly proof by citing how the floors creaked late at night, the way the wind whistled through the house on the stillest of nights, and the most convincing evidence of all: the way that light shined through the second-story bank of leaded windows even during the cloudiest of nights.

Knowing Claire's propensity for storytelling and her stellar imagination, Gayle and Robert smiled benignly, Sam rolled his eyes, and Helen tried to think of a soothing herbal drink for all. Linc told her anything was possible, but no, he was not interested in a séance or a Ouija board. Kathleen explained in her most serious and scientific tone the logic behind the "ghostly" visitations.

In spite of Claire's machinations, or perhaps because of them, life went on in Canfield. We could even say it was a setting to be envied. But, as we all know, an idyllic town or relationship doesn't exist except in the minds of authors and readers.

PART ONE

Above all, watch with glittering eyes the whole world around you because the greatest secrets are always hidden in the most unlikely places. Those who don't believe in magic will never find it.

—Roald Dahl

CHAPTER 1

Linc Hathaway, sheriff of Canfield, began his morning routine by wrapping his red-plaid blanket bathrobe around his spreading waistline. With a lion's yawn escaping from his gaping mouth, he shuffled from the bedroom of his log cabin home into the kitchen. Grunts and groans followed as he reached into the pantry for his most recent acquisition, Black Ivory coffee beans—arabica coffee beans fed to elephants, re-collected from their feces, processed, and sold exclusively to five-star hotels. It was a gift from his son, Flynn, the manager of a hotel in Thailand.

Linc thought of himself as a coffee connoisseur. He scoured the Internet for the most exotic brands but scoffed at the "sissy" ways to make coffee: French press, vacuum and single-cup coffeemakers.

He knew the best way to get that elusive perfect cup. "Yup," he said as he reached for his mother's blue enamel coffeepot.

First, a precise amount of beans were weighed and placed in the coffee grinder. While the beans were being ground, he added filtered water from his reverse osmosis system to the coffeepot. Then onto the stovetop burner it went, and *voilà*—in a few minutes, the best cup of coffee in the world. The most difficult part was listening to the spurting sounds the pot made and knowing he had to wait precisely five minutes and thirty seconds to taste perfection.

Linc surveyed the perimeter of the kitchen. The cabin walls made from handcrafted logs would outlive him—a legacy to be passed on, but to whom? His three sons were scattered around the world and doing a damn good job of making lives of their own. The last thing they wanted was a charmingly rustic—if a trifle drafty at times—log cabin nestled in the hills of Canfield.

His gaze rested, as it did every morning, on the kitchen countertop. A long, flat, unblemished block of rare wood that consistently made his heart skip a beat and his chest swell with pride.

The log cabin and Linc had been together for more than twenty years. *His longest lasting relationship*, he mused. Those before years seemed so far in the past that their memory had become scattered and out of focus.

Perhaps it was his name, Lincoln Abraham Hathaway, that started his preoccupation with Lincoln Logs, or his parents' wishes that he follow in the footsteps of Honest Abe. Linc wasn't sure when the clash between his parents' dreams and his began, but he thought it probably started in ninth grade when he signed up for the high school football team and met Coach Steamroller Cruz, former professional football player and sheriff of Canfield.

His parents didn't mind Linc hanging out with Steamroller. They thought he was a good role model and someone who could write recommendation letters for Linc to the universities of their choice.

Steamroller would let Linc ride shotgun when he patrolled deep into the back hills. Steamroller saw something of himself in Linc at that age: a little flabby, with more than his share of acne and less than his share of friends.

"Mighty nice of your mother to bake her peanut butter cookies," Steamroller said as they chomped away. "Just remember when we get back to the office...what's your first duty?"

"To take the whisk broom and clean up all the crumbs," Linc mumbled between bites.

"Yep. Leave no evidence."

Steamroller motioned to the rolling hills covered in green grass. "Back here, in these hills, are where the sheep ranches are. See them sheep? Happy as can be chewing away on that grass. Little do they know what the future holds for them." He chuckled. "Not too unlike us, piggin' out on these cookies. Some folks have moved from town into cabins up here. Wanted something more private and quiet. But you never know what's going on under-neath—get my drift?"

"You mean like secrets?"

"Yep." Steamroller took his eye off the road and turned to Linc. "See, it's important to know everyone in and out of town. Being a sheriff isn't just about enforcing rules and laws; it's also about understanding folks and helping 'em. And if you know a secret, unless it's against the law, you keep that secret to yourself."

Back at the office, Linc could read magazines until it was time to go home for dinner. Magazines about real life and adventures—*Mechanics Illustrated, True Adventures, True Detective*—that sparked his imagination and his *own* dreams, not those of his parents.

Steamroller sat in his wooden desk chair, rocking back and forth. "Now, I'll tell you a little something, a secret of mine." His voice dropped to a whisper. "Always had a special dream of my own; ain't told no one else, but I trust you."

Linc sat up with rapt attention. A secret...a secret from the Steamroller himself.

Steamroller held the newest *Popular Mechanics* magazine and scanned an article title blazoned across the cover: "Twenty-Three Boats You Can Build."

"One day, I'm going to build my own boat," he boasted, "haul it down to the ocean, and sail the seven seas. You see, the problem with this world is not enough people have their own dreams. It's right smart to have a dream that belongs just to you."

That made Linc think. Why would he want to go to law school? Why would he want to sit in the Oval Office trying to make everyone happy, and running or ruining the world? Those were his parents' dreams, not his.

Steamroller wanted to sail the seven seas. Linc knew what he wanted to be: a cop, or even better, the future sheriff of Canfield.

Linc took Steamroller's advice to heart. He would have his dreams, and he would keep them to himself.

The Hathaway family gathered around the dining room table. His mother's face glowed. "*Three* acceptances!" she exclaimed.

His father stood and thumped him heartily on the back. "Congratulations, son! What's it going to be: Harvard, Yale, or Princeton?" His parents began debating the pros and cons of each university.

I might as well not be here, Linc thought. Suddenly overcome by years of hidden frustration and anger, Linc took his fist, and with his six-foot-two-inch frame and two hundred and fifteen pounds of force, slammed it down on the table. The coffee spilled, his mother's homemade cinnamon cake tumbled, and the acceptance letters scattered. The hopes and dreams of Pearl and Albert now lay on the floor: a collage of cake, coffee, and useless paper.

"Look at what you've done!" his mother screamed.

"I'm not going!" he yelled. "I'm not going to Yale, Harvard, or Princeton. Mother, Father—I don't want to be an attorney, and I sure as *hell* don't want to be president."

"You're upset, Linc. Confused," his father said rationally.

"I know what I want to be. I want to be a cop, and when Sheriff Cruz retires, I want to be the sheriff of Canfield."

"You *what*!" Gasping, his mother clasped her throat with her hand.

"I'll need two years of school, not six. With an AA degree, I can apply to any police department. Then if I work hard—"

"If you work hard, you'll end up where?" his father shouted. "Living and working in a one-horse, one-cell town? You can go anywhere you want. In fact, you ingrate, you can go to hell. But don't expect me to pay for it."

Albert walked over to Pearl and awkwardly patted her on the back. "Look what you've done to your mother. Your mother's a saint and you've broken her heart."

Pearl Hathaway looked up, tears gushing from her eyes. "I almost died giving birth to you and this is how you repay me?"

Linc made his own life; right or wrong, it was his. All things considered, he thought it wasn't so bad.

He met Sharon while he was a cop with the Los Angeles Police Department (LAPD); a whirlwind courtship was followed by a simple marriage ceremony. His parents attended and things seemed to smooth over, especially after they had their first grandson. A lump filled his throat; where had it gone wrong? A marriage that began with passion and hope subtly shifted and changed over the years. Arguments remained unresolved until he and Sharon became two strangers, inhabiting the same space, going through the motions of a relationship.

❋   ❋   ❋

The 1940s porcelain kitchen timer dinged, a callback to the present and a reminder that his coffee was ready. *It's the first sip that will set the tone for the day*, he mused.

His attention shifted to the fifteen coffee mugs lined up neatly on the shelf over the stove, all but one with an image of the King. The first four belonged to a collectible set from 1985, the year Elvis would have turned fifty. *Dead at forty-two,* he tsked. *What a loss.* He reached for his favorite mug, the one sporting Elvis's be-loved 1955 pink Cadillac. Not many people knew that the car was originally blue and had been repainted the custom pink color known as "Elvis Rose," but then Linc knew more about the King than most, including the many conspiracists who continued to speculate on his untimely death.

He held the mug over the sink, carefully filling it from the per-colator. It'd be a shame to waste one drop of this precious coffee or even worse, to spill anything on his countertop. Taking in the aroma, he could tell this would be a good day. *Let it cool for one minute,* he told himself. One minute...it's not so long to wait.

Steamroller retired, built his boat, and sailed the seven seas.

One of Linc's dreams became a reality. He was elected sheriff of Canfield. Money, carefully saved over the years, went toward buying the two-acre lot in the back hills he had come to love. He didn't mind living in the small, rickety cabin that came with the property. After all, it was temporary. And even though temporary turned into years, if there was one thing Linc had learned from Steamroller: if you want something badly enough, it's worth the wait.

Linc showed the sketches of his dream home to his architect, Si-mon Flenders. "I want the cabin to be as authentic as possible. You have my short list: hand-peeled logs and cedar shingles. I don't want any of those, look at the view from the inside, picture windows. I want to step outside onto my porch, relax on a red-wood bench, and take in the beauty of the woods."

"It will be everything you ever dreamed of and then some," Simon said with a clipped English accent. He became thoughtful. "I think the place to start is Spyde's Kitchen Showroom."

The next Saturday, Simon and Linc met at Spyde's in Santa Barbara.

Simon, wearing Harris Tweed slacks and a cable-knit sweater, adjusted his black Ascot cap and began the tour, using his Irish Blackthorn walking stick as a pointer. They strolled up and down the aisles, with Simon delivering a dissertation on each and every type of kitchen countertop material available.

Linc shook his head. "None of this stuff rings true, Simon. A log cabin and tile counters? It's blasphemy. And the wood—it's got no oomph!"

"My sentiments, as well. There's something I want you to see."

Simon guided Linc through a rubber strip curtain into a cold, darkened, cavernous extension of the store. Linc shivered in spite of his heavy sweats. Bricks coated in powdery white efflorescence climbed the walls until they surrounded a bank of wooden windows. The late afternoon sun fought its way through years of grime, managing to cast a single beam of light directly onto the middle of the room, where wooden pallets lay end to end, creating a long, narrow platform.

"What is this place?" Linc said, his voice softening as if entering a holy sanctuary. "And what the hell is that, on top of the pallets?"

"This room was the original warehouse, built more than seventy years ago. And as to what's on top of the pallets, that's why we're here, mate."

Simon motioned Linc toward the center of the room. "Look at this." Simon kneeled and ran his hands slowly over a tree trunk. "It's been whole-tree logged, so we still have the top and limbs intact. It's the *crème de la crème*: the crown jewel of countertops."

"What makes this so special?"

"This one comes with a soul."

"What do you mean?" Linc asked quizzically. "It looks so smooth—like the skin of a newborn baby." His eyes roved over the beauteous specimen in awe.

"I thought you might be interested. It's a Madrone tree. There's something quite mysterious about it, Linc. It grows on the craggy mountainsides north of Canfield. Where other trees can't take hold, the Madrone thrives."

"But, it's so unblemished...unspoiled."

"It's a strange one all right. Every summer it sheds its bark, and what we get is a pristine trunk. We rarely get hold of one of these, but when I heard about it, I had a feeling it might be exactly what you were looking for."

Twice a year, Linc refreshed the countertop with his homemade formula of tung and linseed oils, citrus, and beeswax. Toiling happily, his mind would chant a mantra: *We are one, growing and surviving where others perish.*

Linc took the first delicate sip of coffee. Perfect. Worth waiting for, even if it meant digging through the past.

After getting dressed, he'd get breakfast at the Mountain View Diner in town. Open 24/7. Unless there was something else pressing, he was there 365 days a year. That was the place to gather gossip and, most importantly, the secrets that haunted the residents of Canfield. Everyone in Canfield had their secrets, and Linc Hathaway was no exception.

He walked to his bedroom, avoiding the barest sideward glance at his reflection in the mirrored closet doors.

He had no illusions about what he was. A fairly nondescript middle-aged man. Slightly stooped over. Balding. A spare tire where once muscle had lived.

He showered and shaved. He hated the part that came next—damn uncomfortable, but he had an image to protect. Reaching for his upper-body full-compression men's shaper, he sucked in his breath and closed the zipper. Next, he donned his custom-made uniform, always laundered, starched, and pressed, just the way Mother had shown him. *Almost there*, he thought as he reached for his custom-made Elvis wig, styled after the King's 1950s pompadour, but not quite as flamboyant. He winced in recollection of the cost. *Shit, two at twelve hundred bucks each.* He cinched on his gun belt before looking in the mirror. Smiling at his reflection, he greeted Linc Hathaway, sheriff of Canfield.

CHAPTER 2

*I*t promised to be the kind of day that Californians loved to crow about to friends and relatives living in less temperate climates. During the pre-dawn hours, the ocean fog had glided over the hills, cloaking Canfield House in a gray mist. As the sun warmed the air, the fog gradually dissipated, leaving behind droplets of moisture on the walkways and surrounding foliage.

The daffodils, planted deep beneath the front lawn of Canfield House, had bloomed early this year, laying a yellow coverlet across the earth. Over time, the blossoms had faded and fallen to the ground. For now, the bulbs lay dormant beneath an emerald blanket of grass, waiting for the new cycle of life to begin.

In the apartment over the garage, Helen stirred, trying to shake off the remnants of last night's dream. Her hand reached out to touch Sam. *My husband,* she whispered to herself. She loved Sam; her partner in life, her soul mate. He snored lightly, his lips fluttering comically like the buffoons in those old *Three Stooges* shorts he so adored. She grinned in spite of herself.

Helen hesitated to wake him, but today, she was up for an adventure and the morning was escaping. Touching her lips to his, she said, "Sam, it's a picture-perfect day. Let's go for a ride."

Sam blinked and groaned. He had been planning to spend his Sunday tinkering with his 1959 Chevy Bel Air, a recent acquisition from Linc. A morning kiss with a "go for a ride" chaser meant only one thing: treasure hunting in antique and thrift stores in nearby Ventura.

Helen snuggled closer until the space between them disappeared.

"Let's get dressed and tell the girls," said Helen, playfully running her fingers across the tangle of coarse hair on his bare chest.

Anything for Helen—almost anything. Jolted awake, Sam sat up. "The girls? Do you mean Kathleen and Claire? Two women in their thirties, one a master physician and pushing forty and the other a bona fide nutcase? *Girls*, Helen? *Girls?*"

"Stop now while you're ahead. They're in love and having the time of their lives."

"Just don't forget our plan to have them cook their own meals."

"*Our* plan? It's *your* idea, not mine. And let's hope it doesn't backfire."

"We've been through this a hundred times. How can you expect them to grow up if you're cooking every damn meal for them?"

"They fix their own lunch."

"Yeah, after you've already laid everything out."

"Before this goes any further, I'm taking a shower. Now you can either pout or wash my back."

Throwing the covers aside, Sam grumbled. "You sure know how to get to a guy."

Sam cradled Helen's hand in his as they ambled along the flagstone walkway to the main house. "Look, honey, let's not have this meal business spoil our day. We won't always be around, and we've talked about this being the right time. Gradually— remember, we said *gradually*."

He pulled Helen closer, "And, I want to spend time with *my* girl."

"Hmm," Helen said, opening the back door to the kitchen, "I'll just start the coffee."

"No, Helen, leave them a note. I think they know how to make coffee."

"I know you're right, but this is not going to be easy."

"Hi, guys," chirped Claire as she opened the swinging door to the kitchen. "I thought I heard you."

Helen smiled. "Claire, you look as cozy, as cozy—"

"As a bug in a rug? You like my jammies?"

Claire did a pirouette, ending the dance step with a bow, a toss of her curls, and a dimpled smile.

"My bubba sent them. She wanted Oscar and me to have matching outfits. She had to look all over New York to find the right color, pink of course, with the kitty design. And look, Helen—see how great Oscar looks."

As if walking down the runway of a fashion show, Oscar Tilquist the Third, the Cheshire cat look-alike with more than the proverbial nine lives, strutted around the kitchen.

Claire lowered her voice. "Bubba thinks Oscar is gay, but I know better. I've seen him in action."

Damn, thought Sam. *That cat's got more moves than lives.* "Claire, didn't you have him—"

"Shhh, Sam!" Claire put one finger to her lips. "Oscar doesn't know."

Claire stretched and yawned, then reached down to pet the mewing tomcat as he wrapped his body around her leg. "Oh, Oscar, we do have to see about getting you a real girlfriend."

Sam clenched his jaw. *Good lord, a five-year-old in a thirty-plus-year-old body.*

"I was just going to get some coffee for Kath and me and breakfast for Oscar. So, what's up with you two?" said Claire, holding her hand out for the mug of steaming coffee delivered with a smile by Helen.

❀   ❀   ❀

Claire insisted on Sam and Helen taking her pride and joy, a 1960 VW Beetle convertible, recently rechristened the Yellow Submarine.

Still in her jammies, Claire grinned, her dimples appearing deeper than ever. "You'll love this car, Sam. And as an added attraction—at no extra charge—there's a bunch of Beatles CDs in the glove compartment." *Wow!* she thought. *A whole day without anyone around. Whoopee! Think positive, Claire; I think you're wearing Kath down. Focus on: b.a.b.y.*

Claire reached inside her glove compartment. "Here, Helen, you have to wear this fab and gear Beatles scarf. With the top down, you don't want to ruin your *do!*"

The white scarf, resplendent with headshots of John, Paul, George, and Ringo, and stylized graphics of guitars and records, floated in the morning breeze before settling on Helen's head.

"I love it, Claire," said Helen, tying the scarf under her chin. "I practically cut my teeth on the Beatles music. But don't you think it's a bit much for me? I'm not a kid anymore."

"Oh, pshaw! Let's move it back a bit and get just a wisp of your hair showing. Now, put your sunglasses on."

Standing back to admire her handiwork, Claire said, "Helen, you are a knockout. You have beautiful red highlights in your hair, and with the sunglasses, you are a Sophia Loren in the making."

"It's perfect," said Helen, admiring her reflection in the VW's side mirror. "Where did you find it?"

"At the thrift shop at the far east corner of Main and Fifth."

"It's a gold mine," Helen whispered, fingering the silk. "Look, it's original—and it's still got the fringe."

Sam laughed when Helen insisted on rubbing sunscreen through his thinning hair. "Hold still, Sam. You're worse than a child."

"It's cold," he whined, doing his best little-boy imitation.

"And to think, during your twenty-three years of service, you almost single-handedly protected this country." Her hand strayed from his head to his cheek; they moved closer, their lips touching. "Good morning, love."

"Good morning, my angel."

They drove south, taking the curving coastal route toward Ventura. The road narrowed then climbed until sheer cliffs offered a panoramic view of the sea. The ocean lapped farther and farther away, deepening the beaches and leaving behind shells, seaweed, and tide pools.

"This is some Bug," said Sam admiringly. "I have to admit, Claire sure does know how to have fun." He hesitated. "Helen...this has really been on my mind. Do you think there's something wrong with Claire?"

"Wrong, Sam? What do you mean?"

"Something...um...mental?"

Helen guffawed but quickly became pensive. "I do admit she's a bit on the quirky side, but mentally ill...no. We've all had things happen in our lives that make us a bit...unusual."

Sam looked at Helen, his mouth slackening until it drooped at the corners.

"But, not you, Helen, not you."

"Eyes on the road, Sam." Helen turned her face away and, with a fixed gazed, stared outward to the sea.

As the road began its descent, the cliffs gradually changed to sloping hillsides sprinkled with Mediterranean-style stucco homes.

Sam whistled. "Man, they must have some views."

"Yes, and just look at the hillsides. There's red shank,

manzanitas, lilacs. They've done a beautiful job of planting drought-tolerant vegetation."

"How did you learn so much about plants, smarty-pants?"

"My mother loved to garden. It was her church, and gardening books her Bible. Do you see that plant, the one with the narrow leaves? It's milkweed. Monarch butterflies feed on it and lay their larvae on it. One of my favorites. We can learn a lot from nature— the way everything is linked together."

Sam said, with a catch in his voice, "Sometimes, I think of everything we've missed, all the years when we could have been together. Look at those kids," he said, admiring the surfers catching the last waves of the morning. "Now, *they* know how to have fun."

"I don't know, Sam, it seemed to me, you were having a lot of fun in the shower this morning. Maybe it would have been a disaster if we had met sooner. We needed to be ready, and..."A sudden gust of wind caused the Yellow Submarine to shudder, interrupting Helen's thoughts. "And, we have today. If we're lucky, lots of tomorrows."

Helen reached for the glove compartment and riffled through Claire's CDs. Let's listen to this one," she said, inserting the CD into the player.

"Which one, love?"

"John Lennon's 'Imagine.'"

"You're kidding, Helen! That anti-American song?"

"It's so much more than that. It's about peace, and isn't that why we gave up our personal lives to serve? It's one of my favorites. Listen to the words. Promise?"

"I'm so in love with you, how could I deny you anything?"

"Thank you, darling, that means the world to me."

The air was pure, and the views continued to be unobstructed. By the time they got to Ventura, the surfers had left and sunbathers and families were clamoring for a parking space, unpacking their overstuffed cars, and heading for the beaches.

Helen and Sam parked at Plaza Park to begin their trek down East Main Street, also known as Antique Row. They stopped from time to time to browse through an antique shop or to take in the beckoning aromas from coffee shops, bakeries, and restaurants.

Sam felt his stomach grumble. "Let's stop for lunch."

"Soon. I've got to hit the shop Claire was telling us about." Helen reached into her "emergency" bag and handed Sam an apple.

"What else is in there?" He reached to peek into the black-and-white canvas tote.

"Enough to do an appendectomy," Helen said, pushing his hand away.

Gradually, the aroma of bakeries and restaurants faded and were replaced by the musty smell of thrift shops.

Helen said, "I could shut my eyes and know where I am. Just by the smells."

"What I'm wanting to smell, is lunch."

"One more store, darling. Claire recommended this one." Helen pointed to a thrift store with faded lettering on the window advertising THE BEST PRICES IN VENTURA. She opened the door, stopped for a moment to take in a deep breath. "*Schmata* paradise," she said.

"*Schmata*?"

"A Yiddish term, meaning a piece of old clothing, a rag. Didn't Claire ever tell you about how she got her favorite baby blanket?"

"No, but I have a feeling I'm about to hear it."

"It's a sweet, funny story. Claire was about two and her bubba was cleaning out a hall closet. Claire grabbed this old, threadbare baby blanket and her bubba pulled it away, telling her it was a *schmata*. Claire stomped her foot, grabbed the blanket, and said, 'My *schmata*, my *schmata*!' And that's how Claire got her favorite baby blanket."

"And I'll bet she still has it!"

"Get over yourself, Sam," Helen laughed while playfully punching him on the arm.

They moved sideways through the narrow, cluttered aisles,

Sam moving quickly, Helen lingering at the various displays. She stopped at a table crowded with salt and pepper shakers, wood figures, and glass bric-a-brac.

"Oh my, a cornucopia of treasures." Sighing, Helen let her fingers flit from item to item. "Oh, Sam, look at this alarm clock. I love it," Helen whispered, her eyes going wide at the sight of the bright red fire engine being driven by a Dalmatian. "My father would have loved this." She picked it up, turning it one way and then another. "There's a small chip on the Dalmatian's nose, but Claire can fix it. It'll be as good as new."

Helen caught Sam's frown. "Do you mind? I know it's not your taste."

Sam leaned over, taking Helen's hand in his. "Anything for a fireman's daughter. But only if we can have lunch at the Bumble Bee Cafe."

"You drive a hard bargain."

"And no faces at what I order. Deal?"

"Deal."

They left the musty smells of the thrift shop and joined the throng of customers gathered on the sidewalk and waiting to be seated at one of Ventura's original and most popular diners, the Bumble Bee Cafe. The hostess, wearing black pants and a T-shirt with a bug-eyed, yellow-and-black bumblebee, stood on the sidewalk, writing down names.

"How long?" grumbled Sam.

"Ten minutes, sir." The hostess handed Helen and Sam Styrofoam cups and pointed to a fifty-cup coffeemaker.

Helen reached into her tote and handed Sam a tangerine.

Twenty minutes later, they were shown to a worn, red leather booth with a gray marble Formica top and a booth-sized jukebox loaded with music from the 1950s and '60s.

"Sam, let me have your quarters."

"Don't I get to pick one?" he asked, fumbling in his pants pocket for his change.

"One, Sam. Only one. Which one do you want?"

"'Only You.'"

"Only me what?"

"No, Helen. The song, 'Only You.' The Platters, remember?"

Helen held out her hand for the proffered quarters. "We are so damn lucky."

"I know, I know," he said, gazing into her eyes.

Helen studied the menu. "Have you decided what you're ordering? I'm debating between the vegetarian omelet and the Chinese chicken salad."

"I'm going to have the Polish sausage omelet with potatoes and biscuits. And cream and sugar for my coffee." Sam flashed a challenging grin toward Helen.

"Well, Sam, if you want to be a daredevil, it's your funeral," she said tersely. "I hope it's worth it."

It wasn't, as Sam discovered a few hours later.

CHAPTER 3

Gayle and Robert's married life began in 1979, when they were university students. Their first home was a studio apartment, not much more than one hundred and fifty square feet, with a Murphy pull-down bed and a hot plate for a kitchen.

Robert had to crawl over Gayle to get out of bed, but they laughed and usually ended up making love before dashing for classes; being late didn't seem to carry the mild dishonor it once had.

Their dreams of successful careers came easily. Robert became a prominent attorney, and Gayle, a social worker. Fortune seemed to have smiled upon them. They bought their dream home in a prestigious area, Westwood, California. With four bedrooms, it gave them more space than they had ever thought possible. Robert had his home office and there were two spare bedrooms for the children they planned on having—once they settled into their new home.

Everything had gone their way. Why would getting pregnant be any different?

Six months of trying became a year, then two. Every month, Gayle would look at Robert and shake her head. They began to seek answers to their question: Why couldn't they have a baby?

After visiting doctor after doctor and taking test after test, the end result was that Gayle could not conceive. They tried alternative therapies with acupuncturists, herbalists, and then a month at a Buddhist retreat: meditating, practicing chi gong, and suffering through a vegetarian diet. One evening, during dinner, and after what seemed to be a particularly difficult day, Gayle put down her fork—she thought she would die if she ate one more leaf of kale.

"Robert, I'm done, and I'm going home," she said flatly. "If it's going to happen it will, and if not, it won't. I've cried enough for this lifetime and into the next."

Robert reached for her hand. "I've been hoping you would come to this conclusion, sweetheart," he said plaintively and with tears in his eyes. "We can adopt. Somewhere, there is a child who needs us."

"I know you're right. But, for now, I want to get away from all these vegetables, and exercises. Oh, Robert, can we stop at *McDonalds*?"

After all these years, that defining moment remained fresh in Gayle's memory. *We were so smug, thinking we could have anything we wanted. Fate has a way of teaching us lesson after lesson.*

They went on with their lives, throwing themselves into their careers and then anything that would take them away from their pain. Robert had his distractions: his garden, cooking, and endless projects and renovations to the house. Gayle found hers by becoming a psychoanalyst and shopping. The months and the years went by and the idea of adopting children drifted away, eventually sliding into oblivion.

Gayle continued to remain unfulfilled until that day when Kathleen entered her life as a patient. A waif-like university student so lost inside the closet that she was unaware that a door existed. Kathleen went from patient to friend until she moved in with Gayle and Robert, and they became a family.

❀   ❀   ❀

Lately, that empty spot where memories of sweet babies were meant to reside had returned. It began one night in that twilight space between awake and sleep.

Gayle was drifting off, when a sudden flash of light appeared as if someone had just taken a photo. It startled her at first, and she thought it was simply the beginning of a dream. It repeated nightly, becoming clearer with each passing night. A room with faded wallpaper, a worn wood floor, and an empty rocking chair that moved ever so slightly. As the picture became sharper, she could see herself being rocked to sleep in her grandmother's arms. She could hear Grammy singing a lullaby with words that were beyond her comprehension. What she did understand was the feeling of comfort that came from Grammy's sweet voice lulling her to sleep.

She had Grammy's wooden rocking chair stored in the attic and wondered if the rocker could, like her, be impatiently waiting to sooth a fussy baby.

She began to fantasize about retiring, selling their house, and moving closer to Kathleen and Claire. She could feel their baby resting sweetly in her arms. A chubby, six-month-old little girl with caramel-colored curls falling softly around her face.

It occurred to her, was this...this nightly *thing*...a reminder of time running out? She thought about their house. Did they really need all those rooms? And the garden, so large for just the two of them, a back-breaker to tend.

She mused that it wasn't often that a second chance came about. It was common now for gay couples to have children and, in some states, they could get married.

Robert was convinced that it wouldn't be long before the hate laws against same-sex marriage crumbled.

One day, with a twinkle in his eye, Robert asked her, "Remember that Dylan song you loved so much?"

"Yes, my favorite. 'The Times They Are A-Changin'.'"

"Yes, darling. That's the one. Times are changing, and it will happen."

She sighed. *She needed to let these pipedreams go and return to reality.* She would keep these thoughts from Robert. His life was intertwined with this house, the garden, and his very long list of things to do.

She had her own list. Stephanie, another wounded warrior from Operation Iraqi Freedom, would be staying with them.

It seemed so strange the way fate kept bringing new people into her life. *Was it fate or simply coincidence?* She only knew that if she had not taken that plane to Germany after Kathleen had been wounded, she would have never known about Stephanie: a young girl lying in a hospital bed, alone and without visitors.

The long flight to Germany was followed by the surreal experience of entering Landstuhl Regional Hospital and being directed to Kathleen's room. Until that moment, she had never fully understood the depth and power of denial. Part of her expected to see Kathleen sitting up in bed, greeting her with a wide grin and a bandaged shoulder. The mask of denial was torn off when she saw a pale figure lying in bed surrounded by Frankensteinian machines, tubes, and wires. *How many others,* she wondered, *had walked through these doors and shared the same experience?*

Kathleen turned her head toward the door. She opened her eyes and mouthed a single name. Not Gayle, as she had called her for many years, but Mommy. The one word Gayle never thought she would hear; the word that was said only once but swelled her heart. Gayle held Kathleen's hand and leaned over to hear barely whispered words repeated over and over again: "Next room, Gayle...next room."

Gayle opened the door to the next hospital room to see what appeared to be a child—a heavily sedated child who, she had been told, might never walk again. A nurse stood by Stephanie's side.

"You must be Gayle," she said. "Helen told me you'd be coming in. I'm Nancy."

Gayle gasped. "She looks so young, so helpless."

Nancy patted Gayle's hand. "It's difficult to see them this way. I just got her settled. Gayle, why don't you sit with her? She needs someone to talk to her, to touch her hand. She'll be sedated for a few days, then begin to drift in and out."

"What about family?"

"They were notified."

"And?"

For a brief moment, Nancy looked at the floor. "I can't say anymore. You'll have to read between the lines."

Nancy pulled a chair next to the bed. "Sit," she instructed. "Stephanie will know you're here."

"Nancy, may I ask you a rather personal question?"

"Of course."

"You don't look any older than Stephanie. How do you manage? There's so much damage and pain."

Nancy, caught off guard, drew in her breath. "I don't know that we do manage all that well." A sudden tremor crossed her hands. "Someone has to do it, and I think it's hope that keeps us going."

She cleared her throat. "Keep an eye on this gizmo," she said, pointing to one of the monitors. "This one takes her blood pressure, heart rate, temperature, and oxygen level. I'll bet you'll see some shifts in the numbers. We see it all the time. Any contact, touch, reading to her, or even singing is as healing as anything we can do."

"I don't know about my singing, but I brought a book of poetry with me."

"Then read to her. She'll hear you...she'll know she's not alone."

Gayle sat next to a heavily sedated Stephanie, reading from the book she had impulsively grabbed on her way to the airport. A book that her mother had read to her at bedtime: *A Child's Garden of Verses.*

While Gayle was at Landstuhl, she split her time between Kathleen and Stephanie's rooms. Kathleen was far more conscious and grumbly and quickly getting the reputation of being an uncooperative patient.

Helen opined, "Doctors are the worst, and Dr. Moore is the worst of the worst. Stay next door, Gayle. I'll handle the infamous Dr. Moore."

Gayle continued to read poetry to Stephanie, glancing from time to time at the monitors. Nancy was right; she could see Stephanie's heart rate and blood pressure become more stable, except when she read Robert Louis Stevenson's poem "My Shadow." She didn't understand why, but the jump in Stephanie's heart rate and blood pressure caused the nurses to rush into the room.

When Gayle returned to the United States, she left the book of children's verses on Stephanie's nightstand with a note.

You may not remember my being here. I read to you as you slept, and I'll write to you as soon as I get home.

My name is Gayle Sutherland, and I hope we can become friends.

After Gayle returned home, she would wonder from time to time about the attachment she felt toward Stephanie. On a conscious level, she understood that, in part, it came from being childless. This felt deeper than anything she had experienced. She didn't understand the whys, she only knew she was meant to be in Stephanie's life.

❀   ❀   ❀

Robert handed Gayle a mug of coffee before stepping into the shower. He began to hum, then to sing his daily rendition of "Singin' in the Rain."

Gayle sipped from the perfectly brewed morning elixir and began to apply her makeup using the techniques practiced at Lamont's Cosmetic and Hair Salon. An array of skin products crowded the bathroom counter. No more makeup from the local drugstore. This was a custom-made formula, not with promises of eternal youth, but guaranteed to even out her skin tone and delay the appearance of new wrinkles. She had selected the blend that promised not to settle in the cracks and crevices that were beginning to etch her face.

It took longer these days to disguise the onslaught of time; not only the deeper lines that crept around her eyes and mouth but also the extra padding across her middle that made stretch pants a must-have. *You can't get away from it. I hate this aging process. Kinda makes me a fraud. Teaching classes on aging with grace— yeah, right!* She leaned over to pluck a hair from her chin. *And these damn things, where the hell do they come from?*

Robert, still dripping from the shower, tucked a towel around his waist and wiped the steam from the mirror. "Time to recoat the mirror," he said, leaning over to kiss Gayle. "Big day for you, honey."

"Hmmm...just a presentation on aging. One I've done hundreds of times."

"Just? This one is on PBS. You've hit the big time."

Gayle shrugged. "I'm only one on a panel of six on *Aging with Grace.*"

"That's my girl, forever modest. Sure you don't want me to go with you?"

"No, work in the garden, darling."

He nodded. "It can use some work. No doubt we'll have a bumper crop."

Yesterday he had surveyed the kitchen garden, recently plant-ed with seedlings that were now beginning to grow and thrive. "In two months, it'll be overflowing with vegetables ready to be picked," he predicted. "And about the same amount of weeds."

Gayle chuckled. "That's how life is, isn't it? The good doesn't come easily on its own. We have to ferret out the weeds to dis-cover what's underneath."

"Well said. Remind me again, when does Stephanie arrive?"

"Noon tomorrow, LAX."

Robert hesitated. "Are you sure we're doing the right thing? You barely know her. I thought maybe this would be a good time for us to spend more time together. It seems one of us is always running somewhere. We're both getting older—"

"Robert Sutherland, you're the youngest looking sixty-year-old around! I'm surprised at you. The way you took to Kathleen, the way you made her your own child. And now, here's another kid—"

"Kathleen had no one; Stephanie has a family," he said defen-sively.

"Yes, a mother and father who want nothing to do with her. Good God, Robert, they never called her! Not once!"

"Have you wondered why? There are two sides to every story."

He threw the towel over the shower door and reached for his shorts. "It was different with Kathleen. She was ours for a long time. We knew her—her quirks, even her temper tantrums when she was recovering."

Gayle stared at Robert. Her voice was filled with concern. "Are you okay? It's not like you to reject someone in need. Lately, I feel as if I'm talking to a stranger. You're not keeping something from me, are you?"

"No, everything's fine. I'll start breakfast—bagels, and we've got fresh strawberries."

"From the garden?"

"Yes, peak of the season," he said somberly.

CHAPTER 4

*K*athleen glanced at the clock on the nightstand. *Ugh,* a Sunday and she had been up since 4:00 a.m. Claire had been tossing and turning, mumbling or shouting half-spoken words, then falling back into a deep sleep. Kathleen had to wonder what was going on in that one-of-a-kind mind.

The moonlight was streaming through the window, spreading diffused light throughout the bedroom. She rested on one elbow as she gazed at her one and only. Her love...her life...her major pain in the ass. *I wouldn't change her for the world,* she thought as she took in Claire's angelic look. The softest of caramel-colored curls surrounded her face, while her naturally rosy lips added to the vision of a slumbering child. *When she's sleeping, anyway,* she thought. But awake, a mouth that could pout as often as it smiled, a voice that could lull her into a heightened state of sexual excitement, or a mood that could shift as suddenly as the wind moving from a breeze to a hurricane.

The minutes ticked by. Kathleen counted fifty-nine until the four changed to five, and she began to count all over again. Claire became restless, mumbling, thrashing. *She's having one hell of a dream,* mused Kathleen. Oscar Tilquist the Third, the cat with more than nine lives, moved from Claire's feet, his nightly perch, plopping unceremoniously onto Kathleen's lap.

"Hi, Oscar. Claire's thrashing around getting to you?" she whispered. "She's getting to me, too, in more ways than one."

Oscar's purr was not so subtle. *Get over yourself, sister, and rub my head, please.*

Kathleen stroked Oscar's very round and slightly oversized head, listening to his "motorboat" throttle moving into high gear. *If I were you,* the purring seemed to say, *I wouldn't stop.*

She began to move her hand from Oscar's head toward his back. *Who could resist such an exacting command?*

He arched his back with each caress. *Ahh, perfection at last.*

Her mind wondered to her things-to-do list. She needed to grab a couple of hours today and catch up on paperwork. She broke out in a cold sweat. They had barely made expenses last month. Robert kept reassuring her, "Every new business takes a couple of years to get out of the red and into the black. I have your back, and keep in mind this is a business investment for me. At some point, we'll both see the profits rolling in. Don't forget, you're sitting on ten acres of prime real estate. Patience, Kathleen, patience."

She managed an unseen nod and a raspy, "Okay." What she didn't say was, *Yeah, but I'll bet every new business doesn't have a super nag wanting to have a baby.*

She never realized how ambivalence would enter her life in the form of Claire Hollander. Before Claire, everything had been so structured: foster care, med school, the Army, even her recovery after being injured in Iraq.

Now, she never knew what to expect. Would it be Claire coming out of the shower wearing only the towel wrapped around her head, her nipples becoming erect at the sight of Kathleen's outstretched arms? Moving toward the bed, leaning over until their lips joined, her tongue a familiar tenant in Kathleen's mouth.

Kathleen tried to remember when the baby business first began. *A while ago,* she thought. At first, subtle hints she didn't pick up on or chose to ignore. Then the lingering looks at infants being strolled along the streets by proud parents. Or, the way Claire would stop to gaze inside a store window displaying infant clothing. Long gazes followed by equally long sighs and softly spoken, *oohs* and *aahs*.

Maybe when they went shopping for their mattress. That was pretty direct when Claire flopped down on the queen-sized mattress and box spring set and talked about a family bed. Then there was her humming that treacly old Paul Anka ballad "(You're) Having My Baby," and her weeping when they heard Bette Midler singing "Baby Mine." And through it all, Kathleen either ignored the hint or smiled weakly and turned away.

The unwelcomed and ignored signals finally came to a head last night during their "Let's watch a movie" date night.

"I've picked a great movie for tonight," said Claire, turning on the TV in the solarium.

"What's that, babe?" Kathleen took off her shoes, flopped down on the couch, stretched out her legs, and hoped for a foot rub somewhere along the way. "You picked the movie, I'll pick dessert."

"Maybe we should pass on the movie and go directly to dessert," Claire said, their lips meeting while her hand grazed lightly over Kathleen's breasts.

"Hmm, you sure know how to improve my day."

"Hard one?"

"Super hard. I thought this afternoon would never end. But the biggest downer was, I had to admit Tony Enard to St. Mona's."

Claire said, "The tests came back?"

"Yes, advanced pancreatic cancer."

Tears welled up in Claire's eyes. "He's so young," she said in a near whisper. "He's our age. His wife and kids. Do they know?"

"Jen was there, of course." Kathleen clung to Claire. "The kids don't know. They're only three, six, and eight. How can they possibly understand? Jen will drive home tonight and Tony won't be with her, and the kids will want to know where their daddy is."

Claire held Kathleen closer. "I'm so sorry. I don't know how you do it."

Kathleen said softly, "I don't do it alone. I can because I know when I come home you'll be here. And when you hold me, like right now, it puts me back into balance. I don't say it often enough, Claire-bear, but you mean everything to me. I'm so grateful that we have each other."

"Ditto, my love."

"A movie might help zap the negative energy. How about the movie first? Then, I'll get the fire going in the bedroom; fill the tub and light candles. A long bath...you can even have all the duckies." She smiled at Claire. "Then dessert."

Claire winked. "Sounds perfect. Drum roll time: And the movie of the week is...*Juno*!"

Kathleen's upper lip curled into a playful sneer. "*Juno*? Really? What are we, like, twelve?"

"Oh, shut up, it's supposed to be really good. It's about a teenager who gets pregnant and has to decide on keeping the baby or not. Humor and pathos in one tidy package!"

"Okay," said Kathleen, stifling a yawn. "I hope I can keep my eyes open."

"Hungry?"

"Maybe just popcorn. I had a late lunch."

The red bowl overflowing with popcorn—loaded with butter and salt—sat on the wrought-iron coffee table within reach of both. Claire inserted the DVD, plopped down on the couch, put Kathleen's feet on her lap, and handed her the remote control. It was Kathleen's job to hit the start button. It was a familiar scene; one that got repeated at least weekly, sometimes more often. Sometimes, they watched the movie holding hands; if there was a chill in the room, they wrapped themselves in the pastel-colored throw Bubba had crocheted.

The movie began, and at first, they stayed engaged and inter-twined. Gradually, as the theme of the film played out, they disen-tangled, ending up at different ends of the couch. They sat quietly afterward, unable to do their usual postmortem.

Kathleen broke the dead silence with, "Claire, are you okay?"

Claire shook her head. "The movie really hit me. A young kid like Juno needing to make a decision like that. I never told you this, but I volunteered at Planned Parenthood during college. The movie made me think of...stuff. All kinds of women having to make tough decisions."

"It got to me, too."

Kathleen was making her little girl face, the one that broke Claire's heart. The look in her eyes that said she was reliving a scene from the past, her lips turning down at the corners and trembling, as if she would begin to cry at any moment.

"It made me think of my brothers and sisters," said Kathleen. "All of us scattered and sent to different foster homes."

Kathleen put her head in her hands. "Sometimes, I feel so guilty over not having been able to take care of the twins. I couldn't find any formula, and I gave them milk—just regular milk out of a carton. How do I know if they're okay?"

"Chances are they were adopted by a loving family."

"Even if that's true, it doesn't mean they didn't have some permanent damage. It's like reading a book and the last chapter is missing. It's just so damn hard for me to let go without knowing."

Claire reached over to touch Kathleen's face. "Honey, how long can you go on blaming yourself for something you had no control over? You were just a little girl who needed to be taken care of."

Claire paused, and then spoke plaintively. "Kath, something has been on my mind, well, for quite a while now. What would you think about us having a baby? We go on, day by day, thinking life will go on forever. But it doesn't, and then sometimes it's too late. At least Tony and Jen have their memories of being with their babies, of being a family."

"And now Jen will have three to raise...on her own."

"It's a gamble we take. Sometimes, you just have to take the chance. I'm getting older, and my bio clock is tick-tocking away. Even with all our stuff, I still think we'd make super moms. I want us to be a family, in every sense of the word."

Kathleen stood up and began to fold the throw. "It was sweet of Bubba to make this for us," she said wistfully. When she spoke again, her tone had an uncharacteristic chill. "It's too soon for me. I'm not ready, and I can't promise if I'll ever be ready. I'm sorry."

Claire felt her mood changing from one of understanding to anger. "I'm really tired," she said tersely. "I think I'll pass on the bath and save dessert for another time."

❀   ❀   ❀

Kathleen felt her world collapsing. Her practice was teetering and Claire had pulled away.

Oscar's purring changed to a rumble. "More?" Kathleen asked. Oscar settled deeper into her lap.

"Oscar," she whispered, "I'll bet you have the answers to my dilemma."

Oscar looked directly at her with his luminous green eyes. She thought about her book, *The Adventures of Alice in Wonderland*; a used copy purchased from the library that had opened her imagination to a world of fantasy. She had carried the book everywhere, a talisman and best friend to protect her from a harsh world. A lump rose in her throat as she rubbed Oscar's head, "Damn, if you don't look exactly like the Cheshire cat," she murmured.

Oscar purred. *Of course I do. I am a direct descendant.*

She shivered as the cold penetrated through the single comforter. Reluctantly, she got out of bed to start a fire. She lit the dry twigs, collected from the nearby woods, and watched as the flames sparked upward toward the kindling. The fire sputtered, then leaped, taking hold of the surrounding logs.

Her throat tightened when she remembered the day when they first became lovers. It was in this room on the floor in front of a blazing fire. Blankets and comforters were hastily pulled off the nearby bed to become their pallet.

Now, a recent find of Claire's, a rosewood settee, faced the fireplace. Claire had discovered it on one of their bike rides; to the untrained eye, just another piece of broken furniture left on the curb. She scooped the treasure up, painstakingly refinished the wood frame, and reupholstered the cushions in off-white linen.

Kathleen registered some skepticism that the battered settee could ever be made comfortable and like new again. But only Claire could find a castoff, recognize its hidden charms, and transform it into an object of beauty. They had lugged the restored sofa from the garage to their bedroom, placing it to face the fireplace.

"Try it out," Claire said, gently pushing Kathleen onto the settee. "Now, laugh away, you doubting Thomasina. What do you think?"

"Comfortable and perfect for two. You're amazing."

Claire snuggled into Kathleen's waiting arms. She thought, *There's actually enough room for three. A baby doesn't take up that much space.*

"Remember that hike to Christmas River?"

"I'll never forget it," Kathleen answered.

"Remember who made the first move?"

"I think you did. I wasn't sure about you...a crazy, straight woman," she said affectionately.

"Aren't you happy I was so bold? We'd still be sitting in the truck, waiting for you to make the first move."

"I'll show you how happy I am," said Kathleen. She unbuttoned Claire's blouse, moving slowly, her eyes gazing at the sight of her lover until one by one the garments lay scattered on the floor. "I can't keep my eyes or my hands off you."

Claire felt Kathleen's hands tracing the outline of her face, her shoulders, her breasts. Claire stood, her body illuminated by the flames from the fire. She walked to the bed, beckoning to her lover to join her.

"Take your clothes off...I want to watch you, Kath."

Kathleen turned off the lamps, lit candles, moving around the room until she had returned to the side of the bed.

Claire's lips trembled as she gazed at the sight of her lover, and then changed to a slight smile as Kathleen's clothing fell into a heap by her feet.

Kathleen undid her ponytail, shaking her head until her dark brown hair fell to her shoulders and then drifted, covering her breasts.

"Come here," motioned Claire. Her hands, so familiar to Kathleen, moved slowly over her breasts. She traced the remnants of Kathleen's scar running from her shoulder to her chest, a subtle reminder of having been injured in Iraq.

"Do you remember when we first made love, and I traced your scar with my hand?"

"I'll remember that always. I winced because your hand was so hot. I didn't think about it before, but that's when my scar began to fade. It's barely visible now."

"My hands don't get warm any longer," said Claire mournfully.

Kathleen took Claire's hands in hers and kissed her fingertips. "You're perfect exactly as you are. My Claire...my Claire-bear. She slid forward until their lips met, her tongue tracing the shape of Claire's lips.

Her hand drifted slowly from the small of Claire's back to her shoulders.

"I'm memorizing you," she said with a catch in her voice. "I never want to forget how you feel."

Claire reached up to touch Kathleen's cheek. "This little scar..."

"I fell off my bike. You have three beauty marks on your shoulder."

"You're crying, Kath."

"So are you. It's just...I love you so much, Claire."

"You won't lose me."

"Promise?"

"Promise."

They fell asleep that way, two hearts beating to their own tempo—slowing down and speeding up until they became synchronized as one.

Kathleen eased herself back into bed. How did they get from the place they were in just a month ago, to where they were now?

Oscar reclaimed his place on her belly. She continued to stroke his head, ever amazed at how his purring communicated his feelings: *You got this just right, sister.*

She glanced at Claire, deep in sleep, her arm tucked under her head. She leaned over to whisper, "I love you, Claire. Forgive me, I just don't know...I just don't know."

Claire sleep-mumbled, "Boy or girl, boy or girl?"

Kathleen sunk back into her pillow. "Sweet Jesus, there's no escaping it."

Oscar adjusted his position, exposing his underside. Her hand automatically moved to his plump little tummy. *Light on the touch,* he growled.

Last night—after the *Juno* fiasco—they began to bicker over how many blankets to put on the bed. Claire drew an invisible line down the middle of the mattress. "What's on this side is mine, what's on the other side is yours. And, my side has all the blankets."

Claire shoved a single down quilt onto Kathleen's side of the bed and, with a harrumph, turned over to bury herself under a mound of blankets. Kathleen grabbed the cover, turned on her side, and thought, *Don't wake me in the middle of the night complaining about heat stroke.*

Now, as Claire began to wake from her dream state, she sat up, her face flushed. "Someone must have turned the heat up," she croaked.

Kathleen stifled a laugh. Claire looked as if she had just finished a session in a sauna.

Claire threw off the blankets and, at the same time, cast a sour look Kathleen's way and mumbled, "I'm going downstairs for coffee. Come on, Oscar, I'll get you some breakfast. *Someone* has to take care of you." She left in a huff, throwing another dirty look Kathleen's way.

Kathleen sat up with a jolt, dislodging Oscar from her lap. With an angry mew, Oscar stomped off into the hallway, narrowing his eyes as he glanced at Kathleen. *You've got a lot of nerve to bump me off.*

"Good lord," she spoke out loud, "I've just witnessed a cat having a tantrum. Like mother, like cat."

Kathleen heard muffled voices drifting from the kitchen through the heat registers and into the bedroom. Not clear enough to hear what they were saying but clear enough to know it was Sam, Helen, and Claire. Bless these old houses and their non-technical ways of eavesdropping. She could hear some laughter and breathed a sigh of relief. It seemed that Claire had changed back into her funny, seductive self.

Their life before "I want a baby" was almost ideal, Kathleen thought. But now, she wasn't sure of who would walk back into the bedroom. Would it be the Claire who was laughing and being seductive with Sam and Helen? Or the Claire who was punishing her by withdrawing?

She was beginning to dread her time alone with Claire. *Is this the way a relationship is supposed to be?* she wondered. She had hoped that their reunion with a dance in the solarium and an exchange of belated Christmas gifts would be a fairy-tale ending and they would live happily ever after. Now she knew that was not the end of the story, but rather the beginning of a tale with an unknown ending.

Lately, something from the past had been weighing heavily on her mind. Not a flashback from Iraq, not about money, or Claire's constant "hints" about having a baby, but a shame-filled memory. She had faced most of her demons, but why was there always one more waiting to pop up? This one she wanted to keep to herself. *Not ready to talk about it, damn it...I'm just not ready!*

Claire climbed the stairs, balancing two mugs of coffee. Black for her, cream and two heaping teaspoons of sugar for Kath—a habit she had picked up in the Army after getting one too many cups of stale coffee.

A line drawn down the middle of the bed with her finger, and she was the winner of the covers. She hoped she got her point across to Kath!

What a shitty night's sleep. She was sure she had become de-hydrated and close to indoor sunstroke. It was one of the worst night's sleeps she had ever had.

And that dream that kept repeating itself throughout the night. She was standing in a garage, surrounded by stacks of childhood books. Books that had helped to form her dreams and give her hope. A woman—ugh, it was Kath—crept in and began to steal her books. Her hopes and dreams stolen by the woman who was *supposed* to love her.

She had put on a show for Sam and Helen this morning. Having gone to a clown summer camp when she was eight, she knew just how to do it. That was the summer after her bubba had moved in, and her mother Adele had dragged her to see Dr. Cherry.

Dr. Cherry was the neighborhood pediatrician, an old-fashioned, no-nonsense codger who kept his patients healthy not only with a hundred and one vaccinations, but also by advising parents on raising psychologically sound children, which meant kids who would not argue back.

Sammy Glick, Claire's best friend and another one of Dr. Cherry's victims, had warned her that seeing Dr. Cherry was a fate worse than death. That's what made him behave. That, and a prescription to his parents to give Sammy a *potch in the tuchus* (a swat on his butt) when he wouldn't listen.

Dr. Cherry scared her more than any of the shots he gave her. He was all shriveled up—more the size of a kid than a grown-up—and his hands were gnarled like old tree branches, probably from having given a million shots for at least a hundred years. He had a straggly beard and red splatters on his doctor's smock. Mother had explained it was probably catsup from his lunch, but Claire was convinced it was blood. When he came into the exam room to do her checkup, his jack-o'-lantern smile revealed teeth yellowed over time and the evil glint in his eyes said, "How can I hurt you today, little girl?"

She trembled as her mother dragged her into Dr. Cherry's office. "Ever since your bubba moved in, you think you can get away with murder. Well, Missy, we'll see about that."

She hated when her mother called her Missy. Her name was Claire, darn it, and Bubba had told her it meant Moonlight.

Claire sat across from Dr. Cherry in one of the grown-up chairs. She had worn her tired-looking sweats with torn tennis shoes and a silver-sequined sweater she had found in one of the trash cans left out by the curb.

Bubba had helped her wash the sweater and laid it flat on an old towel to dry. "This is a very beautiful sweater, Claire. A lucky find," Bubba said.

Claire loved the way the sunlight streamed through her bedroom window, bouncing off the silver sequins. The sweater was extra large and hid her budding chubbiness. She smiled into the mirror, appreciating the overall look. She didn't mind that her teeth were screaming out, *braces on the way*!

She thought of the three things she loved best: singing, dancing, and making people laugh. She felt...she felt...just like Bette Midler.

Dr. Cherry picked up his cigarette and put it between his tobacco-stained teeth. Inhaling deeply, he spoke in a raspy voice, "Claire, you are driving your mother crazy."

Claire glared. *Dare she argue with the old poot? Would her answer have her thrown into a closet for the rest of her natural life?*

She smiled at Dr. Cherry in a practiced way that would show off her irresistible dimples. She looked him straight in the eye. "I am a wonderful child, Dr. Cherry, with many talents. My *mother* is the crazy one. I think it would be helpful if you admitted her to Bellevue for a month or two."

She should have added "snooping" to one of her talents. She had heard that line directly from Bubba and her canasta friends on a Wednesday afternoon while Mother was at work. They had laughed, finished eating all the M&Ms, pretzels, and the pound of See's Candies sent by a cousin all the way from California.

Dr. Cherry, at a loss for words, rang for his nurse. "Bring Mrs. Hollander in, please."

Her mother came in, handkerchief in hand, ready to gush tears if needed. She sat down in the chair next to Claire, her eyes averted from her daughter, but focused on the man with the power.

Dr. Cherry cleared his throat. "I have been treating children for over forty years. And, Mrs. Hollander, I have never come across a child I couldn't help. Until now. Your little Claire is..." Claire and her mother waited for his blunt diagnosis: "This girl is *mashugana*. She is the clearest and only case I have seen in all my years of treating children and advising parents."

Her mother sobbed into her dainty hanky.

Mashugana. She had been labeled *mashugana*—the worse possible diagnosis ever created. *Crazy and/or bizarre.*

"What do I do, Dr. Cherry?" her mother said between sobs and nose-blowing.

"Your mother-in-law is living with you, yes?"

"Living with us? She's taken over! Claire certainly doesn't take after *my* side of the family."

Claire rolled her eyes. *Well, thank God for that.*

Dr. Cherry drummed his shriveled Vienna sausage-like fingers on his bony knee. "Perhaps boarding school is the best solution for Claire. I can say no more. You will just have to do your best, and you do have my sympathy."

Adele cried all the way home. Claire wondered; she had heard her bubba use the word *mashugana* in a playful way, but never realized it was the same as saying, *Claire has a fatal illness.*

When they got home, Daddy was sitting in a half-stupor in his favorite chair with his feet resting on the threadbare ottoman. Bubba was fussing in the kitchen, singing at the top of her lungs and sounding exactly like Ethel Merman: *I'm gonna wash that man right out of my hair.* Smells of homemade everything wafted throughout the small apartment and into the hallway.

Hmm, thought Claire, *brisket, mashed potatoes and gravy, peas, and rice knishes.* She rubbed her ever-expanding tummy. *I hope she didn't forget about dessert.*

And that was the defining moment when Bubba stepped in and took over Claire's life. "Boarding school!" she scoffed. "What this child needs is to find a way to express her very unique personality. And I know just the place!"

That summer, Claire attended the Clown School for Mashugana Children and learned two valuable lessons. One was to make 'em laugh, make 'em laugh, make 'em laugh. She took home the gold laughing medal.

The other was, no matter how much she was hurting on the inside, hide behind smiles and jokes. That way, she would always be safe.

Claire stood in front of their open bedroom door. She felt a lump rise in her throat; the steaming coffee had become lukewarm. *Like our relationship*, she thought. She could heat the coffee in the small microwave in the bedroom, but she wasn't sure she could heat up their relationship.

She had pulled another stupid Claire maneuver by grabbing all the blankets. Damn, she hated being mad at Kath. Kath would get that little girl look, all hurt and wounded. She wanted to scoop her up, take her pain away, but she felt angry. Wasn't it normal to want to start a family? Okay, so they both came from shitty backgrounds. At least Claire had her bubba. But, how many nights had she lain in bed sucking her thumb while her mother and bubba fought? Or when her daddy would have a flashback from Vietnam, and Bubba would bathe him like an infant in the old cast-iron tub and sing lullabies to soothe him?

Claire could feel her anger building. Did Kathleen really think she owned the copyright to a miserable childhood? Claire wanted to scream, "Join the fucking crowd!"

She was afraid she would lose it with Kath, the way she had lost it with all of her former boyfriends. And the way she lost it the night she and Kath broke up. If they broke up again, there would be no going back...not for Claire.

She heard the shower running in the bathroom. Kath wasn't humming in her off-key fashion as she usually did. All Claire could hear was the sound of water spraying against the shower walls. At least Kath hadn't completely shut the door. They had decided a while ago that if they needed privacy, the door would be closed all the way. And if it was open even a crack...

She heated the coffee in the "nuker" and pushed the bathroom door open with her foot. Opening the shower door, Kathleen held out her hand.

Claire handed her the mug of coffee and squeaked, "Truce?"

"Only if you get out of those ridiculous looking pajamas and get in here."

She did.

CHAPTER 5

Gayle tested the room temperature by sticking her big toe out from under the covers: *freezing*. Spring weather in Los Angeles was so unpredictable...as unpredictable as their thirty-year-old gas furnace.

How did Monday get here so quickly? The PBS panel on aging was a hit and she had been asked to return as a solo guest on the Tim Weston show. She smiled inwardly, *Quite a feather in her cap. And another undertaking to fit into her overloaded schedule,* she thought as she shivered. *Damn, if it gets any colder in here, I'll need a wool cap.*

Robert was sound asleep—not freezing, obviously—with only a sheet covering him. She made a mad dash for the bathroom, switching on the heater and turning on the shower in one quick movement. She barely made it to the toilet. Was that another sign of this "event" they called aging?

Last week was hectic, preparing for the PBS panel and getting ready for Stephanie's arrival. And this morning...her mind was racing. She had an 8:00 a.m. staff meeting at the Valley Mental Health Center before having to dash to LAX. For a moment, she thought about playing hooky, but her guilty conscious took over.

The center provided counseling for the underserved population and she was one of three therapists who volunteered to supervise interns. How could she not attend?

She stepped into the shower, *Ahh, warm water; heaven at last!* She began to go over the list in her head: fresh linens on the bed, new towels for the bathroom, and every kind of toiletry known to mankind and Lamont.

She had stopped at Lamont's Cosmetic and Hair Salon on her way home from PBS. "I'm stocking up for a guest," she had told Lamont. "Shampoo, conditioner, lotions, and let's not forget sunscreen. Oh, and let's add some of those wonderful elixirs for the face."

Overkill, she knew, but damn, she was feeling anxious; too anxious.

Lamont stood with his hand on his hip. "Twenty questions time," he said in a prissy old maid's voice. "Hair: natural or colored? Curly, straight, perm? Thin or thick? Skin tone? Ethnic origin would be helpful. At least tell me her *age*." He tapped an Italian-loafered foot impatiently.

"You've got to be kidding." She thought about Stephanie. She would be picking her up at the airport and suddenly couldn't remember what she looked like. In fact, what did she really know about her? *It must be my anxiety*, she rationalized.

"Age? Age is all relative," she offered weakly.

Lamont had been cutting Gayle's hair for years and had watched it go from dark brown to its current state of brown-gray.

"Gayle, I'm not asking for Zen philosophy. Just tell me what the gal looks like."

She closed her eyes for a moment trying to remember when she saw Stephanie at Brooke Army Medical Center in Texas. "Hard to tell her age; she looks very young. I'd guess late twenties to thirty. Thin. Very thin. Angular features. Straight, light-brown hair; some reddish highlights. Hazel eyes." Gayle thought for a moment. "The color of dark honey. Quite beautiful, actually."

"You'd make a great witness," Lamont had chuckled as he began to fill one of the shopping baskets with bottles of shampoo, conditioner, and lotion.

"All these?" Gayle said, reaching for her credit card.

"I never have trusted eyewitnesses."

Gayle dressed in her lightweight brown wool slacks, long-sleeved cream silk shirt, beige cashmere vest, and matching leather fringe loafers. Damn, they felt good. Robert would kill her if he knew she had paid $650 for a pair of shoes. What he failed to understand was that there were few things she could purchase that would allow her to feel beautiful. It was down to shoes and handbags. She thought defensively, *At least I didn't buy the bag to go with it, even though I did ask the sales clerk to hold it for me.* "I'll be back next week," she had promised, speaking in a hushed, secretive tone.

The salesclerk had smiled. It was a promise she had heard many a time.

Gayle made her way into the kitchen to find her thermos filled with coffee and a blueberry muffin wrapped in a plastic wrap on the counter, along with a note from Robert.

> *Gayle:*
> *Got up while you were still sleeping and made snacks for you and Stephanie. Sorry about yesterday's doubts. Of course, I'll welcome her.*
> *I found this new guilt-free recipe, for blueberry muffins, low in sugar and fat.*
> *Enjoy!*
> *Love, Bobby*

Gayle scribbled a note for Robert.

> *My darling Bobby,*
> *Thanks for the eats, you thoughtful hunk.*

The guy from Steve's Heating and Air is coming today at 10:30.
Please repair or replace at any cost. Almost froze this morning.
Home around two p.m.
You are my everything.
Love, Gayle

❀   ❀   ❀

Gayle allowed two hours from the Valley to LAX. On a good day, the drive should have taken less than an hour. She wondered if there were any good freeway days left in Los Angeles. Maybe at two in the morning, but even then, there was usually some kind of construction going on.

She sighed. The staff meeting was troubling. Even with the interns carrying a heavy caseload, the center was under-staffed and patients were being put on a long waiting list or referred to out-of-area centers. *Once again, the short stick goes to the ones who need their services the most. Damn, this is a hard profession. Maybe it's time to think about retiring...sometimes I feel so worn out, just so terribly worn out.*

Predictably, traffic stopped as she approached the interchange that would take her to the airport. She tried to focus to keep her attention on the cars in front of her, but her thoughts shifted to Robert. The morning's sweet, apologetic note aside, his recent behavior seemed so *not* Robert. Was he keeping something from her? Could he be having an affair? She laughed out loud. Was he ill? She shuddered. They had promised never to keep secrets from each other. She really didn't count her little secrets like the shoes that adorned her feet today or the thoughts of the matching handbag being held at Nordstrom's. She had to keep the faith in their relationship. Whatever it was, she knew Robert would tell her in time.

She passed the Getty Museum. She and Robert enjoyed lunching in the sculpture garden and the wandering around that followed, viewing the exhibits on American and European photography.

She wondered about Stephanie, *Would she enjoy the museum?* She knew so little about her. Gayle had noticed the way she would skirt around details of her life, even the simple ones. When Gayle asked her where she was from, she answered, "The Midwest." Gayle was curious. "What part?" "Kansas," she replied, then changed the subject. What Gayle did know was that Stephanie loved Italian food, especially pizza.

They would have homemade minestrone soup and lasagna for dinner, salad from the garden, and Italian ices for dessert. Thank God, Robert loved to cook. Perhaps tomorrow, he would make his almost world-renowned pizza. A carefully guarded recipe locked away in his safe. She wondered what else was locked away inside this man she had known for almost forty years.

The traffic slowed, then stopped. *Always at the same place*, she thought, nearing the exit to the airport. A car did a fast lane change and she had to swerve, missing the car by inches. She felt the hot flash start inside her $650 shoes, moving quickly up her body until her head was soaked. *Great*, she thought as she took the off-ramp to the airport, *just what I need: a major hot flash.* She gulped the bottle of ice-cold water that always seemed to help. She began to feel the all too familiar pressure in her bladder. Any thoughts of the museum or secret recipes faded into the background.

She glanced at the passenger seat whose only occupants were a parking pass for the lot directly across from the airport entrance, and a second pass that would allow her to meet Stephanie at the gate.

The line through security was long, but passengers were used to the wait and were going through the process by rote. Recycle bins were filled with water bottles. Jackets and shoes went onto the conveyor belt; laptops were placed in one of the bins. The changes after 9/11 had been met with reactions ranging from "we have to do this" to "this is really annoying," and finally accepted as if it had always been this way—just another day at the airport.

One of the TSA guards saw her gate pass and motioned her to the front of the line. After the security check, she gathered her shoes, computer case, and purse. The TSA guard smiled at her, saying, "Welcome your hero home for us."

My hero. It felt so foreign. She mused, *Was she annoyed with Robert because he had his doubts about Stephanie or because his doubts were echoing hers?*

Perhaps Robert was right to be concerned. After all, Stephanie was a veritable stranger. Their communications through emails, Skype, and phone calls remained casual. What did she really know about her? Outside of the time she had spent with Stephanie at Landstuhl, they had only met once, six months ago, at Brooke Army Medical Center (BAMC) in San Antonio, Texas.

❀ ❀ ❀

Gayle came face to face with Stephanie in the physical therapy department at BAMC. *Impressive,* she thought as she scanned the room. Free weights, weight machines, mats with balls waiting in a nearby bin, treadmills, and parallel bars filled the space. The south wall had floor to ceiling windows with an expansive view of green spaces and nearby hotels.

Exercise charts hung on one wall; the remaining two walls were mirrored from floor to ceiling. There was no way to hide from reality in this room. You looked at a fellow warrior and saw your reflection in their eyes. This was the place where the toughest battles would be fought, where the therapists helped the wounded warriors to discover a new level of physical ability and redefine their identity.

Stephanie was standing at the parallel bars, her arms shaking and sweat pouring down her face. Her light-brown, shoulder-length hair was contained in a single braid, except for a lock that had come loose and drooped over her left eye. The staff had plied her with extra calories, but she remained stick-thin, her bony structure displayed for all to see. It was her light amber-colored eyes that Gayle was drawn to; the color of honey made from the flowers of the blueberry bush. Her mouth had the softness of a child's that lent a glint of innocence to her appearance. When she became taut from pain, her mouth changed to a hard grimace. *Such a sudden, complete change*, Gayle thought. A distortion that showed another side. She intuited, *This is a woman who has had a harsh life.*

"Almost there, Stephanie," said her physical therapist, Joey. "Countdown: ten, nine, eight, seven, six, five, four, three, two, and one! Good job! Any dizziness?"

Stephanie turned her head and saw Gayle. She shook her head. "Joey—first step, please."

"You're only standing today, Stephanie."

She grimaced. "One step—please, Joey." She whispered, "My friend Gayle is here, I want her to see me take my first step."

Joey looked at Gayle and motioned her over toward the parallel bars.

"Hello, Gayle, I'm Joey."

They shook hands.

Joey said, "Stephanie's got good strength in her legs, but now she's got to get her brain and muscles to work together. It's a matter of strength and communication. You can't do one without the other."

Stephanie smiled shyly at Gayle. "Hi, Gayle. Want to see me take my first step?"

"I would be honored."

Joey said, "Looks like I can't win against the two of you. One shuffle, Stephanie. That's your first step."

"Okay, Joey, I'm ready."

Stephanie closed her eyes. "Brain, move my right foot." Nothing. "It's not moving, Joey."

"Slide and glide."

"Slide and glide," she echoed.

"Open your eyes, Stephanie. Look at where your right foot is."

Stephanie broke out into a broad grin. "I did it! Did you see, Gayle?"

Gayle nodded and smiled. She had an overwhelming urge to say, "My baby just took her first step," but checked herself.

"That's great, Stephanie. Mind if I take a photo?"
"Sure!" Stephanie beamed. "Cheese!"

They had lunch at the hospital's cafeteria-style cafe. It was a change for those patients who could manage to leave the hospital floor. For some, coming down to the cafeteria signaled a return to the ordinary.

For others, it was the beginning of a new ordinary: choose your food, struggle to put it on your tray, wheel your chair to a table, and transfer it onto the table. Bright faces lit up at their achievement. Some needed help. One young woman in a wheelchair and with limited use of her hands dropped the dishes on the floor. She bowed her head and sobbed. An attendant came to her side, speaking in a soothing tone, "It's okay, Mandy. It's your first try. Let's go through the line again."

Stephanie chose spaghetti with extra meatballs but stopped abruptly when they approached the desserts. "May I have two?" she asked Gayle.

"After that workout, you may have as many as you'd like."

Gayle suggested moving toward the back of the room away from the crowd. They sat at one of the tables covered with a bright-red tablecloth.

"This is very festive," said Gayle, glancing at the red, white, and blue balloons bobbing against the ceiling. She began to unload the crowded food tray. "Let's see, spaghetti with extra meatballs for you, cheesecake and chocolate mousse for dessert."

"Thank you for letting me have two desserts, Gayle. It's hard to choose."

"Don't I know it."

"You're my first visitor," Stephanie said shyly, taking a tentative bite of chocolate mousse.

"Dessert first?" said Gayle, smiling broadly.

"I couldn't wait. Besides, I'm just testing it. Yummy."

"I do believe in order, but when it comes to dessert, there is *always* room for options."

Gayle glanced at her vegetable salad then gazed at Stephanie's calorie-loaded lunch with a pang of envy. "I'm sorry I couldn't visit you in person sooner."

Stephanie shrugged, "That's okay. We had Skype, that was just like having you here. And they've kept me busy day and night. And four surgeries, but no more. I'm getting better. The best part is I didn't get dizzy. The first few times they stood me up, I got sick to my stomach. But everyone kept saying good job."

"I saw how hard you were working."

"Please, these sadists work your butt off! I'm just kidding. Joey and the other therapists are *saints*, really. I'm really glad you're here, Gayle. I don't remember you being in my room at Landstuhl. Just the book...I read a poem from it every day."

"Do you have a favorite?"

"This food's not half-bad," Stephanie said, slurping up a long strand of spaghetti. "Favorite? Oh, yes. Hands down, 'My Shadow' by Robert Louis Stevenson," she said in a little girl, singsong fashion. "I memorized it."

Gayle was pleased. "My mother read one of the poems to me every night at bedtime. 'My Shadow' was one of my favorites as well. Do you have a favorite part?"

Stephanie put down her fork, took a deep breath, and recited, "'He hasn't got a notion of how children ought to play, and can only make a fool of me in every sort of way.' That's my favorite part. They're the first two lines from the third stanza."

"Why is that your favorite?"

"It made me think," she said furrowing her brow. "Can shadows be real? But everyone knows a shadow isn't real. Isn't that right, Gayle?"

"Maybe to some they are. What do you think?"

"I think a shadow can be real, but not all the time."

Gayle nodded. "Stephanie, do you have any plans for after you're discharged?"

"I don't have a home. I walked out on my parents when I was sixteen and my mother said, 'You walk out that door, you no longer exist.'"

She pushed her plate of spaghetti away. "I have to save room for dessert. Now, which one do I eat first? I know, I'll take a bite of one, then a bite of the other."

Gayle was captivated by the childlike way Stephanie lined up the two desserts, appearing to survey the amount of food in each dish. "It's not always easy to have things come out even," she said seriously. "But back to your question, the social worker found a low-cost apartment for me. Close by, so the van can pick me up for outpatient rehab."

Gayle finished toying with her salad and reached for her ice tea. "I've told you about Kathleen and how she stayed with Robert and me. The VA Hospital is just a few miles from where we live. Robert and I have talked about it, and we would like to have you stay with us while you recover. I think we can offer you much nicer quarters than a cheap apartment. Plus, Robert loves to cook and desserts are one of his specialties." Gayle hesitated. "Funny, isn't it? You and Kathleen were right next to each other at Landstuhl, but never met. Perhaps we can remedy that while you are staying with us."

Stephanie's gaze remained fixed on the two desserts. "You hardly know me," she said softly.

"You hardly know me, either. But what we do know is we like the same poem. That's enough to welcome you into my home."

It felt right to Gayle to reach out and help in spite of any doubts that she and Robert might be having. But this felt so deep, so visceral; she knew she had to do it. She felt it. She believed it.

Gayle watched as the plane carrying Stephanie from San Antonio to Los Angeles taxied to Gate 21 and passengers began to disembark. Tired parents juggled car seats while trying to soothe cranky babies. Other passengers pushed their way through as if the plane had caught fire. She wondered, were they late for a business meeting, rushing because of a crisis, simply tired after a long flight, or hurrying to meet someone...perhaps a lover?

Attendants stood behind a line of empty wheelchairs, their hands gripping the handlebars, anticipating the moment when they might enter the plane to aid the disabled passengers, the last ones to disembark. A veil of uncertainty hung over the waiting area as anxious greeters clustered as close as possible to the gate. Gayle suspected everyone was feeling the same as she, excitement mixed with fear and apprehension.

Passengers waiting to board the next flight sat on hard, plastic seats, their eyes now fixed on the people standing nearby. The attendants began to move the wheelchairs, one by one, directly into the plane.

Exiting first was a young man with a thick, ropelike scar snaking its way down the shaved right hemisphere of his skull. His intense attempt at a smile produced an odd grimace, a tragic by-product of trauma. A woman ran to him, knelt down, and placed her head on his lap, chanting, "Tommy, oh, my Tommy!" He continued to gaze outward to the crowd, unaware that the person he had been looking for and needed the most was already by his side with tears streaming down her face.

"Tommy, it's Mommy...oh, my poor Tommy..."

The other warriors were wheeled out, one by one. Bright smiles and arms extended in greeting blended with tears as "Thank you, God" was murmured over and over again.

Gayle knew this would be the initial reaction: my baby, my spouse is home alive. The other feelings would come later. Frustration, anger, and grief would be followed by the awareness that the person they had sent off standing proud and straight was not the person who had returned. As their beloved had changed, so would they. The utterances of "Thank you, God," would be joined by "give me the strength to cope, to forgive."

Gayle checked her gate pass again. She was at the right gate, but she was beginning to wonder if Stephanie had made the flight. The crew deplaned and the replacement crew boarded.

Gayle scanned the area again, trying to set aside a sudden wave of panic. She began to walk toward the gate agent, whose eyes were fixed on his computer, when she saw Stephanie exiting through the jet bridge, a flight attendant by her side. She was standing, a walker her only support.

Gayle's eyes filled with tears at the sight of the soldier wearing her blue service uniform, her long hair in a French twist and a bright grin that from time to time would become distorted from pain. Stephanie shuffled toward Gayle until they met. Then Gayle's arms encircled and supported her as the attendant brought the wheelchair.

"You've never seen me in uniform and it's the last time...the *last time*." A single tear made its way down her cheek. "I wanted you to see me this way, Gayle, a soldier standing up straight, walking, but I can't make it all the way."

"I'm proud of you, baby. And you will...you will make it all the way."

❀   ❀   ❀

It was a short distance from the gate to the parking lot structure.

"With any luck, it'll take us about thirty minutes to get home," Gayle said, settling into the driver's seat. "I'm going to take the road we used to take, before Los Angeles became nothing but a sea of freeways. Robert packed some snacks." Gayle laughed as she handed Stephanie a Tupperware lunch set. "I should warn you ahead of time, Robert tends to overcook *and* overfeed."

"Can I peek inside?"

"Peek nothing. Graze to your heart's content. I can only imagine what's in there."

"This is like finding a buried treasure." Stephanie's eyes goggled. "Oh my God! I can't believe it!" she said, taking out container after container. "Sandwiches with the crust cut off...grapes, no stems. And how did he know? My favorite dessert, lemon squares."

"Another thing you should know: My Bobby's psychic."

Stephanie flashed a wide grin. "Seriously, Gayle, Robert really did this?"

"Yes, and as you'll soon find out, I can barely boil water."

"They fed us on the plane but, I'll tell you a secret, Gayle: I'm still hungry. And the way I am about dessert—gotta have a bite of it before anything else."

Stephanie popped open a bright-green Tupperware container, plucked out a lemon square, and tossed it into her mouth. "Mmm, better than sex, as they say. Anyway, we flew first class and they made this big announcement and thanked us all for serving. The whole plane applauded. Not one boo. Do you know what's funny about me getting almost blown to smithereens, Gayle?"

"No. Is there a joke in there somewhere?"

"Big one. I didn't tell you this before because I've been ashamed. I was wounded on the first day I got there. We were sent on a supply convoy and got ambushed. Six hours after landing: *BANG!* I got it, but good, and I got a Purple Heart. People call me a hero, but I didn't do anything but show up."

"I think showing up, as you call it, is in itself a great act of bravery."

"I didn't wear my medal but, if you'd like, I'll show it to you later."

"I'd like that very much."

Stephanie turned back to the Tupperware lunch set. "Wow, this is amazing," she said, opening another of the bright-green containers. "Do you want anything, Gayle?"

"No, I'm fine. If I ate all of Robert's snacks, I wouldn't fit in this car."

"Gayle, can I ask you a question?" Stephanie took a bite of turkey sandwich. "Sinfully good! The bread is homemade, isn't it?"

"Yes." Gayle turned to Stephanie. "Was that your question?"

"Can I have two?"

"You can have as many as you want. Shoot."

"Okay, I've never known a therapist before. Well, during rehab, we had group therapy. But not really. I mean it's not like being alone with one."

"I do admit we are a bit of a different breed."

"I read a book on dreams while I was in the hospital. About what different things mean: *Dream Symbols,* it was called. So, for example, if I dream about a tree it could mean growth. Do you think that's true? Can I read a book and understand my dreams?"

"I think dream books can be helpful, but what I believe is that each symbol in a dream has a special meaning known only to the dreamer. And sometimes, a dream can be a wish or an old memory trying to come to the surface, or even about something we fear might come true."

"So, it could be like that song from *Cinderella*: 'A Dream Is a Wish Your Heart Makes'?"

"It's a possibility. After all, if it's in a Disney film, it has to be true." Gayle thought about winking, but wasn't sure if Stephanie would understand. In some ways, she seemed to think in a very concrete way, much the way a small child would.

"Do you want a lemon bar, Gayle?"

Gayle smiled. "Yes, I would love one, but don't tell Robert."

Robert heard the thump, thump, thump that signaled a car had entered the brick driveway. A sound that might not be discernible to most, but Robert had laid and leveled every brick with his own two hands. *After all these years the ground settles, elements slowly erode the most even of surfaces,* he mused. *Maybe that's what happens to relationships; the subtle wear and tear from the years and you end up with a bumpy surface.*

It was so different when they were first married and life was an unexplored adventure.

❀   ❀   ❀

Gayle peered over her textbook, *Relationships: Make 'em or Break 'em.*

"I have a very important question to ask you, Robert. So important it may impact the next sixty years of our married life."

Robert hid his urge to smile. "I'm all ears," he said in the most serious of tones.

"Are you aware of what really kills a relationship?"

He drew Gayle closer. "Not enough lovemaking?"

Gayle playfully slapped his hand. "Ha! You can't keep up with me as it is."

"Okay, I give up. What?"

"Knowingly keeping secrets from your partner,"

"Is that what—" he looked at the author's name on the spine of the book "—Fritz Hafner says?"

"More or less. Robert, have you told me everything of substance that went on in your life? Because I have—even my most shameful secret. Remember when I told you I wet my pants in second grade?"

"Yes, I do. And how did you feel afterward?" he asked, using a term close to Gayle's heart.

"Much better. I was so ashamed I hid it from everyone for all these years. And to trust you with it...it told me how much you really loved me. I want us to make a promise that we will never withhold anything from each other. Not now, not ever. No matter how painful." She put the book down. "Promise?"

"I do," he said seriously.

"Now, what do you think is the second most important thing that kills a marriage?"

"Not enough lovemaking?"

"This time you got it right," she said, throwing Fritz Hafner to the floor and reaching for Robert.

Sooner or later he would have to talk to Gayle about his struggles. It was obvious he had his doubts about Stephanie, but there were other things weighing on his mind, but with Gayle gone so much of the time...there never seemed to be a right time. Would there ever be a right time? He hoped Gayle would be as understanding as he was when she had confessed her most shameful secret.

Life is filled with bumps, he mused. *Either we repair them or adjust to them. Not too different from the driveway.* Perhaps he would leave the bricks in their natural, uneven state as a reminder.

He wrapped the lasagna snuggly in foil and popped it into the refrigerator. The *I Love Lucy* inspired kitchen table with its yellow Formica top and matching vinyl chairs was set with glasses, lemon slices, and sweeteners. Gayle would like that he used the bright-red silverware and cloth napkins. It was a beautiful setting, and he wanted to please Gayle.

He put the pitcher of ice tea in the middle of the kitchen table, noticing the way the sun was streaming through the garden window, shedding light into every corner of the room.

He went to the front door to greet Gayle and Stephanie.

"Thanks for the snacks, Robert," Stephanie said, holding out her hand.

"'Fraid a handshake just won't do it," he said, hugging her gingerly. "I thought you and Gayle might be hungry."

Gayle looks really stressed out, he thought. Maybe it was just the long day. He couldn't put his finger on it, but something wasn't feeling right.

"I've been rethinking our dinner dessert," he said, shaking off his unease. "Thought I'd bake a scrumptious chocolate cake with filling between the layers. Stephanie, why don't you choose the filling?"

She thought for a long moment. "Robert, can I ask you a question?"

"Of course."

"Do you think we could make it two flavors instead of one?"

"You mean three layers and two fillings?"

She nodded excitedly.

"What flavors would you like?"

"Lemon, Robert. Lemon and raspberries."

"Why, I do believe I can manage that."

Gayle reached for Stephanie's soft-sided, plaid carryon. "While Robert's busy in the kitchen, let's get you settled into your room. Are you okay on the walker?"

"Yes, I'm fine as long as it's short distances. The docs want me to use it as much as I can."

"This is it, Stephanie. It's a shame to waste the fresh air," said Gayle, opening the bedroom window.

Stephanie stared at the double bed with a white wicker headboard, a matching desk and chair, and a hard rock maple chest of drawers. A white chenille bedspread with a floral pattern covered the double-sized mattress.

"Oh, Gayle, it's the nicest room I've ever had," she said.

"Robert refinished the dresser," said Gayle, rubbing her hand over the top. "He does so many things around the house. I keep his 'honey do' list pretty much full."

"It's very pretty." Stephanie opened a drawer. "I don't think I can fill half the drawers up."

"At some point we'll go shopping." Gayle lowered her voice, confessing, "It's one of my favorite hobbies. Now, come see the bathroom."

Stephanie shifted her weight and walked slowly to the bathroom. "It's handicap-ready."

"I told you about Kathleen living here with us when she was recovering from her injury. We had it designed with a walk-in shower."

Gayle pointed to the open bank of shelves. "Extra towels are here, and," she said, remembering her excursion to Lamont's, "plenty of lotions, shampoos, and conditioners. Don't forget the sunscreen—you are very fair."

"I won't forget. It's perfect." Stephanie wiped a tear away. Steadying herself with one hand on the walker, she leaned over and rested her head against Gayle's chest. "Thank you, Gayle."

"I'm glad you like it," said Gayle, returning and then releasing the hug. "I do want you to feel right at home. Are you sure you don't need any help?"

"I'm fine. With the grab bars, I can take my own shower, and if I sit on the bed, I can even reach my shoes. The docs say it's good to do—increases my flexibility when I stretch." She became thoughtful. "I might need help with a top. Sometimes, it can be hard for me to lift my arms high. It's from tensing up when I grab the walker."

"I'll be here to help. Just yell out."

"Could I take a nap, Gayle? Just lie down on top of the covers, if that's okay. I haven't slept in a real bed for a long time."

"Of course. But, why on top? Let yourself feel the comfort of the sheets." Gayle turned down the bed, exposing the linens. "I'll get you an extra blanket. Late afternoons can get a bit chilly."

"Gayle, do you think I could have two blankets?"

A shiver made the hair on Gayle's arms stand up. "Two it is."

❀   ❀   ❀

Robert was taking the cake pans out of the oven.

"Smells luscious," said Gayle.

"One of our tried and true favorites. How is Stephanie?"

"She seems fine."

"Then, why are you making your 'something's wrong' face?"

"And what exactly is that face?"

"The corners of your mouth droop and one eyebrow—" he reached over to trace her right eyebrow "—goes up."

"Damn, Robert! Is nothing sacred?"

"Not after all these years. Come outside so we can speak privately," he said, handing Gayle a red metal colander. "You'll hold, I'll pick."

They stood on the brick patio. "The garden is magnificent!" Gayle sighed, taking in the splendor. "I forget how healing it is for me. It's our bit of paradise, isn't it? Remember how much Kathleen loved it out here?"

Robert put his arm around Gayle's shoulder. "Yes, that was a wonderful time. Kathleen was so open to learn about life...about everything."

"You were the perfect dad for her. Remember when you and Kathleen refinished this wrought-iron table?" Gayle moved her hand over the table's filigree. "So intricate," she said softly.

Robert nodded and cleared his throat. Words he wanted to say—and that should be said—couldn't come out. *The time's not right. Not now when Stephanie just arrived.* "That was a special time for all of us."

Robert walked toward the vegetable garden. "I'm no professional, but it strikes me that Stephanie's a bit off. Her demeanor—well, I wasn't sure if I was speaking to an adult or a five-year-old."

"Don't forget what she's been through. But you're right, she does seem to be regressed, almost infantile at times. Perhaps, it's just the unfamiliar surroundings or the trauma."

"You're the therapist, but it seems beyond that. Was she diagnosed with post-traumatic stress disorder? And what about the time you spent with her at the hospital? And all the time you've spent messaging back and forth—didn't you notice *something*?"

"Whoa, Robert. One question at a time. We're not in a courtroom, and I'm beginning to feel like I'm on the witness stand."

"Sorry, I guess I'm just overly concerned."

"We have enough lettuce. How about some of those wonderful-looking asparagus?"

Robert nodded. "Sure. No witness stand. Just tell me your thoughts on Stephanie in your own way."

"All right. Let's go back to square one. First, she was not diagnosed with PTSD. Second, she was in a hospital setting where everything and every minute were structured. She had some horrible wounds. I had a talk with her physiatrist. She had a ruptured bladder, and there were bone shards embedded in her spinal cord. It's a miracle she lived, and they were quite certain she would never walk again. I don't know anyone who wouldn't regress after that experience. And now she's in a strange home, with strangers."

"All right, I'll give you that." Robert turned to put the asparagus in the colander. What do you suggest we do?"

Gayle set the colander down. "I love the different colors of the lettuce. Just look at how everything blends. There are no wrong colors, just as there are no wrong people. We wanted a child more than anything, but did we ever consider what we would have done if our child was born with, or developed, a disability?"

"I would imagine we would have cried and then given it all the love we had in our hearts."

Gayle nodded. "And that's exactly what we're going to do with Stephanie."

Stephanie squirmed around on the mattress and fluffed the pillows.

"HE, I like the thinner pillow. Which one do you want?" she whispered.

"The thicker one?" She moved the pillow to the other side of the bed.

"This is the best bed we've ever had. Remember that tiny twin bed at home? And you would pull all the covers off me. Now, we have two covers so we don't have to share."

"And did you notice I got you your favorite dessert filling? HE, you can say thank you."

"You're welcome. Just promise me one thing. Don't hog the bed."

And with that, she turned on her side, covered her head with the blanket, and fell into a deep sleep.

CHAPTER 6

Sam thumped the alarm's off button. Jeez, wasn't that clock ridiculous enough without the sounds of a fire engine roaring down the street with sirens screaming, bells clanging, announcing *this is a five-alarm fire...this is a five-alarm fire*? Why couldn't they have an alarm clock that woke them up to music or sounds of birds chirping? This one reminded him too damn much of his days as a recruit, when the drill instructor would come in at 5:00 a.m. clanging two garbage can lids together as if he was a cymbalist in a classical orchestra.

Ten more minutes, he thought as he put his hands under his head, pointing his toes toward the ceiling while stretching his legs out straight. Helen began to stir, and as she did every morning, moved toward Sam until her head rested lightly on his shoulder.

A smile flitted across his face as he felt her breath moving against the hair on his chest. *It tickles,* he thought as he stroked her head with his hand; he would never tire of the feel of her.

The day the accursed alarm clock entered their lives would always rest in the deepest recesses of his mind; a fleeting memory that he knew would pop up at the most unexpected times and make him smile. *Memories were like that,* he thought. Meant to be a reminder of how very precious each moment was with Helen. It seemed petty to be annoyed over something so small as a Dalmatian driving a fire engine.

There were times when he would worry about how many more years they would have together. What if he lost Helen? How could he manage without his lover, his wife—his best friend?

Rather grim circumstances had brought them together; Helen would say it was destiny. But whatever it was, he would never forget the way they met and the gift of love he received.

Sam boarded the C-17 medical transport plane that would carry Kathleen, along with other wounded troops, from Iraq to Ramstein Air Base in Germany. Injured by "friendly fire" would be the official cause of her injury. Stabbed by a soldier high on drugs? He knew that would never show up in any report. He shuddered at how close he had come to losing his best friend.

He watched with amazement at the way the transport medical staff worked to keep the more seriously injured troops alive. Although Sam had worked the same way as a physician's assistant, it was a surreal experience for him to watch it happening in the air. *Ninety-five percent chance of survival if they made it this far,* he thought. Someone's son, daughter or spouse would be alive because of them. He wondered, *Did the public really know the truth?*

His heart leaped when he saw Helen for the first time. She opened the door to Kathleen's hospital room in Landstuhl, Germany, wearing her teddy bear scrubs. Her hazel eyes sparkled when she smiled, and he felt an immediate attraction when they shook hands. *Damn, and here I thought the days of being thrown completely off balance by a simple touch were long gone.*

They made an instant connection: two lifers who had served

through many wars, each time returning home to find no one waiting for them.

Helen and Sam went to a favorite spot of theirs, a small clearing surrounded by lofty pines at the edge of Palatinate Forest.

They held hands as they walked toward the single picnic table.

"Our lucky day," said Sam. "The weather is perfect and we're alone." Sam took off his backpack and laid it on the table.

He reached for Helen, whispering, "I'm in love with you."

She laughed. "After just three weeks, Sam? Be careful, I don't want my heart broken."

"It's real, Helen. I knew it the minute I saw you."

Helen spoke softly, a slight tremor in her voice. "I think we're way too old to have a whirlwind courtship. I'd like to think of it as more of a gentle breeze."

"Nothing gentle about what's going on between us." He moved closer and took her hand. "Whatever you want to call it as long as it means being together." Sam leaned over and kissed her.

"That's a Category 5 hurricane," she said, catching her breath.

Sam looked down at the ground, and then raised his eyes to meet Helen's. "I've only got one week of leave left. The three weeks have flown by...I know it isn't a very long time, but damn it, I know I'm in love, and I know I want to spend the rest of my life with you."

Helen stroked Sam's cheek. "I do love you, but we know so little about each other. You have to know, I had something happen to me, a long time ago; it's a memory that still hangs around. Not all the time, but at the oddest times. I don't ever want to talk about it. I just want you to know if I seem—" Helen struggled to find the right word "—if I seem *unavailable*, it's not about you."

"I get it. We're not coming into this like a couple of twenty-year-olds. We each have a long history." He became quiet. "I told you I was married once. But I didn't tell you much about it. We barely knew each other, and we had to get married. Marie's her name, and I have a son, Thomas. He wants nothing to do with me. It's also something *I* don't like to talk about. It's old baggage and maybe we have to leave those memories packed away in their suitcases."

Helen said, "I suspect, between the two of us, we've got enough luggage to take us around the world. I'm willing to leave well enough alone if you are."

Sam got down on one knee and took Helen's hand, "Marry me?"

She smiled flirtatiously. "Yes, oh yes, Sam."

And that's where they left it, an agreement not to pry, not to dig into the past.

Sam never told her about the times he would cry when he was alone, remembering a ten-year-old Thomas looking at him with eyes turned hard with rage, and speaking the last words Sam would hear from his son, "I hate you."

Helen wondered why something that happened so many years ago continued to torment her. She had shared her secret with one person, Alice Foster, a perfect stranger at the time. Sometimes, she thought, shame can be so pervasive that there is no place deep enough to hide it or nothing powerful enough to bring it into the open. It felt as if a chip had been placed in her brain and was set to replay a scene from her life when she was fast asleep and helpless to stop the haunting memories.

It was 1980 and Helen's first day as a high school freshman. Her mother drove her to school, kissed her lightly on the cheek, and said, "Remember, no dating and one extracurricular activity required."

Helen hadn't given much thought to dating and wasn't sure about an afterschool activity. She saw the sign-up sheet for the musical production of *Oklahoma!* She had a pleasant voice and sang every week in the church choir. *Why not?* she thought with a shrug and wrote her name down for Thursday's tryouts.

❦　❦　❦

The auditorium was filled with aspiring singers and thespians. Helen had chosen to sing "People Will Say We're in Love." When she was called up to the stage, Mrs. Lawrence, the director, said, "This song is meant to be performed as a duet." She looked at her list of candidates. "Glenn...Glenn Forrester?"

A gangling boy stood up, rubbing the peach fuzz under his nose bashfully with his index finger. He had hit his growth spurt, but his weight had failed to catch up. His thick blond hair was cut short and parted to one side, a sign, Helen surmised, of his conservatism. But his *eyes*. Helen was certain she could lose herself in those deep blue eyes. And the way he smiled—a welcoming lopsided grin that took her breath away.

Mrs. Lawrence said, "Glenn, you're down for the same piece. Why don't you sing it with Helen?"

A wide grin crossed Glenn's face as he gazed at Helen. His reply set the audience tittering. "Shucks, Mrs. Lawrence, it'd be my pleasure."

Helen felt her face flush and wished the earth would open and swallow her up. *God, why was she wearing her white blouse with a peter pan collar instead of her pale rose sweater set? She looked like a child! An absolute child!*

They stood next to each other, their hands occasionally touching as they shared a single copy of sheet music. They didn't sing as if they were playing the parts of Curly and Laurey: They *were* Curly and Laurey. Glenn was awarded the role of Curly and Helen

did indeed find her place in *Oklahoma!*—the chorus just suited
her fine.

In spite of the three years difference in their age, Helen's parents
allowed her to date Glenn as long as they were chaperoned. The
duty and the power fell to her sister, Doris.

"Mother, please!" Helen pleaded. "Hell's bells, this is like going back to the Victorian days. The next thing I know you'll be
fitting me with a chastity belt!"

"Watch that tart mouth, young lady! The next thing *you* know,
you won't be going out at all."

Her mother held her arms out to her. Helen rested her head on
her mother's shoulder. "Ever since you were a baby you couldn't
stand to wait for anything. Be patient, honey—a little bit at a time.
Trust has to be earned."

Helen and Glenn began to map out their life on their third date.
Helen bribed Doris to sit on the other side of Farrell's Ice Cream
Parlor at Ford City Shopping Center.

"You can wear my *special* sweater set one time."

Not one to miss an opportunity, Doris said, "Ha! I'm risking a
month's allowance if we get caught. Three, or no deal."

"Any spots and *you* pay for the dry cleaning. Deal?"

"Deal."

Occasionally, their hands would find their way across the table
and their fingertips would touch.

Glenn cleared his throat to control the crack in his voice. "I'm
certain to get into the University of Illinois. They've got one of the

best colleges of veterinary medicine in the country, and it's only a few hours from Urbana to Chicago. I've been taking advanced science courses so it will only take me six years to become a veterinarian, not eight."

Helen said nothing. She just gazed into the blue wells of his eyes.

"Uh, Helen, there's something else I want to tell you." When she still didn't answer, he plunged ahead. "Helen, I'm in love with you. Will you wait for me?"

Helen heard *that*, all right. She squeezed Glenn's hand in response and mouthed a silent, "Yes."

"I've thought it all out," Glenn said. "We can see each other over the holidays, and maybe at some point your parents will let you visit me at school. Chaperoned, of course. And after I graduate, we can get married and be together during my internships. Helen, will you marry me?"

"Oh, Glenn, of course I'll marry you and I'll wait...for as long as it takes."

They dreamed of the perfect future. The perfect church wedding surrounded by happy friends and family, followed by a small, but perfect, house in the suburbs. Eventually, they thought, having three children would be just— perfect. Everything was discussed in great detail and nothing was left to chance—even down to the number of pets.

"Lots!" they both said. After all, Glenn would be a DVM, and Helen, his loving and doting wife.

Helen discovered that falling in love had opened new doors to a previously unknown talent. She might have been best suited for the chorus of *Oklahoma!* but she found her true calling as a matchmaker. She wasn't sure how it began or where it came from, but after she fell in love with Glenn, she could look at two people and know instantly if they belonged together. It was that certain gleam in their eyes that first caught her attention. After a while, she began to sense their energy fields and if she concentrated, she could see two separate auras connecting and merging into one.

She spent the next three years of high school getting decent grades, enjoying her fame as a matchmaker, and waiting for Glenn's frequent calls and letters.

They became informally engaged, but her mother said, "You are far too young to wear an engagement ring." Instead, Glenn had placed a petite diamond ring on a slender gold necklace and, with trembling hands, closed the clasp around her neck.

Her parents beamed. Her mother said, "When you graduate, you may have Glenn place the ring on your finger."

Throughout the day, she would touch the ring as a reminder of the love they shared.

The years flew by and Glenn came home for Helen's graduation. She didn't finish at the top of her class—her grades were only fair—but she overflowed with kindness and love. Glenn and Helen stood on the quad, surrounded by friends and family. Helen took the ring from her necklace and handed it back to Glenn. He asked her once again, "Helen Martin, will you marry me?"

She didn't hesitate to say yes, and Glenn slipped the ring on her finger.

She thought about college, but Glenn said it might be best for her to get a job, live at home with her parents, and save everything for that day when they would become one.

For the next year, she worked diligently at Weston's Insurance Company. Her first position was opening and sorting the mail. Her supervisor saw how energetic and friendly she was and transferred her to customer service. She liked it there; she could talk easily to customers and, while they were sometimes angry and even nasty, she seemed to have a knack for soothing them.

She was busy, working as much overtime as possible, watching her savings account grow week by week, and planning for their wedding. Glenn's calls and letters began to come less frequently. When he called, he seemed more distant. She asked, "Is everything okay, Glenn?"

"Finals," he said. "I'll be home on the twentieth. Then I'm all yours."

She shared some of her fears with her mother. "Mama, I'm worried about Glenn. His calls...he seems not as close...more distant."

Her mother reassured her. "It's nothing to be concerned about. He's working hard, and that's what a man is supposed to do. You just have pre-wedding jitters."

She fantasized about their reunion. She would see him across a crowded room, his blue eyes focused on only her. As they moved toward each other, he would hold out his arms to pick her up, twirl her around, and kiss her with all the ardor of a lover long separated from his beloved.

Oh my, she thought, how she wanted their children to have Glenn's blue eyes.

❀   ❀   ❀

It was the final fitting of her wedding gown and pre-wedding chatter filled the air. Helen was as beautiful and happy as any bride-to-be. Her face shone with the glow of youth, her eyes sparkled with the eyes of love, and her bright smile dimmed everything around her.

Her mother, bridesmaids, and maid of honor circled around the star of the event. Helen was anxiously waiting for her fiancé Glenn to return home from college, waving his diploma in Doctor of Veterinary Medicine with excitement. The very thought of his broad grin flashing across his face was overwhelming.

"Helen, this is the last time I'm going to tell you," the dressmaker, Mrs. Jensen, said. "If you want the hem to be even, I need you to drop your hands to your sides and stop all this fidgeting."

"Sorry, Mrs. Jensen." Helen dropped her hands, pulled her shoulders back, and tried to keep her head straight.

"Excellent," said Mrs. Jensen. "Now, don't move."

When her sister Doris came flying into the bridal shop, waving a letter from Glenn, Helen felt the weight of worry floating away.

"Open it, open it!" chimed Doris and Helen's mom.

"Not until I'm done with the fitting," she said, wanting to hold onto the excitement for as long as she could. "Oh, Mama, this is the perfect dress. I love the pearl bodice. Do I look fat?" she asked, suddenly frowning.

"Helen, you look like a healthy young woman who is fairly bursting with happiness."

"That means I'm fat. I just know it—I'm fat!"

Mama spoke sharply. "Now you listen to me, young lady. You don't want to end up like your cousin Leticia."

"Leticia?"

"Yes." Mama whispered in her ear, "Aunt Betty found her eating and throwing up. She's in the hospital."

Helen froze.

"And that's not all," Mama continued. Her whispering became softer, so that Helen had to strain to hear.

She whispered back, "What! Before they were married?"

Mama nodded. "You don't want to follow in those footsteps. And someday you'll be a mama yourself. Healthy mothers have healthy babies."

Helen nodded, a little giddy from the adult information that Mama would not have shared in the past. She swelled with pride at the thought of being initiated into the married women's club.

Mrs. Jensen, with pins in her mouth, mumbled, "Stop fidgeting, Helen! We're almost done, if I don't swallow these pins first."

Helen stood perfectly still on the dressmaker's stand, trying her best to imitate Glenn's lopsided grin; she loved him so. *A letter from Glenn!* She couldn't wait to read it.

Struggling up from her arthritic knees, Mrs. Jensen pronounced her lone French word, *"Fin,"* with flair and a wave of her hand. All of her customers loved to hear that word. It was a special gift from Mrs. Jensen and only used after the final fitting.

Helen looked at her reflection; she looked like a bride in every way. Her adolescent acne was gone, her eyes moist and shining, her brown hair had just the right amount of bounce.

Now, she motioned to Doris for the letter. Could anything ever be this grand again?

Hands that shook from excitement fell limp as tears dampened a hastily written note. Not a love letter as Helen had expected, but a brief message telling her that Glenn had fallen in love with someone else. The last line would remain etched in her mind:

I'm sorry, Helen, but it's for the best.
Glenn

❀   ❀   ❀

One part of Helen's wedding fantasies came true. She was the talk of the neighborhood, not because of a perfect wedding, but because she had been jilted. With a figurative scarlet "J" blazoned across her heart, shame now filled the empty crevices where love had once resided. She would have no one alongside her to plan a future or to say the words, "in sickness and in health." There would be no one to take care of her—not now, and, she thought bitterly, not ever. She would learn to rely on the one person she could count on: herself.

Helen enrolled at Chicago State University to receive a BS degree in Accounting. She would work with numbers. She envisioned sitting at a desk in a small windowless room, surrounded by steel-gray file cabinets, a typewriter and a calculator her only friends and company. Could anything be further away from people and the pain they caused?

The years went by and gradually, friends began to stay away—their phone calls went unreturned, wedding RSVPs were mailed back with "decline with regrets" checked. Birth announcements followed, with photos of a new family: mother, father, and infant. All were thrown unceremoniously into the trash can—at first with painful sobs filled with envy; then after a while, methodically, awarded only a quick glance from a woman whose talent as a matchmaker had left her as quickly as it came. She wondered if it was because her heart had turned to stone.

The university was holding its annual Spring Career Fair at Jacoby Dickens Center, a massive athletic building large enough to accommodate the most ambitious of career fairs.

Her class on Resume Writing was canceled and attending the job fair became a mandatory assignment.

Helen packed her Maxine Robinson women's leather briefcase with personalized business cards, a stack of resumes, and pens. She thought, *What a waste of time. I've already got the perfect job.* She had been offered and accepted, an accounting position with the local branch of the Bank of America. What could be a better fit for a jilted bride? She saw herself as an old maid, living in a studio apartment with a hot plate and a cat. Wasn't that the grim fate of every jilted bride who became an old maid?

She would attend the job fair, make a quick pass-through to drop off the required number of resumes, and take in a movie. *Fatal Attraction* was playing at the Rialto. *A perfect title for the story her life,* she thought.

⊛   ⊛   ⊛

It was difficult to recognize the interior of the gym. Helen had to strain to see the bleachers; they had been cleverly hidden behind white and evergreen curtains. A glance at the floor revealed traces of basketball court lines and the stubborn scuff marks of athletes' sneakers.

Helen melted into the crowd, moving from booth to booth, from company to company. Some display booths bragged about all the benefits of being an employee: health insurance, life insurance, vacations, upward mobility, and most importantly, becoming part of a company family. Others had opted for simple tables with trifold brochures showing happy people sitting behind desks or in small offices showing their progression from clerk to occupying an office with their name on the door. Phone companies, insurance companies, and banks—one had a poster showing a woman breaking through the proverbial glass ceiling. While Helen thought "fat chance," she did smile at the recruiter and left her resume. She began to randomly leave her resumes, jotting down the name of the companies, not really interested in any of them, but she did have to write a paper for class, after all.

At the very end of the gym, backed up against the cement block wall was an Army recruiting booth with a banner reading, BE ALL YOU CAN BE. It was a simple booth, with historical recruiting posters pinned to cloth walls and the American flag displayed in a flag stand. The blurb on one poster caught her attention, a woman in a World War II uniform—YOU ARE NEEDED NOW: JOIN THE ARMY NURSE CORPS. Needed now? How long had it been since she was needed by anyone...for anything?

There were three recruiters, two men and a woman. The woman, wearing her green service uniform, held out her hand as Helen approached.

"Hello, I'm Lt. Alice Foster, United States Army Medical Corp."

Helen liked that Lt. Foster's handshake was firm, exuding warmth and confidence. She had never felt a woman shake hands that way.

"I see you're looking at the Army Nurse Corps poster. Kinda draws you in, doesn't it? Five hundred and forty-three women died in the line of duty during World War II. Brave women back in the day. Not only on the front lines, but also having to fight the discrimination of being a woman."

"So many? I didn't know that."

"Most don't."

Lt. Foster looked at the business card Helen had given her. "So, Helen, what brings you here? As you can see, we aren't exactly winning a popularity contest."

Lt. Foster scanned the gym filled with students milling about; occasionally a scowl and a dirty look would float her way. "I'm ready for a break. Want to join me? A bit of lunch? A cup of coffee?"

Alice held up a paper sack. Homemade egg salad on rye. I add chopped olives," she whispered as if giving away a national secret. "And the best cup of java you'll find anywhere."

❀   ❀   ❀

They sat at a table near the concession stand. In spite of the crowds milling about, the potted palms surrounding the dining area gave it an aura of privacy.

Alice leaned back on the white resin low-back patio chair. "Helen, you look like you're carrying a heavy load. Can I share that load with you?"

Helen held onto the Styrofoam cup of coffee and began talking. For the first time since she had been jilted, she talked about her pain, her loss, and her shame. "I feel so worthless, and now I've boxed myself into an office job. Before, I thought I might teach, but now, I just seem to need to be alone."

Alice looked at Helen with piercing eyes. "Sometimes, the way out of our own pain is by helping others. The Army can offer you a career. I can guarantee you'll get the finest training available in nursing."

Lt. Alice Foster's dark brown eyes fixed on Helen's. "Become an Army nurse; you are desperately needed."

Needed? Finally, someone wanted her, needed her. A smile crossed Helen's face. "I do think I've found where I belong."

The happiest day in Helen's life was the day she raised her right hand and swore to uphold the Oath of Enlistment:

"I, Helen Martin, do solemnly swear that I will support and defend the Constitution of the United States against all enemies, foreign and domestic; that I will bear true faith and allegiance to the same; and that I will obey the orders of the President of the United States and the orders of the officers appointed over me, according to regulations and the Uniform Code of Military Justice. So help me God."

In spite of their difference in rank and age, Helen and Alice became good friends. Deployed to different parts of the world, they stayed in touch by letter, phone, and, eventually, email. Everything Alice had told her was true: She was needed. She served in field hospitals in war zones and military hospitals around the world. How many during her first ten years of service? Six? Seven? So many...so very many.

She began to think about what it would be like to return to civilian life and move closer to her family. By now, there were nieces and nephews to love. She could settle down; perhaps buy a small house with a garden. A home of her own with a garden filled with organic vegetables and flowers.

She talked it over with her best friend and mentor, Alice Foster; now Colonel Alice Foster.

"Alice, I'm thinking of not re-enlisting."

"I'm surprised. I always thought of you as a lifer."

"It's the impermanence of it all. And, Alice, I'm starting to see people as body parts. Jesus, I never thought I would say that out loud."

"It happens to the best of us. You've been on the front lines too long; it's time for a change. The Army is like a small town in a lot of ways. Things get around: good and bad. What I've heard about you, the way you are *with* the troops—we'd hate to lose you. What you have to offer is a talent; now let's put it to use. What would you think about becoming a physical therapist? You'll still see the injuries but, with the excellent bedside manner you have with patients, you'll get to see the looks on their faces when they take those first steps or lift a cup to their lips. Whaddaya say, Helen?"

"I say you've got a golden tongue. Sign me up."

September 11, 2001, started out the same as any other day. Helen was finishing her shift at Landstuhl Military Medical Center when news of the attack was announced. They all knew what would follow; it was inevitable. Another war, more casualties, and more pain.

She thought about her life. Fate had stepped in and placed her where she was destined to be. She went from jilted bride to college student to Army nurse, and now a new career as a physical therapist.

From time to time, she would wonder where fate might lead her. She had no idea that one day she would open the door to a hospital room to find a new family waiting for her: Kathleen, Gayle, Robert, and above all, Sam. And that one day, she would find herself guided to a small town in California called Canfield.

❀   ❀   ❀

Helen grunted, opening her eyes just a crack, just enough for a sneak peek at Sam. She liked to watch him that way. She knew if he became aware of her watching, he would also sense her longings and want to make love to her. But not today. Today promised an onerous task; one that she was not looking forward to, not at all.

She moved into Sam's open arms, resting her head on his chest; a sigh signaled that she was waking up.

Sam cradled Helen in his arms. "Today's the day, kiddo," he said, leaning over to give Helen her morning kiss. "Helen..."

"Hmm?" she murmured, wanting the kiss to linger.

"Nothing. Just, Helen."

She pulled Sam even closer, reading his mind. "I know, Sam, I know."

"Sweetheart, I've got to get a run in. Mondays are always so crazy. I'll make it a short one...just to get the kinks out."

"I hope we're doing the right thing, Sam. This, 'cooking your own meals business,' doesn't feel right to me."

"Jeez, Helen. We've talked about this ad nauseam. I thought we were on the same page. We need more time together. I want to be able to take you out to dinner or go away for the weekend without you filling the fridge up for them. If Kathleen and Claire want a relationship, you have to help them grow up. Between you and Gayle, you've created two infants."

"You're right. Two women who have never had their own children, fussing over them like mother hens. Guilty as charged. And as far as Claire's concerned, that's her persona, but don't sell her short. And I love to spoil Kathleen a bit; she's never had a chance to be playful and dependent before. It just seems so close to Kathleen's birthday, and it's such a big one. The big 4-0. Maybe we should put off this announcement until after her birthday."

"Another three months? I want more time with you, and they need to learn how to cook and take care of themselves." Sam's voice softened. "And besides, you're going to do this gradually. You'll see; it'll be fine."

He leaned over to kiss her before getting up and reaching for his Army sweats. "I love it when you're tough. Only you can help these kids to grow up."

Lingering in bed alone was never one of Helen's favorite things to do. *Agh, this is not good,* Helen thought as she threw the covers aside and got out of bed.

❀   ❀   ❀

Sam jogged down the winding driveway toward the road that led to Christmas River. Usually, he fell into a zone; a mind clear of thoughts and worries. Usually, but not lately.

No sirree, he thought. *Ain't gonna happen.* Exactly what his dad would say to a young Sam. He was years and miles from the farm and the fundamentalist church they had attended every Wednesday and Sunday. He hadn't been in a church since he left, except for a few weddings and christenings and all too many funerals. Now, the scenery surrounding him was his church.

He stopped and leaned against a clump of beech trees. Beginning as one tree damaged by a fire years ago, new stems had grown from the roots of the parent tree until a cluster of small trees had formed.

He removed a crumpled letter from his pocket and stared at it, his bottom lip quivering. He heard himself addressing someone he hadn't spoken to in years.

"Lord? It's me. Samuel Hughes. I'm feeling like one of your lost sheep, Lord. I'm struggling with something, and I've got to share it with someone. I've fought in many wars, I've seen hell, and I've looked deep into my soul to accept Kathleen and Claire as a couple. Not too bad for a guy who was raised with so much hatred. I've tried to remove the parts of me that are so angry. But it's so deep and I can't stand the pain. Please tell me what to do...could you send me a sign?" He chuckled. "A burning bush would do. See, I got this letter from my son, Thomas, and I don't know what to do."

He read the letter out loud.

Dad,

I'm writing this letter to ask you for your forgiveness.

I'm in prison for dealing drugs. I won't make any excuses for what I've done.

I've hurt a lot of people and I'm trying to make amends.

I'm sorry I told you I hated you.

I'm getting out in two years. Would you write to me?

Or, even better, come to see me?

Thomas

"I thought after I retired, I'd finally have some peace and love in my life. And now, *this.*" He released the crumpled letter and let it fall to the ground. "A drug dealer for a son and I'm supposed to forgive just like that?"

Sam sobbed, his head resting against the interlaced trees. "Oh Lord, the years have been hard, and I'm so drained of strength. I don't have any more to give. Please, God, show me the way."

CHAPTER 7

"Rise and shine, Superdoc," said Claire, standing next to a half-awake Kathleen.

"Umm..." Kathleen said groggily. "You got up before me."

"There's a first time for everything."

Claire swooped down to kiss Kathleen. "Good morning, love. This is for you."

"Another present? You're spoiling me rotten," she said, shifting her weight and sitting up. "Where did you get this paper?"

Kathleen turned the box in different directions. "Hey, it's made of our photos—places we've been, things we've done." She turned the box over. "Cool! Here's the one when we went to see *Young Frankenstein.* And where did you get this one?"

"You mean the river rafting trip? Someone on shore snapped it."

"Remember how scared you got? You were bawling like a baby."

"Oh, I was just pretending."

"Sure. I love what you've done with the photos," Kathleen said softly.

"Never doubt my creativity."

"*Puh-leeze,* as if that's possible," Kathleen giggled as she rattled the box. "Whatever's in here can't top the paper."

"Open it!" urged Claire.

"I don't want to tear the paper," Kathleen said, moving her fingers carefully around the seams of the wrap, then peeking into the box.

"Take it out, silly."

"It's the red backpack from L. L. Bean! It's perfect! Exactly the one I wanted. Remember the Superdoc cape you gave me?"

Claire said dreamily, "I'll never forget that Christmas. You danced with me for the first time—wearing a tux with tails and a top hat, no less."

"That was really daring of me, wasn't it?"

"I'll tell you what's really daring about you."

"Tell me," said Kathleen, reaching up and pulling Claire on top of her.

"Putting up with my moods."

"Oh, I hadn't noticed," Kathleen replied playfully.

Claire straddled Kathleen. "Jesus, Kath, I get turned on when you sleep naked, but when you're wearing your boxers and tank top, I'm like super-horny. You've become so butch...ummm, let me take that back—*butchette*."

"Flattery will get you everywhere."

"Open the backpack! There's something inside that I think you will really, really like."

"It's heavy. I can tell it's a book. Oh, Claire! Where did you find it? The *Kama Sutra for Us*! Yippee!"

"This relationship," said Claire, "is not going to end in Lesbian Bed Death."

Kathleen began to open the book.

"Uh-uh. No sneak peeks. We're going to start with page one and work our way through together."

"Work? So much for spontaneity."

"So it's spontaneity you want, eh?" said Claire. "Keep digging."

Kathleen glanced at the clock as she dug down and lifted out a soft, tissue-wrapped package. They had an hour before breakfast. She thought, *Who wants to follow a schedule at a time like this?*

A scent of strawberries drifted upward as she began to open the package. An out-of-character thought entered her mind: *Whatever is in here, it's just like Claire to get her favorite flavor when she knows mine is chocolate.*

Kathleen dangled a pair of edible panties in the air. "Oh, my God, it's what I have always wanted, my whole life. But, Claire," she pouted, also a newly acquired characteristic, "I love chocolate, not strawberry."

Claire caressed Kathleen's face, leaning over until their lips touched. She murmured, "Kath, they're not for me to wear. Put them on, put them on!"

They walked downstairs holding hands, pausing every few steps to move closer, to touch their lips. "That was an hour well spent," Kathleen murmured. "Do you think it will show?"

"Ha! As if Helen and Sam are virgins."

"TMI, TMI." Kathleen's stomach rumbled. "Damn, I'm hungry."

"Remind me to ask Santa for a metabolism transplant. It just isn't fair. You can eat anything and stay skinny as a stick, and me, well..."

Kathleen pulled her closer. "Babe, every curve of yours is luscious. You're in a class beyond compare."

"Ha! Just wait until *I* turn forty and blow up."

"Biology is not destiny. Just because your mother was...was..."

"Obese?"

"Doesn't mean you have to be."

"Really, with my metabolism and Helen's cooking? Mmm, I smell breakfast cooking. Oh, Lord, Helen is making chocolate chip pancakes. I don't stand a chance."

"Helen told me this would be a special breakfast because she has a surprise."

Helen was bustling around the kitchen as she did most mornings. The coffee and fresh fruit were on the table; chocolate chip pancakes, melted butter, and pancake syrup were being kept warm in the oven. Sam kissed Helen on her neck, while his hand deftly opened the oven door and reached for a pancake. "Just what I need after my run."

A swift tap on Sam's hand with a bamboo spatula was followed by a scowl and a smile. "Wait your turn, mister. Ladies get served first in this kitchen."

Kathleen hugged Helen. "Those pancakes smell awfully good. And prepared just the way I love them."

Helen sat down and, mindful of her latest diet, placed half a pancake and a cup of fruit on her plate. She glanced at the oven clock. "It is eight—patients will begin to arrive in an hour."

Digging into the pancakes, Kathleen said, "Anything special I should know about?"

Helen went over today's schedule in her mind. "We need to cover several things. First, the Farley family is scheduled for physicals at nine."

"What! The whole family?"

"All seven."

Kathleen stopped eating. "Good Lord, all seven at once?" She began speaking in her take-charge physician voice. "Sam, you take Sloane." Kathleen thought a minute. "He's been on prostate watch. Get a PSA test. Helen, I'll see Lynn. Make sure the room is set up for a full GYN exam. Claire, Lynn needs to be scheduled for a mammogram, and you'll need to follow up with her. Last year she was too busy to keep her appointment. This year, tell her I'll arrange a police escort if I have to."

"What about the unholy five?" asked Claire between bites of pancakes.

"Good luck on that one. Try to keep the office in one piece. Helen, will you get height, weight, eye, and hearing tests on the kids? I'll take the girls. Sam, you get the boys."

Sam stammered. "Three? Three Farleys all at once?"

"They're inseparable. Last year, I did it as a group. That way I only had one exam room to put back together. Sloane and Lynn are fasting. As soon as they walk in they'll start sniffing out breakfast. Don't let them eat a thing while they're here. Oh, and Helen, draw blood as soon as you can."

Helen nodded. "I left a gap until ten. The whole town shudders when they leave their llama ranch and come into town."

"If things calm down at all, Claire, try to hit Brett Garvey's insurance company. I've got to get him into an inpatient weight-loss program. He's at the point of no return."

"I'll sit on 'em." Claire sat back in her chair and sighed. Best pancakes ever. "Helen, where did you learn to cook?"

"By my mother's side. Ever since I was five. If the Farleys haven't put a clog to your digestive system, whose turn is it to clean the kitchen?"

Claire said, "It's Kathleen's. And, Dr. Moore, if you hop right to it, you'll have enough time."

Kathleen groaned.

Claire's brow furrowed and her hazel eyes darkened. "Don't look at me! I cleaned up yesterday."

"Yes, but yesterday we only had bagels and coffee."

"It's still a day."

"Jesus H. Christ," said Sam. "You too are like a couple of squabbling infants."

Helen banged her hand on the table. "Enough! Claire, you take the turn."

Kathleen smiled smugly.

"And this is a perfect time for me to give both of you a very special gift. Dr. Moore, defender of the sick, if your patients only knew. And Claire, the whiz kid at all things except cooking and cleaning."

Kathleen looked at Helen with wide eyes, now filled with mirth—not the eyes of pain that Helen had come to know so well.

Helen handed Kathleen a small package, and Claire a large box.

"I got the bigger one," mouthed Claire.

Kathleen grinned. "For me?"

Helen replied, "*Kath*, you have caught Claire's personality, and I'm not sure it's flattering on you. Actually, they're for both of you; let's say to share."

"Kathleen, you open yours first."

"Oh, Helen...it's your cookbook, *By My Mother's Side*."

"Is my chicken soup recipe in there?" said Claire, putting on bright-yellow dish gloves.

Helen said, "Oh, it's in there all right. Open it to the dedication."

To Kathleen and Claire.
May your adventures include cooking your own meals.

Claire paled. "Seriously? I thought this was one of my employee benefits. I'm afraid to see what's in the other package."

Unable to move and frozen into a position of shock and terror, Claire's hands shook as she tore away at the paper. "A crockpot? This sounds really serious."

"When does this start?" Kathleen croaked.

"I want to give you both time to adjust to the idea. I think after your birthday party in June. We'll have cooking classes once a week, and we'll start with Helen's super-salad. On to the next item on the agenda, Dr. Moore's fortieth birthday party. Sam and Robert will be taking care of the barbeque."

Sam said, "Chicken, hamburgers, and hot dogs. June barbeque food."

"How many are we?" Helen began to count: "We're four...Devon and family, that's five. Linc's coming. And Gayle and Robert, that's three."

"Three? You can't count, woman," said Sam, snatching another pancake before Helen could stop him.

"Yes, three. I spoke to Gayle this morning. Stephanie's coming, too." Helen grabbed the plate from under Sam's nose, his fork still in midair. "You've had enough, Sam. They think it would be good for Stephanie to socialize a bit more. Robert and Gayle will stay with us. Hmmm, Stephanie may be a bit of a problem, though. She's using a walker, and Gayle wasn't sure if she could climb the stairs."

Claire said, "We can put a folding bed in the solarium, unless Sam wants to carry her up the stairs the way he carried me." She looked at him seductively and sighed. "Sam," she purred, putting on an exaggerated Southern accent, "you were exactly like Rhett Butler carrying Scarlet up that long, long staircase."

"Oh, Claire. I learned my lesson about carrying damsels up the stairs. By the way, where was Stephanie hospitalized?" Sam asked.

"Brooke Army Military Medical Center," replied Helen.

"I was assigned to their burn unit. Two years," Sam muttered.

Kathleen looked surprised.

"Before we met, Doc. There are some things we don't like to talk about, not even with our best friends." A dark cloud flashed upon Sam's face. "Let me tell you, Brooke didn't release her without her being able to climb stairs. We'll shadow her, but if she got through Brooke, she'd be strong…Army strong." A memory of the burn unit flashed through his mind, followed by a shudder that went undetected.

Helen said, "And speaking of Army strong—Dr. Moore, there are some rumors flying around town about you and Claire, let's say, getting ready to plant the garden."

"How does anyone know?" said Kathleen, choking on her last bite of pancake.

"This is a small town, and when a certain someone is all dreamy-eyed and starting to buy baby clothes, you can guess the rest. I thought you should know because patients will be asking questions and giving their homespun advice, along with congratulations."

Kathleen glared at Claire, who responded with the sweetest, most innocent smile she could muster, considering she was probably in a shitload of trouble.

"What's that rattling sound?" said Claire, pulling a diversionary tactic.

Sam jumped up. "Good God! They're early."

Kathleen threw a dirty look Claire's way. "Isn't the front door locked?"

"Apparently not," said Helen, just as the kitchen door swung open and five fearless, freckled-faced Farleys—topped with ginger-red hair—appeared. "We smelled pancakes all the way down the road," they said in unison.

Unruffled, Helen automatically reached for five paper plates. "Hold out your hands," she commanded.

The thought of pancakes won over their natural aversion to soap and water. They held out their hands for Helen's inspection.

"The five of you march into the bathroom, scrub those hands with soap, and then, if you pass inspection, you'll get your pancakes."

Kathleen sat at her office desk; she had a few minutes before examining Lynn. Helen had delivered two helluva surprises. Maybe it *was* time for her and Claire to grow up and do their own cooking. But, this baby thing...and now the whole town knew about it. How long had Claire been planning on having a baby? Obviously longer than she had suspected. How could she have been so oblivious to what was going on around her? She remembered the night they had watched *Juno*, but their truce didn't last long and completely fell apart while they were sharing a pint of ice cream.

Kathleen opened the freezer door to get their favorite dessert, Neapolitan ice cream. *Ugh!* she thought. *A 1970s kitchen in a Victorian house.* The attempt to modernize by the previous owners had only served to make the yellow, green, and orange nightmare stand out.

They sat at the kitchen island on mismatched stools found at a garage sale.

"I hate this kitchen," Kathleen said, holding out her hand for the pint of Neapolitan ice cream. Claire passed it. They had been sharing the ice cream for the last ten minutes, keeping in mind their cardinal rule: Kathleen gets the chocolate, Claire gets the strawberry, and they share the vanilla, one teaspoon at a time.

"I can strip the wallpaper," Claire said, referring to the gold, orange, and brown striped wall covering.

"Not good enough," Kathleen groused. "It'll still have the Formica countertops on top of fake wood cabinets. Only an atomic bomb would improve this hellhole."

"I have the solution," said Claire as she finished the last bite of ice cream and passed the empty carton to Kathleen.

Kathleen glanced at the skimpy remnants, performing a final scraping as she raised one eyebrow. "Okay, what's your solution?"

"Simple. We stay out of the kitchen. Helen does all the cooking and *maybe* we can get her to serve us in the dining room; like in the old Victorian days."

Kathleen burst out laughing. "We wouldn't live to see the next meal. No, Claire, when we're out of the red and, really in the black, I want to demolish the kitchen and recreate Canfield House just the way she was—but with modern appliances, of course."

"Sometimes I think you love this old house more than me," Claire pouted. "You want that kitchen more than a baby."

Kathleen stared at Claire, taking her in. A lump began to rise in her throat and she struggled to speak. "That's not fair. There are different ways to love different things. You helped me figure that one out. A baby is not a toy, and it's not a cat, either. I'm just plain not ready."

"When will you be? Six months? A year?" Claire began to push. "I don't want to grow old never having known what it's like to feel life inside me. Maybe you don't care, but I do. I think we're at an impasse. It reminds me of just before we broke up."

"Is that a threat?" Kathleen said defensively, watching the last dribble of ice cream melt and drip from her spoon.

"Not a threat, just a reminder of how damn scared you get. Remember when you told me you didn't know how to do a relationship? Remember how you couldn't come out of the closet? Then when you did, everything was fine. What the hell is this really about?"

Kathleen could feel the ice cream wanting to come back up. "Give me some time, Claire. Let me get my practice built up. There's expenses, and remember, I can't *give* you a baby. We have to get a sperm donor and what if you need in vitro? How do we pay for that? And what if something goes wrong? What if something happens to you? I can't lose you...not again."

Claire pushed her chair back and put her arms around Kathleen. "I can be such an asshole. I don't know how, but we need to get through this. Just keep in mind—tick-tock, tick-tock."

CHAPTER 8

$\mathcal{K}$athleen watched the sun setting as she drove the coast road from St. Mona's. *What a day,* she mused. She would have Claire cancel Lynn Farley's appointment for a mammogram. Lynn was pregnant and her obstetrician would want to make that call. She could only imagine Claire's reaction.

The afternoon was taken up by continuing education on HIPAA compliance and changes in Medicare coverage. Had she heard any of it? Just enough to know that there would be more and more paperwork. *Treatment by numbers,* she thought. *A robot could do it.*

It felt good to see some of her old buddies from the emergency room. Keith Omafu was now chief of the Division of Emergency Medicine. Glenn Marston, physician assistant, had been so impacted by the fire that he had entered medical school to become a pediatric plastic surgeon. And Nancy Wright, the LVN and ER clerk, still ran the ER as efficiently as ever.

She sat next to Cheryl Troop; they hadn't seen each other since that night of the fire when Cheryl appeared like an angel from heaven. Those kids would have never survived if it hadn't been for Cheryl's knowledge of pediatrics and the ability to coordinate transportation to burn centers in Los Angeles.

She thought about the night of the fire, and the way she had slipped into a black hole. She hadn't hurt herself since then, the way she had that night. But, during the most stressful of times, she felt the pull to reach for the scrub pad and alcohol until the pain changed from emotional to physical.

She found her throat tightening and tears began to leak down her cheeks. She reached for a box of tissues, put her hand deep inside, and felt around the sides and bottom hoping to find at least a single tissue. She threw the empty box on the floor and wiped her tears with the back of her long-sleeved shirt.

She wanted to make Claire happy. Was that possible? Would she ever be ready to be a mother?

She thought about how different she and Claire really were. Gayle had once told her that sometimes we are drawn to the person who challenges us, makes us grow. If that was the case, she must be six inches taller.

She was still fuming at Claire for throwing their breakup in her face. Would that be used as a weapon every time she didn't get her way?

She pulled into the gravel driveway, stopping for a moment to gaze at Canfield House with its arched entryway and rounded solarium. It was hard for her to believe it was hers—well, not exactly hers since the bank really owned most of it.

Summers were filled with tourists attending the Festival, shopping along Main Street, or camping along Christmas River. Maps of the area were offered at the old stagecoach stop, now serving as the Visitors Center, an attraction in itself. Tourists would wind their way around the area, much the way Kathleen had done when she first came to Canfield. Some would park on the driveway to take photos of Canfield House, and a few had even asked for a tour.

She *had* fallen in love with a stately Victorian Queen Anne. Did Claire actually see it as her rival? Who would have ever thought that a kid who went through the foster care system would have become a physician with a house that was coveted by many?

The kids who had laughed at her all through school, would they be laughing now? She thought about what Father Andrew would have said, *Pride goeth before a fall.* Her momentary sense of triumph plummeted as she opened the car door and walked up the pathway to the house.

❀　❀　❀

Kathleen was hit by the smell of popcorn coming from the solarium.

"Hi, Kath," Claire's voice greeted her, muffled by the munching of popcorn. "Come here, come here," she said excitedly, "you have to see this! I think I've found a solution to our problem."

"Which problem is that?"

"The tick-tock problem. Sit!" She motioned to the couch. "I made us popcorn." She handed Kathleen the blue-and-white-striped bowl.

Kathleen looked inside. "Thanks," she said sarcastically. "It's empty, unless you want to count the half-popped kernels swimming in that buttery muck at the bottom."

"Sorry, I guess I got carried away. I'll make you your very own as soon as we watch this segment."

"Segment of what?"

"A bit on the grumpy side, are you?" she said, noticing Kathleen's angry expression.

"A bit? More like pissed off. Claire, we have to talk. Seriously, none of the whining shit allowed." Kathleen plopped on the other end of the couch with a disgusted sigh.

"Stop whining yourself and give me your feet!" Claire barked.

"Can I just chill for a minute?"

"Quit stalling. Gimme!"

Reluctantly, Kathleen put her feet on Claire's lap.

"You have beautiful feet," said Claire, taking off Kathleen's shoes and socks. "They match the rest of you perfectly."

Kathleen sighed, giving in to Claire's touch. "Please don't do 'this little piggy.'"

"Relax, I promise not to," said Claire, applying the foot massage technique she had learned in massage school.

"That feels *soooo* good," said Kathleen with a deep cleansing breath.

Claire said, "I think I have found a solution to our problem, and I do admit I have been just a teeny-weeny bit of a nag. So, I happened to flick on PBS, and they have this show on couples counseling with an amazing therapist. Kath, she's created a six-session program for couples that really works! She gets incredible results, and I think we need to resolve this issue before I bust a blood vessel. And the best thing is, if we become members, we'll get a chance to win a free program. Just imagine sitting across from the very famous Dr. Imajean Friend for six whole sessions. It's an opportunity not to be missed!"

"Sweetheart, I am so therapied out. I don't think I can face another therapist."

"You have to admit, we do have this major stumbling block to a complete and idyllic relationship. And her name, Kath...I'm telling you I have really good vibes about this."

"And, what exactly is her name?"

"Dr. Friend. Imajean Friend. Get it?"

"Don't stop rubbing," Kathleen commanded. "Oh, God, Claire. Ima Friend!"

"It's destiny, Kath."

"And how much is the PBS membership?"

"Don't worry; I've already paid for it."

"Aren't you out of money at this point?"

"Just. Bubba sent me a hundred bucks to buy you a birthday present. So, happy birthday, Kath."

CHAPTER 9

*O*majean Friend, Ph.D., sat behind her desk, rocking back and forth, thoughtfully stroking her chin. Dr. Friend had been raised in a rather unusual home. Her father was an engineer, her mother a cognitive-behavioral researcher. Both believed in raising children according to the theory of operant conditioning made famous by B.F. Skinner.

B.F. Skinner was convinced that it was far more productive to study observable behavior than it was to explore the internal world. His operant conditioning theory was based on the concept that rewards increase positive behavior, and losing privileges can reduce or eliminate negative behavior.

When Skinner's wife was expecting their second child, he designed a crib that would create the near perfect environment for the infant and greatly reduce the mother's workload.

The air crib was a metal crib with a ceiling, three solid walls, and a safety glass window that could be lowered to move the infant in or out. The temperature was maintained at seventy-eight degrees, the humidity at fifty percent. There were even built-in toys to keep the infant occupied and stimulated. The air crib was the perfect metaphor for the parenting advice of the day: Don't spoil your baby by too much cuddling.

Imajean was not, as urban legend seemed to insist upon, kept prisoner in the crib. She had a full view of the outside environment, was taken out regularly for holding and playing. And, because the crib was temperature—and humidity—controlled, she could sleep in only a diaper. An expanse of sheeting was on a roller—similar to the roller towels found in gas stations. Her mother only had to turn the roller to have Imajean sleep and play on a clean sheet (after Imajean was removed from the crib, of course).

Her parents were kind, read to her, integrated playtime with educational toys, and kept a very clean house.

Imajean was homeschooled for her first eleven years. When it came time for middle school, her parents felt she needed more exposure to the outside world, and Imajean entered the public school system. She was ready; her parents, ever diligent, had been preparing her for the last two years. She understood it was a difficult transitional time for most of the kids; they did not have the benefits of being raised by parents who believed in childrearing through operant conditioning.

They explained to Imajean that she would have to be very selective in her choice of friends. Imajean complied, choosing only Marilyn Hammer and her twin brother Fred. Marilyn and Fred had also been homeschooled, and they formed a brainy, aloof clique of three. They weren't bullied, because to the other kids they were simply invisible.

One day, they went to the movies and Fred leaned over and kissed Imajean. It felt as if someone had taken a soft piece of unbaked bread dough and placed it against her lips. She said nothing to her mother because there was nothing to say.

A few weeks later, they went to the movies again. And this time, Marilyn leaned over and placed her lips on Imajean's. While Fred's lips felt like unbaked bread dough, Marilyn's felt like freshly baked cinnamon rolls. Once again, she said nothing to her mother because there was nothing to say.

Imajean took school very seriously. Her parents had explained, in a very kind way, that her job was to learn, just as it was Daddy's job to be an engineer and Mommy's job to understand human behavior. Imajean took her task to heart and became the top student in her class. She had one overriding interest outside of school: poetry written by Elizabeth Barrett Browning. After a while, she no longer needed the books—having memorized Miss Browning's every word—but clung to the worn vellum pages as if a deeper meaning would be revealed through touch and sight.

When she first read Miss Browning's poem "A Dead Rose," she thought of herself. A basic instinct seemed to be dead inside her, never to bloom. She was kissed by a boy and kissed by a girl, and yet had no feelings at all. Wasn't she supposed to have the tingling sensations that started inside her head and traveled downward to that special spot between her legs? The kind of feelings that appeared whenever she read poetry?

When those feelings first began, she wondered if she was having a migraine or even a stroke. Then her hand traced the sensations until it drifted to what she came to think of as the magic spot. She knew what it was; hadn't she received an A-plus in physiology? What she didn't understand was how she could only be aroused by poetry and not by a person.

Perhaps, after all, she had been kept in the crib too long.

Imajean followed her mother's path by becoming a research psychologist, working in a laboratory studying the behavior of rats. It was purely happenstance that Imajean became an expert on counseling couples.

She was a doctoral student supplementing her allowance by analyzing dissertation data. She was analyzing a questionnaire when one question popped up with an unheard of positive response rate of ninety-eight percent: *Do you keep secrets from your partner?* She called it to the attention of the author, who simply shrugged her shoulders and said, "I'll be glad when this damn project is done. These dissertations are only exercises in futility."

Imajean thought differently; a ninety-eight percent positive response was downright freakish. The dissertation might be pointless, but the responses to the question were not. After thoroughly checking and rechecking the data, Dr. Friend began to think about secrets. She didn't have a partner and she had never dated, but she had kept secrets from her parents. She never told them about that little device she had purchased and had mailed to a private post office box. The one that late at night after reading a romantic poem would find its way to her magic spot.

She mused, *Even the animals in the lab kept some secrets.* Basic ones, of course, like hiding food to survive. Could humans have simply evolved to a more sophisticated method of survival? And had it now become so complex that it actually worked against the original intent?

She began to obsess about couples and the secrets they harbored. After her long day in the laboratory, she went home to a sparse dinner and spent the rest of the night reading books and research papers on relationships and couples therapy.

Completely enamored by other people's lives, she forgot that she had never had one. After ten years of research and many "first drafts" she published her book: *Six Steps to a True and Honest Relationship.*

Dr. Friend worked with a precise formula, not unlike her research in the laboratory.

Step One: Compare and discuss your top five concerns.

Step Two: Explore healthy communications.

Steps Three and Four: Individual sessions on sharing your secrets.

Step Five: Discuss the outcome from sharing your secrets.

Step Six: Plan for the future.

She found it worked. Statistically, eighty-five percent of her couples reported an improvement in their relationship following her treatment program. It wasn't long before her grateful clients began to refer to her by the genial sobriquet of Dr. Ima Friend.

❀   ❀   ❀

Her book had been on the *New York Times* best seller list for ten weeks, inching its way up until it was in third place. PBS Santa Barbara contacted her for a guest appearance. It would be her first public presentation, but she felt ready to share her find with the world.

❀   ❀   ❀

Dr. Friend dressed in one of her nicest outfits: a stone-colored, long-sleeved blouse, dark-gray slacks, and sensible pewter-colored leather loafers. When she walked into the studio, Julie, the makeup artist, turned pale as a sheet.

"Oh dear, matchy-matchy won't work. You'll fade into the gray background. Sit here," she said, motioning to the red salon chair.

Julie stood with her hand on her chin, studying Dr. Friend as if *she* were a rat in a laboratory.

"You have lovely hair, Doc," said Julie, running her hands through it with a professional's detached adroitness. "It's thick, with just the right amount of wave. If we part it on the side, like this—now, your high cheekbones show."

Dr. Friend never knew she had high cheekbones or that her hair was anything but something that sat on top of her head.

Julie became the grand-wizardess, moving quickly between the array of cosmetics and Dr. Friend—blending, applying, dabbing, sponging, and brushing. She stood back and smiled.

"Well, I'll be!" exclaimed Julie. "You look a bit like Audrey Hepburn."

Dr. Friend had no idea who that was, but knew she was being complimented, and dutifully smiled—despite her distaste for having her face used for this woman's blank canvas. And those ticklish tools! She didn't like to think what unsanitary conditions they'd probably seen.

Julie leaned against the counter, gazing at Dr. Friend, "You need something to offset all that gray."

Julie removed her Diane von Furstenberg ombré scarf, in shades of light pink to purple, and placed it around Dr. Friend's neck. Dr. Friend shuddered at the thought of something going from a stranger's skin to *her* skin without being thoroughly washed or dry-cleaned. She made a mental note to take a very hot shower when she got home and to pay particular attention to the germs that might be lurking on her neck and in her hair.

When she saw herself in the mirror, though, Dr. Friend had to admit she liked what she saw.

"What did I tell ya?" said Julie proudly. "Audrey Hepburn, right?"

"Er...right."

"The scarf is yours to keep," said Julie. "Good luck on the show."

Her presentation was a hit and the list of new subscribers to PBS went over the station's goal. PBS was thrilled and so was Dr. Friend. Now, she had to pick the lucky winners. She took a pen, closed her eyes, and began to move the pen round and round, ready to let it fall where it may. She stopped suddenly and looked at the list. Why leave something as important as this up to chance?

She studied the names and addresses. One couple popped out: Dr. Kathleen Moore and Claire Hollander. Kathleen Moore, that name was familiar. Ah, it was at St. Mona's Winter Fundraiser. They were sitting at the next table and looked as if they were having fun. She had watched as they danced together, then, when they got back to the table, the shorter one took off her shoe and was playing footsie. The dark-haired one, which she now presumed was Dr. Moore, pretended annoyance, but didn't push her foot away. And she had that look in her eyes, the kind that said *wait until I get you home.*

The physician sitting next to Dr. Friend pointed them out. He confided quietly, "That's Canfield's beloved doctor, Kathleen

Moore. She used to work here in the ER, then had some kind of a collapse—a flashback to having been wounded in Iraq, or so the gossip goes. A big loss for St. Mo's. And her partner, Claire Hollander." He had lowered his voice but couldn't help from chuckling. "One of a kind...one of a kind!"

She circled their names. Satisfied that she had made the best selection. Dr. Imajean Friend picked up the phone to call the lucky couple.

CHAPTER 10

$\mathcal{K}$athleen took a quick shower, debated about using makeup, and ended up using just a tad. She had laid out her going-to-see-Dr. Imajean Friend outfit on the bed: a pair of silk-like black slacks, a soft white shirt, and a cashmere poncho, in a neutral ecru called Campiollo.

Claire was waiting downstairs, fuming. She was wearing hiking boots, jeans with holes in the knees, and a light-blue cable sweater.

Kathleen thought, *Well, aren't you the dyke in training.*

Claire thought, *Back in the closet, eh, Dr. Moore?*

They hugged briefly, exchanging the phoniest of pleasantries, "You look nice."

"Did you send in your intake form?" asked Kathleen casually as they made their way to the car.

"Of course. Why would you doubt me? And what about you, Ms. Perfect? Early, I bet."

"On time. Let's stop this snarling at each other, okay? Jesus, I can hardly wait to get into Dr. Friend's office."

"You and me both, sister."

They drove in silence, taking the narrow, winding road from Canfield toward Santa Barbara. They reached the coastal route just as the sun dipped below the horizon. It was a moonless night, and the only light came from the few stars peeking through the cloud cover. The black highway stretched like an endless tunnel before them.

Claire rested her head on the window, gazing at her reflection. "I have PMS," she said, half to herself.

"I'm sorry," said Kathleen, not unkindly.

They were silent for the rest of the trip, each lost in their own thoughts.

Am I being unreasonable? We've broken up once, and I told Claire then I didn't know how to do a relationship. I'm so sorry I've hurt her, but a baby? And is this how she'll be every time she doesn't get her way?

Claire's mouth quivered. She hated being this angry with Kath. *I think I'm just crazy. My mother always screamed at me,* "Mashugana," *one of the six Yiddish words she knew.* "You're crazy!" *Maybe my mother was right. I wouldn't blame Kath if she told me to pack my bags and get out.*

They used the after-hours entrance. The guard sat at a small table in front of the door and buzzed them in. He turned the visitors book around for them to sign; they signed their names on separate lines.

"Fifth floor," said the guard.

They were two strangers standing at opposite ends of the elevator.

Claire pushed the button that would send them to the fifth floor. *I'm not budging. If it's no baby, it's no Claire.*

Kathleen shut her eyes and leaned her head against the wall. *Another one of Claire's screwball ideas. And if she throws a tantrum, I'll be the one to walk out.*

They watched as the floor light indicator lit up: two, three, four, five. The elevator gave two bumps before it settled down and the door opened.

The stale air from the sealed building hung over them like a shroud. They followed the signs pointing to Dr. Friend's suite, walking on cheap tweed carpeting past oak-stained doors with plaques announcing the name and specialty of the tenant. One office after another: physicians, accountants, dentists, psychologists, social workers, and marriage and family therapists.

This is how we run our world—compartmentalizing everything from our neuroses to our taxes, thought Claire, whose cold feet were turning to icebergs. *Back in the day, my bubba would sit us down with a bowl of chicken soup, give us a bop on the head and say, "What's wrong with you two?" I want my bubba.*

Except for the plaque next to her office door, Dr. Friend's suite was indistinguishable from the others. While other tenants had chosen a soft script, Dr. Friend had selected bold, square lettering. When she had rented the suite, some ten years earlier, the office manager had tried to convince her that a soft script would be more welcoming.

"Lucida Calligraphy is very *friendly*, Doc," he said, pleased with his play on words.

His pun went unnoticed, and Dr. Friend simply stated, "Copperplate Gothic fits my product."

Kathleen opened the office door to the waiting room.

"Do you want me to press the call light?" Claire said with a quiver in her voice.

Kathleen shrugged and sat quietly on one of the Naugahyde chairs. She absentmindedly thumbed through a shabby *National Geographic* from two years ago. Claire sat staring into space.

Dr. Friend opened the door to her inner office. Tall, thin, and angular, she towered over Kathleen and Claire, her spindly limbs suggesting a bare tree in the dead of winter. "Hello," she said, peering over her tortoise shell half-glasses. Kathleen noted that her left eye had a slight drift.

She was wearing all brown except for the ombré scarf, which now seemed to be plastered to her neck.

No flair, thought Claire.

Nice. Understated, but nice, thought Kathleen.

Dr. Friend's office was as monochromatic as her wardrobe. She had selected an ergonomic adjustable-height desk that could, at the touch of a button, be moved up to accommodate either a standing or sitting position. There were two taupe leather recliners that afforded perfect lumbar and neck support, and a single brown-and-beige tweed sofa with throw pillows in ecru and dark brown. She thought she did nicely with the paint, having selected a color called neutral sand.

Claire and Kathleen sat on the tweed couch, as far apart as they could, each leaning against one arm.

Glancing around the office, Claire thought, *Sterile!*

Neat and orderly, were Kathleen's observations.

Dr. Friend started out conversationally. "Did you find the office okay?"

Kathleen nodded. "Yes, your directions were excellent."

"How was the drive from Canfield?"

Claire stifled a yawn.

"Just a bit under an hour," Kathleen replied. "No traffic this time of night. And thank you for seeing us this late."

Nodding, Dr. Friend turned to Claire. "Claire, I understand it was your idea to put your name in the hat, so to speak."

Suddenly overwhelmed by her aching heart, Claire blurted out, "I think we're in real trouble, Dr. Friend."

"I'm so sorry to hear that," the doctor said sincerely. "My goal is to work with you and see if we can't get past the main issues that are causing your distress. I work on the premise that each person in a relationship may be holding onto a secret or secrets that have not been shared with their partner. Hiding parts of ourselves does not mean that it has disappeared. It only means it has gone underground and may keep us from having a full and intimate relationship."

Dr. Friend paused. "Having said that, I do not believe that all secrets should be shared. What you disclose to me, or with each other, is going to be your decision."

Dr. Friend laid Kathleen and Claire's intake information on her otherwise bare desk. "Thank you for sending me your Top Five Concerns. I find that by having them early, I can gain an understanding before we meet. I must say I was taken by yours. Number one and number three were identical. That's a very good start," she said encouragingly.

"The others varied to a degree, but not to a large degree. Number one was about whether or not you would have a child. And number three was about—"

Claire and Kathleen both muttered, "Ice cream."

"Yes, ice cream. A bit unusual, but apparently critical to the well-being of your relationship. Did you discuss or share the Top Five with anyone?"

Kathleen shook her head, a single tear rolling down her cheek.

Claire said, "I shared with Oscar." She reached for a tissue.

"And Oscar is?"

"My cat."

Kathleen began to cry.

"Kathleen, if your tears could speak, what would they be saying?"

"When Claire and I broke up, she left Oscar with me. I took care of Oscar, and he slept with me. I thought he was *my* cat, too."

Dr. Friend was intrigued. "Go on."

"If—and it's a big if...will a baby be *ours*? Or just *Claire's* baby? Claire can't share. It's like the chocolate graham crackers. *Someone* gets up in the middle of the night and eats the last one and then leaves the empty box with only a few crumbs in the bottom."

"Oh yeah, and what about the ice cream?" snarled Claire. "I saw you sneaking into the strawberry when you were supposed to be eating chocolate."

"As if you weren't double dipping into the vanilla."

"And what about being forced to fix dinner?"

Dr. Friend scanned the list.

"That was number four on Claire's list and number five on Kathleen's."

Claire looked up at Dr. Friend. "And that was Sam's doing."

Kathleen nodded. "Helen would have never done that on her own. And here I thought Sam was my best friend."

Claire said, "By the way, Dr. Friend, would you like to purchase one of Helen's cookbooks, *By My Mother's Side*? All profits are going to Canfield's annual festival."

"Of course, I'd be happy to, but let's not get sidetracked off the subject."

"Claire's famous for that," Kathleen mumbled under her breath.

"What did you say?" roared Claire, rising up off the couch.

Dr. Friend thought, *I'm breaking new territory with these two. I can see a second book hitting the* New York Times *best seller list.*

"Could you tell me more about being forced to cook your own meals?" Dr. Friend asked, noticing perspiration was beginning to gather in her armpits.

Claire replied, "Having meals prepared by Helen was one of my employee perks and now... *Now* we're going to be *required* to cook our own meals and Kathleen can't cook *at all*."

"*I* can't cook? You can cook one thing and that's usually sent to you *frozen* by Bubba."

Dr. Friend, bewildered at the fast turn in the conversation and her loss of control over her very well thought-out process, thought back to a textbook she had read on layers of feelings. "I do believe I see glimpses of your caring beneath the anger. And did you know that anger could be the symptom of pain from the past?"

Dr. Friend spoke very seriously, "Secrets, Claire and Kathleen, are like cancer, working beneath the surface. I think you both care about each other deeply, and I suspect that under the anger is pain, and under the pain lies a deep, dark secret."

Looking unobtrusively at her watch, she breathed a quiet sigh of relief. *Thank God,* she thought, *the hour is almost over.*

"This has been a most productive session, and our next appointment will focus on healthy communications. I'd also like to schedule your individual sessions. I want to see you both on the same day, and I must caution you not to discuss your private session until after I have met with each of you. Kathleen, evening appointments seem to work best with your schedule. What about you, Claire?"

Kathleen nodded and Claire said, "Anytime during the day will be fine."

Dr. Friend wrote down the dates and times and handed them plain black-and-white appointment cards. "My, but the hour does fly, doesn't it?"

"Tick-tock," said Claire.

Kathleen snarled, "One more tick-tock out of you..."

Dr. Friend stood up. "Before you leave, I want to see you hug, and when you hug I want you to say to each other, 'I'm a friend.'"

Claire's eyebrows shot up. "*Seriously?*"

"Yes, seriously," responded Dr. Friend. "It's about closure. A nice hug and look at each other and say, 'I'm a friend.'"

They hugged, tentatively at first, and then as they felt the warmth from their embrace, they relaxed, melding into familiar curves.

They looked in each other's eyes.

Kathleen had forgotten how Claire's eyes sparkled with mirth and how her lashes curled.

Claire noticed the way the color of Kathleen's eyes dulled when she was hurt and brightened when she was happy.

Kathleen murmured, "I'm a friend."

Claire put her head on Kathleen's shoulder, taking in a scent that swelled her heart. "I'm a friend, too."

Holding hands, they said good-bye to Dr. Friend with a very friendly wave. They got as far as the hallway and then burst out laughing.

"God, that felt good!" said Kathleen.

"Wanna stop at the ice cream parlor? We should get a pint of each flavor and eliminate that item from our list. What else was on your list?"

"Not telling. But it had to do with popcorn kernels."

CHAPTER 11

Claire settled into her yellow Bug for the hour drive to Dr. Friend's. She tried to concentrate on the road, but her mind drifted to the stash of baby clothes hidden in the spare bedroom that doubled as her office. Sometimes, late at night, after Kathleen was in a deep sleep, she would sneak out of bed, cross the hallway to the bedroom, and open the dresser drawers where the clothing was tucked away under her T-shirts and sweaters. She would lift them out, one by one, holding them against her cheek, feeling the softness of the material, and imagining how their baby would look in them.

Claire smiled at the thought of dressing their little boy or girl in the green onesie with yellow teddy bears. She could feel the warmth of its tiny body, the fragrance of that sweet baby scent. She could see a chubby infant with big wide eyes and hair...her fantasy stopped suddenly—not as curly as hers, she hoped. The fantasy began again. A chubby infant slept peacefully in her arms, a halo of ringlets falling loosely around its face. *Much better,* she thought.

She wasn't sure how or why this obsession began. Perhaps it was seeing one patient after another coming into the office, a wide grin plastered on their face and one hand on their tummy. She only knew that once it started, it had a life of its own.

"I'm going for a drive to Santa Barbara," she announced casually one Saturday. Kathleen was sitting at her desk, surrounded by files, taking notes, updating charts, and returning phone calls. She nodded and returned to her paperwork. No one would think it was out of character; they all knew how Claire loved to scour the thrift shops looking for the "find of the century."

"Not much luck today," she said upon returning, showing them something that she had bought to camouflage her real finds secreted in the trunk of her yellow Bug. It wasn't long before she stopped going to the thrift stores; after all, *their* baby would deserve the very best. Now, she strolled boldly down State Street joining the crowds of shoppers going in and out of high-end infant wear and toy stores.

She became more daring and went into the Baby Makes Three store in Canfield. "All my friends are having babies," she said, oblivious to how thinly disguised her cover-up really was.

The store clerks knew Claire and they knew Kathleen—how could they not, since they were practically joined at the hip—and the look in Claire's eyes led them to reach for their phones and share the latest gossip.

She mused, *So, now Kath knows and she hasn't shown a bit of interest in seeing our baby's layette—all the way from newborn to twelve months sizes.*

Completely lost in her thoughts, she took the wrong turnoff to Dr. Friend's office.

Claire looked at her watch. Damn, ten minutes late for her appointment. She bypassed the elevator and dashed up five flights of stairs. She was panting and felt her heart racing when she opened the door to Dr. Friend's office and pushed the call button.

Dr. Friend, half expecting a last-minute cancelation, breathed a sigh of relief. She had become unusually attached to Claire and Kathleen; not at all like her, and probably not in the best interest of helping them through their dilemma. She had heard many couples bickering over small and what might seem unimportant issues to the untrained mind. It was the way they interacted when they did their "I'm a friend" hug that allowed her to see true love. The way they clung to each other, she could tell their love was deep. It didn't predict success, though...no, success would come from them being able to trust each other and work through the shame of their secrets.

A welcoming but inscrutable smile crossed her face as she opened the door and made eye contact with Claire.

In spite of her anxiety at being late—and dreading a psycho-babbly interpretation of *why*—Claire scanned Dr. Friend's outfit. A navy-blue suit with a navy-blue mock turtleneck and sensible navy-blue shoes.

I'll have to take her shopping, Claire thought. She had taken Kathleen to the discounted designer clothing store, the Dungeon before their Christmas party. If it could work with Kathleen, it could work with Dr. Friend. Claire's mind began to race with thoughts of a transforming color scheme.

Claire blurted out, "I'm sorry I'm late. I got confused and took the wrong exit."

Claire settled into one of the recliners. *I shouldn't have said that. OMG, will she make an interpretation?* She liked Dr. Friend, but she couldn't help but wonder what she had gotten herself—and Kathleen—into.

Dr. Friend smiled benignly and sat opposite Claire. She leaned over toward her side table and straightened the already anal-retentively straight pens and pads of paper.

Monochromatic and OCD, Claire thought, pleased with her diagnosis. She noted that Dr. Friend was wearing the same ombré scarf. Claire had a fleeting thought: *Is that the only scarf she owns? I should have brought her a present. A different scarf, but what colors?*

Claire began to relax into the comfort of the recliner. She knew how therapists worked and she would play the game, only telling Dr. Friend what she wanted to hear. She wanted an A-plus in Dr. Friend's class, and she wanted a baby. She would use all her God-given wiles to win her over.

"Claire, I noticed in your intake that you have been in therapy before."

"Yes, when I was twelve and my father died. And, more recently, I joined a support group at the LGBT center."

"Can you tell me what it was like for you after your father died?"

"I was always pretty chubby, but I became a compulsive overeater. I discovered a stomach could hold an entire Boston cream pie."

Dr. Friend's eyes widened.

"And my grandma and my mother had lots of fights over me, and then I was sent to a fat kids camp for the summer." She added defensively, "But I worked all the steps."

"The twelve steps?"

"No, Elisabeth Kübler-Ross's steps, one after another: denial, anger, bargaining, depression, and right into acceptance."

Claire chose her most seductive smile, the one she hoped said, *I'm okay. I'll be a terrific mom.*

Dr. Friend rocked slightly back in her chair. She reached for her cup of tea and took a sip. She closed her eyes for a moment. "Elisabeth was a courageous woman. She went where others feared to go, into the deepest emotions of death and loss. Fear can keep us trapped," she mused. "And most of us carry at least one secret that we keep to ourselves; sometimes not even remembering it for years at a time—a secret with immense power over us and our relationships. It poisons love and destroys the most important thing in our life, our ability to love unconditionally."

Dr. Friend was surprised to hear the depth of her own interpretation. Never having had a relationship or real friends, perhaps it was all those years spent reading love poetry that gave her the ability to identify with Claire. Clearly, it couldn't have come from watching all those rats trying to find their way through mazes.

Claire felt the color drain from her face. She hoped Dr. Friend didn't notice. "I'm the most open person you will ever know. I like to tell it like it is—straight out. No secrets in my life." She forced a smile.

Dr. Friend rocked back and forth. "Hmm." She repeated the pensive utterance until it became a soft, sweet melody that seemed to send a message directly to Claire's heart.

"Everyone keeps some small secrets," said the doctor at length. "And after all, why not? The secrets that I believe are damaging to your relationship are those that fill you with shame."

Claire could feel her breathing change. Not meditative breathing, but shallow breathing followed by flashes of unwanted memories.

"Um, I'm feeling a little queasy. Is it okay if I stop early?"

"You've only been here for ten minutes."

"Ten?" Claire wiped her brow with a tissue. "Dr. Friend, when you talked about the importance of confidentiality, you really meant it?"

"Yes, with the exceptions we discussed earlier."

"Child abuse, elder abuse, danger to self and others?"

"Yes, and you do have an outstanding memory."

She's on my side! She likes me...she really likes me.

"So you won't accidently leak it to Kath? I mean, I really get it that secrets can harm a relationship. But, I've really worked this one through. It's in the past...the far past. It happened so long ago." Claire wiped away a tear.

"I do believe that secrets shared with that special person in our lives can deepen the relationship. It can be a risk, and it means you will have to fully put your trust in Kathleen. It will be up to you to decide if you feel safe enough to share your secret with her."

Claire's lips drooped and began to tremble. "I haven't told anyone because it was kinda my fault. You see, I was the chubby kid that made people laugh. My bubba overfed me—in my bubba's time, a fat kid was a healthy kid. The kids in school called me Tubby the Tuba. Then in third grade, I found out I could make people laugh. I used to sing this song, 'Pickle in the Middle with

Mustard on Top.' And I would tap dance, and everyone would laugh, even the teachers. I was the class clown."

"Interesting. It is said that clowns are funny on the outside and sad on the inside."

"I never liked clowns. They scared me. My bubba took me to the circus once, and I cried the whole time. That was before I went to clown school," she added.

"Clown school?" Dr. Friend's mind reeled.

"Umm, Dr. Friend, are you a hypnotherapist, because I think I'm about ready to spill, and I want to know if you have me under some kind of spell."

"No, Claire. No spell, I think you are just ready to...umm...to *spill*, as you say."

"Maybe, because I want to do everything to make this work between Kath and me. Okay, take a big breath and start spillin'."

Claire leaned forward in her chair, her eyes focused on the floor.

"I went to Brooklyn College to become a teacher. I used to drink a lot back then. I was really a goofy kid who just wanted to have fun. I had lost all that weight and guys started paying a lot of attention to me—flirting, asking me out."

Dr. Friend kept a stoic expression. *No, I really don't know.*

"I was pretty smart and the classes weren't hard for me. Statistics, maybe, but the rest of them, I could coast through. We used to spend Friday and Saturday night bar-hopping. I would sleep in on Sunday and recover."

Claire reached for a tissue and dabbed her eyes. "This particular Friday night, we were at our favorite bar, Sam's Joint. It's a real dump and packed to the rafters on a Friday night. I had two margaritas and the night was still young."

She looked up staring at the wall where Dr. Friend's diplomas and academic certificates were neatly lined up. *Could someone who is so obviously the poster child for obsessive-compulsive disorder have a clue about getting out of control?*

"I'm not much of a drinker now," she said ashamedly. "I mean,

Kath and I have a small glass of wine with dinner sometimes, but that's about it. Live and learn, I guess."

Claire's eyes moved from the wall to Dr. Friend.

Dr. Friend's expression remained neutral. Her only movement was the pencil occasionally gliding across the pad of paper resting on her lap.

Claire breathed in deeply. *Shit, no clue about what this shrink is thinking.*

"Well, this guy came over to me and we started talking. Just idle chitchat and pickup talk, and I thought he was cute. He had on Dockers and a long-sleeved brown cashmere sweater and brown loafers. I'll never forget the way he looked—squeaky clean, not the kind that usually hung out at Sam's Joint. The kind I could bring home to meet my grandma. We talked a lot about our interests. He told me he was majoring in business, and I told him I thought I would teach history.

"I've had lots of thoughts about doing different things. I've got a license to teach and certificates as a masseuse and a dog groomer. Never could stick to one. I feel like a failure," she added with a shrug. "Well, back to my story. Sam's was getting more crowded and wild, and it was getting late. I told him I'd be right back, to save my place, and went to the bathroom. The bathroom line was super long."

Claire paused to blow her nose. "I was gone for about fifteen minutes. When I came back, he stood up and held my chair. He was a complete gentleman. I finished my drink, and then he said, 'May I drive you home?' I thought that was so sweet.

"I stood up, and suddenly I felt really woozy. The room was spinning, and he took my arm and said, 'Time for you to head on home.' I couldn't talk; my tongue was thick, and my words wouldn't come out. I remember stumbling to his car. He held my arm and helped me up the steps and into the elevator. I was all confused. I thought I was home, but it didn't look like my apartment."

Claire began to sob. "Oh God, this is really hard to say."

Dr. Friend stopped jotting down her occasional note. She knew that any movement on her part could disturb the space that Claire had entered.

After a moment, Claire's sobbing became gasps and gradually stopped. "When I woke up, I was lying in a strange bed—naked. I had bruises on my breasts and thighs and bleeding from... I looked...I looked as if I had been, had been..."

"Raped?"

Claire began sobbing. "It was my fault. The apartment was empty. I saw a note on the nightstand: *Had a great time. Be gone by 3:00 p.m. My wife will be home by then. Here's money for a cab.* There were two twenties next to the note. I threw on my clothes and went home. I soaked and I scrubbed, and I knew I couldn't tell anyone. And I couldn't feel clean.

"My periods have always been irregular, so it wasn't unusual for me not to have one. Six weeks later, I started feeling queasy. Sick to my stomach. I went to the women's health center at school."

Claire wrapped her arms tightly around her chest, tears flowing freely down her cheeks. "This hurts...this really hurts. I didn't know what else to do. Twenty years old...a man I didn't know... It would have been a *shanda.*"

Dr. Friend looked at her quizzically.

"A scandal. A black mark on the family. Bubba would have been so ashamed." Claire looked up, her eyes widening in spite of the tears.

"I had an abortion and now I want a baby...and Kath really doesn't. And now, I buy baby clothes and sneak them in. She hasn't even asked me about what I bought or wants to see them. I think she's too scared and worried about money, and I know she can't rest until she finds the twins she got separated from. I get that, but I think God is punishing me. At the time I had the abortion I thought, it's only bits of tissue. Now I think I took a life— my baby's life."

"That's a very painful secret to have carried alone for all these years. I want to thank you for trusting me with it."

Claire reached for a tissue and blew her nose loudly. "God, Kath is going to know I've been crying. My nose is going to look like a circus clown's!"

"I doubt it," said Dr. Friend, her voice softening. "It seems to me, that part of your wanting a baby is to heal the past. But, I'm wondering, are there other reasons?"

Claire stopped crying and looked up, her eyes connecting directly with Dr. Friend's. "I want a baby because, because...we'll be a real family."

Dr. Friend nodded. "That is a perfectly normal and unselfish desire, Claire."

"Is it? Kath doesn't seem to think so. Oh, Dr. Friend, sometimes I feel so bad about the abortion. I wonder what the baby would have been like. He or she would be a teenager now. I took its life, and I don't think God will ever forgive me."

Dr. Friend leaned forward in her chair. "You've blamed yourself all these years?"

"I should have known better."

"Did it ever occur to you that you were drugged?"

Claire hung her head. "No," she spoke softly. "I don't know why, it never occurred to me."

"It makes me wonder if you don't blame yourself for other things that happened in your life, too."

"Things?"

"In your intake, you described a great deal of turmoil in your home between your mother and grandmother—your bubba as you call her. And your father?"

Claire became thoughtful. "The fights between my mother and my grandma were about me...and my dad, he did drugs, but I know now he had PTSD from serving in Vietnam."

"I want you to think about this in a different way, Claire. What were they really fighting about? Was it really about you? Or were you the camouflage? Sometimes one person in the family is selected to be the center of negative attention. Instead of dealing with the pain, the family feels safe by focusing on one person and laying the blame there."

"You mean like a scapegoat?"

"Exactly like that."

Dr. Friend lifted her tea from the cup holder, moving her thumb slowly up and down the handle. She became lost in her own feelings. She had never felt such an overwhelming sense of compassion for another human being. She felt a tremor in her lips when she spoke.

"You're not a bad person, Claire. You did the best that you could at that moment. Sometimes we need to forgive ourselves so that we can move on and forgive others."

"Do you mean I need to forgive myself so I won't be so pissed off at Kath for little things? Like swiping the last spoon of ice cream?"

"Something like that...something like that."

Claire slipped into the bathroom, shutting the door quietly behind her. She looked at her reflection; her usual smile was absent, the corners of her mouth drooping. A feeling of sadness and unworthiness traveled throughout her body and settled in her heart. She could see the pain in her eyes; the gold flecks that sparkled through her hazel eyes had faded. The painful, overcast look reminded her of her mother. She had worked to develop the one side of Claire; the part she wanted everyone to see. The one that told funny stories, danced and sang, and made people laugh. She wanted to hide the other Claire, the woman who was filled with painful memories of a mother whose eyes never shined with a look of love.

Was it her fault? She had flirted with that man in the bar. He seemed friendly, safe. They liked the same things. She had no reason to distrust his motives, and when he offered to take her home, she thought... No, she *didn't* think—and that's what was making her so angry.

And what about the baby? It was a mere fleck of inchoate life, but no one could deny it would have been a human being.

She stared at her reflection. *Oh, snap, I'm beginning to look like my mother!* Her eyes were shaped the same way, and her hair had the same amount of curl. Did that mean she was like her mother? *After all, she did have her DNA.*

She remembered something some of her psychology friends would chant and laugh about: "Mirror, mirror on the wall, I'm like my mother after all."

CHAPTER 12

$\mathcal{K}$athleen opened the door to Dr. Friend's waiting room. *What a name*, she thought. *Did she become a therapist because of her name or in spite of it?*

Oh, well...Dr. Friend was her third therapist: first Gayle, while she was a student at UCLA, then Kevin after she and Claire had broken up, and now Dr. Friend. No first name here. A cure in six sessions? She chuckled out loud. Not much could happen in *only* six sessions. Why, she was almost a professional patient, possibly only second to Woody Allen. *A piece of cake*, she thought.

Her childhood had been filled with distortions, fantasies, and secrets—lots of secrets. Gayle had reminded her more than once, "It's a means of survival and not out of the ordinary for children trying to cope in a stressful environment."

That changed when Claire came into her life. When she and Claire would go to bed, they would wrap their arms around each other—two women in love, their bodies so closely meshed, that feelings and memories would change into words to be shared with complete and utter trust.

She had told Claire almost everything. It was the *almost* that was beginning to bother her. Could Dr. Friend be right about keeping secrets?

❀   ❀   ❀

Kathleen sat on the couch across from Dr. Friend.

Dr. Friend asked, "How was your day?"

"Very long and difficult. A patient died this morning," she said softly.

"I'm so sorry."

"It was a long battle. I've seen a lot of death, in Iraq and now. And my father."

"What about your father?"

"He committed suicide."

"How old were you?"

"Nine. That's when I got into the foster care system."

Dr. Friend wrote the number nine on her pad. She gazed at the number. *So young.* She looked at the woman sitting across from her. Her eyes that had been so alive during the first session now seemed unfocused, as if she was staring at something from the distant past.

"What happened after your father died?"

"My world fell apart. My mother had a breakdown." Kathleen reached for a tissue. "I tried to take care of the kids, but a neighbor reported us to Child Protective Services, and we were all placed in different foster homes."

"You lost touch, then?"

"Yes, for years. My brother Devon and I reconnected a couple of years ago, and he's found most of the kids. Some stayed in foster care, others were adopted. We haven't been able to find the twins, Charlie and Rose. They were babies, just months old."

She wiped the tears from her eyes. "You'd think it would stop hurting after all these years."

"Kathleen, what is the *it*?"

Kathleen was taken aback by the question. *The it?* "I guess there's a whole list of its. I'll be forty in a few weeks. I know Claire wants a baby, but it scares the holy crap out of me. I think that's the biggest *it*."

Dr. Friend leaned forward, her hand stroking her forehead. "I'm wondering if something isn't getting triggered with Claire's wanting children. You lost both of your parents after your mother had the twins, and in such a tragic way."

"Yes, and that scares me. What if something happens to Claire, the way it happened to my mother?"

"The circumstances sound quite different to me."

"What if I can't take care of Claire and the baby? I'm hanging by a thread financially. I don't think Claire really understands. She's never been so poor that she's shivered in the cold or went to bed hungry."

Kathleen shifted, her eyes staring at the floor as she spoke. "Don't get me wrong. I love my practice, my home, and family, especially Claire." She looked up, her eyes now focused and filled with tears. "I don't know what I would do if I lost Claire."

"Can you tell me more?"

Kathleen lowered her voice to a near whisper. "She makes me feel important, as if I really matter."

"And you don't think you do? Matter, that is?"

"I struggle with it. I've had issues around feeling special, so I might get a little emotional talking about it."

"That's quite all right. Could you tell me more about how Claire makes you feel special?"

"She started calling me Kath. She's funny...she got me a cape with Superdoc written on the back. She'll massage my feet at night. She'll tell me when we're in bed that I'm special, in lots of different ways. This is a bit embarrassing. By any chance, have you read sonnet forty-three—popularly known as 'How Do I Love Thee'—from Elizabeth Barrett Browning's *Sonnets from the Portuguese*?"

"Yes, I'm aware of it." *I've read it at least a thousand times.*

"Sometimes Claire can be so silly. If I've had a really hard day, she'll treat me as if I'm a little girl. And she'll say, 'How do I love thee? Let me count the ways... Then she'll start counting, one, I love your nose. Two, I love your toes...and if I'm really tired she'll give me a foot massage, and she starts doing this little piggy. I know it's silly and regressive, but damn it, it's comforting."

"It sounds quite charming."

"She loves me, I know that, but lately...we've just been snarling at each other like rabid cats."

Dr. Friend nodded. "During your initial session with Claire, we talked about how secrets can impact a relationship."

"I think I've told Claire all there is to know about me. She knows about my life, everything we've talked about just now. And, I've had a lot of therapy along the way." *See, I really believe in this process.* Her eyes wandered to the clock sitting on Dr. Friend's desk. *Damn, it's only been fifteen minutes.*

"I see your eyes are roaming to the clock. Any reason?"

"Oh, no. Just a hard day. The death of a patient is always difficult; I don't think any doctor really gets over it. And, I've been doing evening house calls to the elderly, homebound patients. Nothing else." Kathleen squirmed and felt her face flush.

"No secrets, then?"

"Well, maybe one," she admitted. "Dr. Friend, I've read your book, and I think I understand your theory. But I'm not sure it's always a good thing to share everything with your partner. Why dig up old..." She tried to think of the perfect word. "...garbage."

"I don't disagree, and I discuss that very subject in my book. If memory serves me right, Chapter Thirty-Seven. Some secrets can be risky and even damaging. But, what if sharing your secret brought you closer? I know Claire has her quirks, as we all do, but overall do you find her to be compassionate and understanding?"

"Claire has the most tender heart, but when she's on a mission...I'm not so sure."

"Of course, it's your decision to share your secret with me or Claire. If you are struggling with something, it will help me to understand your dynamics."

"I don't have to tell Claire?"

"Only if you decide to."

"For your ears only?"

"Yes. What you say here stays here."

"Just like Las Vegas."

A small smile played across Dr. Friend's otherwise unchanging, somber expression.

Kathleen said, "Sometimes I feel so overwhelmed with shame. I think about who I was before I could accept being gay. Hiding, sneaking, and always filled with shame. When I was in the Army, the 'don't ask, don't tell' policy was in full force. But sometimes the impulse to be with another woman overcame my fear of being caught."

Kathleen waited for a clue from Dr. Friend. *Was she friend or foe?*

"I couldn't stop myself from going to a bar. That urge to be touched—I couldn't resist it. I knew every time, I was putting my career in jeopardy, but I couldn't stop. Sometimes, I would take a woman back to my hotel, and sometimes I'd go to their room, and sometimes..." She stared off into space. "Some of the bars have private places, a storage room or just a dark corner."

Kathleen looked up, expecting to be judged. She was surprised to see that Dr. Friend's expression remained unchanged.

Dr. Friend said, "Wanting to be touched is the most important need in humans, and in animals, too, I might add. Are you aware of the study of the Romanian orphans?"

"Yes. I haven't thought about it for years, not since my sophomore year at UCLA. Orphans were basically warehoused. They received enough food but weren't touched or played with. Some died from the lack of human contact. We watched a documentary in class. I found it so upsetting; I don't think I slept well for days." Kathleen began to weep softly.

Imajean Friend leaned forward. "Do you have any memories of being held as a child?"

"I do. I remember my mother holding and singing to me. And my Da used to tell funny stories. That was before he lost his job and everything changed."

"As an infant and young child, you learned what it was like to be held and loved. And why would that need disappear, simply because you grew up and were gay? You got caught between a social dictate and the strongest of human desire: to be touched and loved."

"I felt promiscuous during those years; I never thought there would be someone for me...just for me. A friend *and* a lover. Then Claire came along. And for the first time I had everything."

Dr. Friend removed her glasses. Her eyes glowed with understanding. "Do you think of yourself as promiscuous now?"

Kathleen felt her shoulders slump; she brought her knees up and hugged them, making her body into a defensive ball. "Sometimes it scares me, because I want Claire so much. And Claire, well she's very open and creative. I want to be, but I'm worried I might not be enough for her...that she'll tire of me and leave."

"I want you to think about what it would feel like to share your secret with Claire. To take the risk that she will understand and still love you. I wonder, Kathleen, if the situation was reversed, would you still love Claire?"

Kathleen's expression changed to one of surprise. "I never thought of it that way. Yes, I would love her no matter what."

"Then perhaps that's a thought for you to hold on to. If you can understand anything, perhaps Claire can, as well."

Dr. Friend looked at the clock. "I see our time has ended."

Kathleen stood, they shook hands, and Dr. Friend showed her to the door.

Dr. Friend picked up the notepad from her side table. Alongside her notes, she had doodled two hearts connected by an arrow. Something about Claire and Kathleen had touched her in a place that had never been touched before.

She locked the office door, kicked off her shoes, lay down on the couch, and wept.

CHAPTER 13

There was a weariness that crept throughout her body. A familiar companion of late; she was fatigued, her chest was tight, and her joints ached. She opened the front door, purposely left unlocked by Claire, and went directly into her office. The room was cold and dark except for the desk lamp that illuminated a small area. She found a note from Claire.

Kath, couldn't keep my eyes open, went to bed to read.

She turned the lamp to bright, went over tomorrow's schedule, and checked her messages: only two, and nothing critical.

She cast her eyes upward and thanked any god, goddesses, or angels who might be listening.

Mrs. Olson, ninety-three years old, couldn't sleep and wanted to know if she might have a tablespoon of brandy with her tea. Kathleen called, told her to take two tablespoons, and to sleep well.

Brett Garvy complained of a stomachache. No matter how she tried, she knew Brett couldn't handle his obsession with food on his own.

"Well, Doc," he confided, "I was following that cooking show—Southern cooking at its finest: fried chicken, mashed potatoes with gravy, fried green tomatoes, turnip greens, and ice cream and cake for dessert. And just a little popcorn while I was watching *Guess Who's Coming to Dinner.*"

In spite of her concern, Kathleen couldn't help but stifle a laugh. "Brett, by any chance did you have a bowel movement sometime this evening?"

"Uh, you think I should, Doc?"

"Remember when we spoke about the natural movement of food?"

"Must have forgotten that one," Brett said sheepishly.

"What liquids have you had today?"

"Coffee with breakfast, and then diet soda...maybe six. I'm trying to stay away from sugar, like you said."

"I want you to drink some hot water, maybe three to four cups, and see if you feel better or if you get any *action.* Call me back if your stomach doesn't settle down."

"Thanks, Doc. Feeling better already."

She hung up the phone and thought about the day.

Tony Enard's mother had called early that morning. "Tony always thought of you as his doctor and his friend. He asked if you would be here to say good-bye with the rest of the family."

She stood by Tony's bedside in a sterile-appearing hospital room but filled with the greatest abundance of love and caring she had ever experienced. His mother held his hand and sang his favorite childhood lullaby, "Hush, Little Baby." His wife, Jen, lay on the bed next to him, whispering what only Tony could hear.

She knew as she watched Tony take his last breath she was meant to be there with his family. Every experience, no matter how difficult or painful, had brought her to this place to be with the people meant to be in her life. *Especially Claire.* She was destined to be with Claire. The Claire who made her feel alive and loved; the Claire who could change from hot to cold in a single breath and absolutely drive her crazy.

She went into the kitchen and saw two apples waiting on the kitchen sink along with a paring knife. Eating apples in bed had become one of their nightly rituals.

Claire had shown her how to cut an apple into quarters. "No one ever did this for you before?" she had marveled. "I'll do it this time, and then it's forevermore your job." She did her best Barbra Streisand imitation from *Funny Girl*, doing a pitch-perfect Bronx accent when she said, "Can you imagine? I'm showing a doc how to slice an apple."

Reverting back to Claire, the teacher, she instructed Kathleen on the fine art of apple peeling. "Now, after you have all the skin off, cut the apple in quarters and use your paring knife to scrape out the seeds and core."

Kathleen looked at Claire with a familiar longing. "An apple a day won't keep *this* doc away."

They shared one-quarter of that apple in the kitchen, each taking a bite from the end until the last bite was taken and their lips met. She thought of all the little things that went into making them a couple—a couple with memories and history.

The session with Dr. Friend had left her vulnerable and exhausted. She climbed the stairs, holding onto the banister with one hand and balancing the plate of apples with the other.

Memories of Claire were in every crevice of Canfield House, but most of all, they resided in her heart.

She remembered returning from her evening house calls to find Claire sitting up in bed, her Kindle resting on her knees, her back supported by rainbow-colored pillows. At first, Kathleen was uncertain about the use of so many bright colors: red, orange, yellow, green, blue, indigo, and violet. They were a full-frontal assault on the eyes.

"We should always have a rainbow nearby to remind us that we have found our pot of gold," Claire said seriously. She would look up at Kathleen, patting the bed as a signal to come to her. Kicking off her shoes, Kathleen would slip under the covers. "I shouldn't be doing this," she would say, handing Claire a slice of apple.

"Five minutes, Kath, just five minutes." Five minutes would turn into twenty, and Claire would begin to doze on her shoulder. Kathleen would whisper, "Honey, I have to pee."

"Can't you hold it?" Claire would whine.

"Five minutes more, but at your own risk," she would say, seeking Claire's mouth.

Now, Kathleen climbed the stairs filled with trepidation. Would Claire accept her after she revealed her secret? She thought Dr. Friend was right about how her shameful feelings had kept her from fully being able to love and trust. Was that also true for Claire?

❀   ❀   ❀

The room was dark except for the moonlight showing through the sheer curtains.

Earlier that morning Claire had informed her with a crack in her voice, "It's a blue moon, and it only happens once in a blue moon."

"Every thirty-three months to be precise. We get two regulation full moons in one month," said Kathleen in an officious way.

Claire was on her side, tucked in a fetal position, seemingly asleep, her rainbow pillows scattered on the floor.

That's odd, Kathleen thought. *Asleep already? It's only a little after nine.*

Concerned, she leaned over to feel Claire's forehead. *Fever? Was she sick?*

Claire groaned.

"Honey...are you okay?"

She shook her head. "Oh, Kath, it's that Dr. Friend. Why did I ever let you convince me to go to that, that cannibalistic, narcissistic, horrible Ima Friend?"

"I convinced you?"

"Oh, Kath. You know how hard it is for me to take the blame. Do you mind?"

"My sensitive, fragile, Claire. I know you, most of you...inside and out. Quick to chase the rainbow, but furious when you can't get to the pot of gold."

"You do get me."

"Why, yes I do." Kath held out her arms.

"How was yours session?" asked Claire, her voice muffled against Kathleen's chest.

"About as good as yours. Do you want to share?" Kathleen said, using one of Dr. Friend's favorite buzzwords.

"You'll hate me."

"You'll hate *me*. Claire, I want to see your face. I'm not confessing to the top of your head."

"Close the drapes first."

"Then I won't be able to see you."

"That's the point."

Kathleen moved to the window. Fast-moving stratus clouds obscured the moon and stars. "It might rain," she said before freeing the drapes from their tiebacks. The drapes spilled across the window, hiding any remaining light and darkening the room.

Kathleen eased onto the bed. "I've been thinking about that song 'Blue Moon'?" She hummed the melody. It's been running through my mind all evening.

"I love that song."

"Me, too."

"Claire, let me hold you," Kathleen said, opening her arms. "You're the one who comforts me. Let me give instead of taking."

Claire crept into her open arms, resting her face against Kathleen's breasts. "Oh, Kath, I'm so ashamed. Do I have to look at you?"

"No, Claire-bear. We can both close our eyes. Who goes first?"

"Want to toss a coin?"

And so they shared their secrets, their feelings of shame and longings throughout the night. And as the sun began to rise, they shared their bodies as they had shared their secrets: with complete abandonment.

Before they fell asleep, wrapped in each other's arms, they stood at the window gazing upward as the sun and the moon shared a clearing sky.

PART TWO

"Reach high, for stars lie hidden in your soul.
Dream deep, for every dream precedes the goal."
—Pamela Vaull Star

CHAPTER 14

*O*majean woke to the smell of the salt air rising from the sea and the sound of her white mini-blinds moving against the aluminum window frame: clink, clack; clink, clack. She stretched, her feet sticking out from the end of the too-short twin bed.

It was the same bed her parents had bought her after she graduated from the air crib.

"Extra long mattress—we knew you'd be tall," her mother said as she helped Imajean pack for her move into her own home. She lowered her voice, "You take after my Aunt Neddie. She was about as tall as you, six feet two inches in her stocking feet. So tall, no boy would date her. That's why Neddie stayed an old maid all her life. She was very much a loner except for one friend, Minnie. They used to pal around all the time. In fact, now that I think about it, they shared a home for many years."

Her mother began to fold some towels, a little on the threadbare side, but still usable. "Two old maids, making the best of it, I suppose. Father and I had a discussion. Imajean, we'd like you to take all your bedroom furniture. No sense in unnecessarily spending money. And we'll be making this room into a den."

"Thank you, Mother." Imajean leaned down to kiss her mother's cheek.

Her mother tilted her face up. "You made a good investment in that condo. Perfect for a single woman."

After all these years, she remained in the same bed she had slept in since she was three, and used the same French provincial desk, with its curved iron legs, as she had used in middle school.

She became aware of something new: the movement—the aliveness—that surrounded her oceanfront condo. She heard the waves beating against the beach and the seagulls—how could she have missed their squawks and squeals as they argued over a bit of food?

She wondered, with a sense of uneasiness, what was happening to her.

Imajean felt a sudden chill and closed the bedroom window. It was Friday, and her schedule was unusually light. *In fact,* she thought with a start, *I have nothing to do today, nothing at all.*

Somehow, she felt more adventuresome. Why not do something unplanned; perhaps even risky? She hadn't traveled and she hadn't dated. Certainly there were other kinds of exhilarating experiences. She thought of Kathleen and Claire and how every day was filled with some kind of excitement, even if it was only playing this little piggy or hiking down to Christmas River.

She began to follow her usual morning routine. Breakfast consisted of four ounces of raisin toast, black coffee, and four ounces of orange juice. She stopped. Black coffee? *Ha!* she thought. *No more!* She topped her coffee with heavy cream and three heaping teaspoons of sugar. She would stop at the market today and buy something sinfully good: croissants! She smiled at the thought of the treat, slathered with butter. She was feeling a sense of daring, along with a sense of danger. Was she stretching too quickly out of her well-confined boundaries?

Imajean settled into her conservative, black, four-door Buick sedan and drove to the Paseo Nuevo Mall in Santa Barbara. She purposely got there before the stores opened, first to avoid having to park in a compact-car-only parking space and, most importantly, to not get swept up in the frenzy of out-of-control shoppers. The entire notion of going to a mall was stressful enough.

She blanched at the parking lot sign: 75 MINUTES FREE, MAXIMUM $25. Not one to pay unnecessary expenses, she set her smartphone alarm for one hour. An hour should be more than enough time to do a quick inspection of the stores and then, as she knew she would, return posthaste to her car.

She couldn't remember when she had last walked into a mall. Her sparse wardrobe, from top to bottom, had all been purchased through catalogs. She thought it was Claire Hollander and the bohemian way she dressed that had awakened what she considered to be a sleeping giant into motion. She became drawn to clothing advertisements and, most shameful of all, waited eagerly for Claire's appearance, wearing what she came to think of as the costume of the week.

Claire and Kathleen had driven separately for last week's appointment. Kathleen had come from St. Mona's and apologized for wearing scrubs. Claire was dressed in a full-length patchwork skirt in blue and avocado, a white poet's blouse, long dangling Gypsy earrings, and embroidered flats in colors that matched her skirt. They hugged when they first saw each other. Kathleen had smiled, quite lovingly she thought, when Claire said she had spent the afternoon writing poetry.

Today would serve as a quick pass-through for Imajean. Step one: she would only look in the windows. *Baby steps*, she kept telling herself. Baby steps toward any change.

She thought Paseo Muevo was the perfect choice for her adventure, so much nicer than an indoor mall with store after store packed into floor after floor. Shade trees, fountains, and every kind of geranium that would grow in the seaside community surrounded the pink Spanish-style architecture. Park benches and outdoor tables and chairs made a comfortable rest stop for shop-till-you-drop shoppers. Clearly, Imajean did not fit into that category.

Early morning walkers, wearing sweat clothes and sneakers, moved at a comfortable pace, talking and laughing, enjoying each other's company as much as the fresh ocean air. She felt a pang of envy. Outside of Fred and Marilyn from middle school, she had never experienced the benefit of friendships. Occasional luncheons or business dinners never seemed to go anywhere or get repeated.

She stopped outside of Annie's Boutique and stared at the window display. She was drawn to the mannequin dressed in a gray tuxedo-style jacket, black pants, and a white blouse.

A large-boned woman in her early thirties was finishing decorating the display window. She smoothed the outfit Imajean had been admiring, stepped back, and smiled with satisfaction at her creation. She stepped down and began to ready the store for customers. She waved at the tall, thin, rather forlorn-looking woman staring at the display. Imajean froze...should she run? The woman turned on the inside lights, unlocked the front door, and motioned Imajean inside.

"Hello!" she said, smiling broadly. "My name is Lezlie with a Z. How may I help you?"

Imajean blanched. She had no intention of needing help...for anything.

Lezlie studied Imajean. *Brown wide eyes and well-defined cheekbones. Those eyebrows have to go, but her eyelashes! Women would kill for those lashes. By God, there's an Audrey Hepburn hiding inside this tight-assed woman. And I'm the one to set her free.*

"Oh, I was just admiring your window display," Imajean sputtered.

"Red is your color," said Lezlie, with an authoritative ring to her voice. "Here, allow me to show you."

❀   ❀   ❀

Imajean spent the rest of the day under Lezlie's careful tutelage as she selected outfit after outfit. Imajean dutifully tried on all of them, all with a hint of red in the fabric.

At first, Imajean flinched at undressing in front of another woman. Then, toward the middle of the day, she began to relax. Perhaps some part of her was feeling freer. Or perhaps the appearance of canapés with caviar and smoked salmon, accompanied by crystal glasses filled with white wine, helped. Imajean had never experienced such a devotee of haute couture as Lezlie.

Lezlie loved nothing more than a total makeover. After all, hadn't she recently completed her own perfect makeover? From Lester with an S to Leslie with a Z.

"Think simple, but elegant. Timeless styles are the way to go. And, my dear, red *is* most definitely your color," Lezlie said to her student, who was by now entirely under her spell.

Lezlie sent for a makeup artist she knew, both professionally and personally. After a quick but thorough assessment, Paulette said, "Haircut, eyebrows, waxing, facial, massage, and makeup lesson." Imajean made an appointment for the next day. She was putty in their hands.

"I see you like scarfs," said Lezlie after noticing how the ombré scarf seemed to be glued to Imajean's neck. "Never underestimate the power and magic of a scarf, and I have the perfect one for you."

"I never realized there were so many ways to tie a scarf," Imajean said, staring at the black and white lace scarf trimmed in red, while her eyes roamed to the booklet, gifted to her by Lezlie, *You and Your Scarfs: One Hundred and One Knots.* "It's a bit overwhelming."

"I think I know the perfect knot for you." Lezlie's hands moved deftly in what appeared to Imajean as a blur.

"What is this one called?" asked Imajean.

Lezlie stepped back to admire her handiwork. "It is one of my personal favorites. It's called loosely-wrapped."

❀   ❀   ❀

Dr. Friend was delighted to see the call light turn red. That would be Kathleen and Claire. *What a pair,* she thought. The very antithesis of everything she had learned in her Behavioral Psychology classes. The fact that they had actually completed five sessions and were returning for the grand finale was proof positive that her *Six Steps to a True and Honest Relationship* was a success.

She adjusted her new frameless glasses and slipped on her red blazer. She went into the bathroom to glance in the mirror. She smiled at her reflection and carefully adjusted the black-and-white lace scarf, trimmed in ruby red.

A bright, open smile greeted Claire and Kathleen as Imajean waved them into her office. Kathleen and Claire exchanged shocked looks, each with a raised eyebrow that said, *Are we in the right office?*

Imajean had, by now, returned to her professional demeanor. "Our wrap-up session is a time for us to go over anything that's on your mind and tie up any loose ends." She unconsciously touched the knot on her scarf.

Claire raised her hand.

"Yes, Claire?"

"I'd like to say, I really like your outfit, and your haircut is, like, *wow*! Could I get the name of your stylist?"

Kathleen rolled her eyes.

"Why, thank you, Claire. However, I'm not sure that would be quite professional." She thought a moment. "Of course, I can't stop you from going to the Paseo Nuevo Mall and entering Paulette's Health Spa." She hesitated, thinking about the four stylists that worked there. "Say hello to Paulette for me. Now, onto business. During your previous session, you agreed to come up with a list of your own baby steps along the path toward achieving your primary goal of having a baby. Shall we begin this session with—"

Kathleen interrupted. "I'm asking for three months before we begin the um...project. And," she said, looking directly at Claire, "*no* more tick-tocks."

"Project?" Claire was beginning to steam. "You're calling our baby a freakin' *project*?"

"Kathleen," Dr. Friend intervened in a soft, seductive voice that was hitherto unavailable, "can you say the word *baby*?"

"Of course I can." Kathleen burrowed into the tweed couch that she was sharing with Claire, hugging one of the square brown pillows tightly against her chest. "B...b...b..."

"Breathe, Kathleen," Dr. Friend said encouragingly.

Kathleen nodded. "I can do this. B...b...ba...ba..."

Dr. Friend nodded. "Almost there."

"Bay...bay...baby. There, I said it! *Baby*. I want three months while we work on our steps *and* before we try to have our baby. And no more tick-tocks."

She gazed at Claire. "Our baby," she said softly, reaching out for Claire's hand. "I really do want our baby, Claire. I want to watch as our baby grows inside you, and I want to feel it move when I put my hand on your belly."

Claire moved closer until there was no distance between them. She took Kathleen's hand and placed it on her belly. "Oh, Kath, it'll be right here. It will be ours, I promise. And I promise to be more mature."

Kathleen chuckled. "One baby step at a time."

For the first time in all the years of her practice, Dr. Friend went over her fifty-minute hour. *The hell with the tick-tocks,* she thought. The two hours went by quickly as they mapped out, as Claire insisted on calling it, their Six Steps to Babyhood. "If Dr. Friend's six-step program worked for us," she proclaimed, "then our six-step program should work, too."

They decided to go somewhere away from the house once a week and discuss this latest adventure, baby step by baby step. Using, of course, I-statements and, as Dr. Friend added, a boat-load of empathy.

After they said good-bye and did a group Ima Friend hug, Dr. Friend sat at her desk and swiveled around in her desk chair. "Whee!" she said softly. She put a copy of Claire and Kathleen's Six Steps to Babyhood in their file:

Step One: Finding the lucky donor.

Step Two: Getting ourselves ready, physically and emotionally.
Step Three: Buying baby furniture.
Step Four: Managing financially.
Step Five: Help, support, and babysitting by others.
Step Six: Learning to cook.

She added a brief note to their file: I am delighted at the progress made by Kathleen Moore and Claire Hollander. Couple has reached a new level of communication and understanding.

CHAPTER 15

Living with Gayle and Robert was the happiest time in Stephanie's life.

Gayle fussed over her and even tucked her in at night, and Robert was teaching her how to cook. Robert did most of the cooking, but when it came to waffles, Gayle was the expert.

"This waffle iron belonged to my mother," Gayle had told her, showing her the ancient oblong iron, so well-seasoned over time that the griddle had turned a fine black. "I remember when my mother got it as a Christmas gift. She was so very happy. Can you guess why?"

Guessing games, thought Stephanie. Both Gayle and Robert liked to play them.

"I guess...because she could make waffles with it." *Well, duh.*

"Yes, and—" Gayle paused for effect "—the griddle could be flipped over for making grilled cheese sandwiches, one of my mother's favorites. I think we had grilled cheese and tomato soup every Friday night after that."

She liked it when Gayle or Robert would tell her something about when they were kids. It made her feel as if they really were a family. Sometimes, she even pretended that Gayle and Robert were her mom and dad. She knew it was pretend, but it made her heart feel happy.

She spent three days a week at the VA Physical Medicine and Rehabilitation Services. The van picked her up at 8:00 a.m. and got her home by 5:00 p.m. It was a long, hard day and there were days she didn't want to go, and days when she got angry and told her physical therapist Madeline to go away and leave her alone. Even though she sometimes got angry, she had loved Madeline from the very first day she had met her.

Madeline was muscular, with dark-brown skin, close-cropped hair, and the Marine Corps emblem of the eagle, globe, and anchor tattooed on her right upper arm. Madeline saw Stephanie staring at it. "Official emblem since 1955. *Semper fi!*" she said proudly. She lifted her tank top to show a second tattoo with her name, social security number, blood type, and religion. "This is my meat tag," she said, pointing to her rib cage. "In case that's all they found, they would know who I was and make sure I got the last rites," she explained.

"Now, Stephie girl, I've gone through your file, and you aren't even supposed to be here, let alone be walking. That tells me you're a fighter, and now we're a fighting team. Tell me your goal?"

Ugh, another goal, she thought. Since she got wounded, that's what everyone wanted: a goal. She looked at the wall near the parallel bars. Canes of every type and description were housed in a wooden display case.

"A cane...Madeline, I want to graduate to a cane."

"Okay, we'll make that your first goal. Do you want to know what my goal is for you?"

Stephanie shrugged. *Working me into an early grave?*

"Watching you throw that cane away. Now, I won't work you any harder than I would work myself. And I work really, really hard."

Stephanie had already figured that out by the sculpted look of Madeline's body.

The first day was spent in assessment. Afterward, Madeline and Stephanie walked out to the patio and sat at a white plastic table, shaded by a faded blue umbrella.

Madeline handed Stephanie a chocolate and peanut butter shake with a terse command, "Drink!"

Madeline settled into one of the chairs. "You can't beat this West Los Angeles weather. No smog and ocean breezes every afternoon. I'll take you on a tour of the grounds one day. There's a lot of history on this chunk of land. It all began in 1887 as a home for disabled vets. There are some incredible old buildings around here, including a chapel built in 1900. But first things first, Steph—we've got to put some weight on you."

"I eat a lot."

"You'll eat more. I checked your range of motion against your last assessment at Brooke and it's much improved, but your core muscles..." Madeline shook her head. "More sit-ups for you, Stephie girl. You did fifty at Brooke; I want you to start here with seventy-five. We're going to focus on overall flexibility, balance, and strength. I'm going to watch you walk out of here on your own two feet, standing straight...military straight."

❀   ❀   ❀

She felt herself getting stronger. Madeline plied her with extra calories, and she was up to one hundred sit-ups. Sometimes her muscles hurt so much she felt like crying. But, she remembered Madeline telling her on the first day they met, "No pain, no gain."

When she faltered, Madeline would say, "Look at the cane display, Steph. One of them has your name on it."

The VA van stopped in front of Robert and Gayle's. Stephanie always felt happy to see her very favorite spot: the front lawn planted with groups of birch trees.

"They are planted in threes," Robert had explained, "for symmetry."

Like a family, she thought, *a mommy, daddy, and little girl*.

She had a big surprise for Gayle and Robert. It had been a month since she had started rehab and today, Madeline told her she could start to practice with a cane. She was so excited she told Madeline she would keep it as a surprise for Gayle and Robert. "When I'm ready to say good-bye to my walker, I want to step out of the van with my cane and say, 'Surprise!'"

She used her key to open the front door and made her way to the kitchen, where she knew snacks would be waiting. Sometimes, it would be fruit and yogurt or cookies and milk. Since she had been staying with Robert and Gayle, she had gained five whole pounds.

She carried her snack outside and placed the ice-cold glass of milk and oatmeal cookies on the wrought-iron table. Robert had told her how he and Kathleen had worked together to refinish the table. She would be meeting Kathleen soon since she was invited to her birthday party. It would be her first birthday party since...ever! She was thinking hard about what to get Kathleen for a present. She really didn't know much about her. She knew she was a doctor, and she knew she had someone to love, Claire. She felt a pang in her heart. She wondered what it would feel like to have someone in her life to love her that way. A real someone—not like HE.

The fresh air and the hard work with Madeline had made her sleepy. *Nap time!* she told herself. Naps were always nicer than nighttime sleep. At night, the Dream would bother her, but nap times were peaceful. She would listen to music on her iPod; she didn't want anyone to know that it was baby lullabies that would keep her brain at rest.

Before she drifted off to sleep, she thought about the way Madeline encouraged her when she thought she couldn't do another sit-up or stretch her arms any further. "It isn't just your legs that we have to work on. You've carried yourself so stiff; you've locked most of your arm and shoulder muscles. It's up to you, Stephie girl. Only you can get yourself back to normal."

No one had ever called her Stephie. Madeline made her feel special. But, *back to normal*? She was never normal. Everyone had told her so, one way or another. Even Santa.

Daddy said it was going to snow *and* they were going to see Santa Claus. She loved it when it snowed. Not because of the snow—it was way too cold for her—but because Mommy would give her warm baths at night. She could play with her plastic fishies and pretend she was a fishie, too. She knew what she wanted to be when she grew up: a mermaid.

Mommy dressed her in heavy black stirrup pants, a white cable-knit sweater, knitted by Mommy, and an embroidered emerald-green coat with a black velvet collar.

"Mittens for your hands," said Mommy. "It'll be cold in the car."

Mommy buckled her up and Daddy stuck the "Baby on Board" sign on the rear window. She hated that sign. She was no baby— she was four, going on five.

They drove downtown to Jones' Department Store. Daddy put her on his shoulders so she could look at the store window filled with Christmas decorations. This year, Mommy said, the decorations would be about *Miracle on 34th Street*. She had watched the movie with Mommy and Daddy. Mommy had whispered tearfully, "There really is a Santa Claus. Susan got her heart's desire: a real family and a home."

If Susan, the little girl in the movie, could get her heart's desire, why couldn't she? All she had to do was be a big girl, sit on Santa's lap, and tell him what she wanted for Christmas.

The elevator was filled with exhausted, cranky parents and overly excited children. "Make room, make room!" someone shouted, pushing their way into the overcrowded elevator. The small space filled with the dank odor of wet coats and body heat.

The doors opened to the third floor: Toy Department and Santa Claus. The elevator emptied as quickly as it had filled. The older kids made a beeline for the Toy Department while moms and dads ushered the littler tykes toward the long line leading to the North Pole.

Mommy held on tightly to Stephanie's hand. "Stay with me, I don't want you to get lost."

She waited patiently until Santa's elf picked her up and put her on Santa's lap. Santa said, "Ho, ho, ho! Smile, little girl," and a bright light flashed, making her blink.

"What is your name, little girl?"

"Stephanie."

"And what do you want for Christmas, Stephanie?"

She looked at him with a solemn expression. "Fishies, I want two little fishies...in a bowl. And fishie food."

Santa glanced toward Stephanie's mommy who was shaking her head and mouthing, "No."

"Don't you want a Cabbage Patch Doll or My Little Pony? Why, you can see them right here at Jones' Department Store." Santa leaned over and whispered, "That's what all the other little girls want."

Stephanie shook her head. "Fishies. I want two little fishies in a bowl." She was adamant. "And *fishie food*."

Which, she wanted to add, was what Santa's breath smelled like.

Three solemn people rode home in their 1980 four-door, bitter-sweet-red Ford Fairmont, with the idiotic "Baby on Board" sign still affixed to the rear window with a suction cup. The radio was off, and no one was in the mood for singing Christmas carols.

Mommy tried to talk to her. "Stephanie, sometimes little

fishies don't like to live in a bowl. And they die. Then you would feel very, very sad."

Stephanie slumped as far into herself as the seat belt would allow. She drifted to another place, where HE was waiting for her. "Told you so," he taunted. "No little fishies for you, cry baby."

She heard Daddy whisper to Mommy, "She's gone inside again. Damn it, Lois, it's not worth it. The kid wants two goddamn fish for Christmas. So what? I say let her have 'em if it'll make her happy. It's better than one of those creepy Cabbage Patch Dolls."

"I don't want her to feel bad when they die."

"And making the poor little thing withdraw is *better*, I guess?"

Mommy was saying something, but the sounds began to fade. Stephanie had disappeared inside her womb-like sanctum with HE.

❀   ❀   ❀

That Christmas, she got puzzles, a book she wanted, *A Christmas Carol*, the classic Candy Land board game, and a pink My Little Pony. She said "thank you" and tried to smile. *No fishies. Maybe I was bad, or Santa really wasn't listening*, she thought.

Daddy went into the kitchen to get a cup of coffee and came back carrying a clear bowl with pink and purple rocks in the bottom, fake plants, and two little guppies.

"Santa thought they would be safer in the kitchen," Daddy said.

"Ohhh, thank you, Daddy, thank you, thank you," she said, hugging him tightly.

A sweet smiled crossed Daddy's face. "What will you name them?" he asked.

"HE and SHE."

Friday was Stephanie's favorite day. No school tomorrow and reruns of *Flipper* were on.

Mommy let her sit all by herself in the family room, in Daddy's favorite chair, right smack in front of the TV set. Mommy kissed the top of her head and handed her a small bag of Froot Loops and a glass of milk.

"Special treat," she said, "enjoy the show. I'll be in the kitchen if you need me."

"Thank you, Mommy," she said as she held the snack-sized plastic bag in her hand.

She counted the colors, one at a time. It bothered her that they never came out even. She would eat them in order: first red, then yellow, and saving her favorite, orange, for last. She felt like a very big girl—almost ready for kindergarten.

She wished she could walk into the television and be next to Flipper and Sandy Ricks, his little freckle-faced boy companion. She would jump into the ocean and swim with Flipper. He would be the same big, smart fishie with the funny laugh, and she would be a mermaid.

After the show, Daddy read her a story, and Mommy listened to her prayers and tucked her in. She never told Mommy that she always prayed for her fishies to turn into a dolphin like Flipper and that one day she would wake up and be a mermaid.

Mommy and Daddy must have thought she was sleeping because they weren't using their secret voices. She could hear them getting ready for bed in their room, right across from hers. If she closed her eyes she could imagine Mommy cleaning her face with Pond's cold cream, which smelled so good, and Daddy taking off his socks, tossing them on the floor, and cleaning the fuzz between his toes, which didn't smell so good at all.

Mommy said, "Phillip, I had a conference with Stephanie's preschool principal, Mrs. Roland. She has some concerns."

"What kind of concerns?"

Mommy started to cry. "Mrs. Roland said Stephanie is bright off the charts. She's reading—not just words, but everything. She picked up a National Geographic and began reading it *and* comprehending it. But, Mrs. Roland said she's troubled about the way she is with the other kids. She even gave me a list." She handed the paper to Daddy and turned her head away.

Daddy read the list out loud.

Often speaks without inflection.
Trouble making friends.
Doesn't seem to understand what other kids want.
Sometimes appears confused and anxious.

"Lois, what the hell does this mean?" Phillip said angrily.

"During 'Feelings Time,' they sit in a circle and express their feelings: sad or glad or mad. She just sits, inside herself like she does, and now the kids aren't playing with her at all. Mrs. Roland said she's not qualified to make a diagnosis, but she fears something may be terribly wrong. She gave me the name of a psychiatrist."

Phillip lowered his voice to a near whisper. "'Feelings Time'? Come on, give me a break. A psychiatrist? And then what? Fill her full of pills? Make her dopey? Make her feel even more different?"

He patted Lois's shoulder. "Did you tell the old biddy about HE?"

"Yes, and she said it's very common for children of this age to have imaginary friends. But Phillip, she's saying our Stephanie is not normal."

"Bull. That's what I think of you, Mrs. Roland: full of bullshit. Our Stephanie is just a little bit shy. Good lord, she's just turning five. I'm not having a daughter of mine labeled and doped up. Goddammit!" he cursed, opening his arms for Lois and letting her sob against his chest.

Stephanie scrunched under the covers. Daddy never said the G-d word unless he was... She thought of a good word to use: furious.

She could hear him shouting, "Tell Mrs. Roland *no*. End of story: no!"

Both HE and she were afraid. Mommy was crying, and Daddy was furious. They made a plan to try to play more with the other kids, and to stop talking to each other while they were in school. HE came up with an idea. HE whispered to Stephanie, "You have to swear an oath—under pain of death—you will never mention me again to anyone. Remember, Stephanie, under pain of death."

She remembered.

❀　❀　❀

Things changed for Stephanie at Happy Brook. HE was very quiet, and Stephanie stepped out of herself and into the world of pre-school.

❀　❀　❀

Mrs. Roland was a full-figured woman who wore her hair in a bun and thick, horn-rimmed glasses to correct her stigmatism. She thought of herself as being extraordinarily devoted to her students and took her chosen profession seriously. She used her vacation time to attend seminars on childhood development and tried, always, to put the children first. What better legacy to leave to the world than to aid in the development of the next generation?

It was the end of the semester and the summer break began next week. She smiled at the thought of the little ones, the graduating class of 1985, wearing their maroon gowns, with matching mortarboards and beige tassels. They were well prepared for the next step in life: kindergarten.

Mrs. Roland sat at her desk writing personal notes to each and every parent. She came to Stephanie's name and became perplexed. She had recently attended a lecture on Asperger's syndrome and, while she recognized she wasn't qualified to make diagnoses, she thought of Stephanie throughout the lecture. *The poor child needs to be evaluated,* she thought.

She wrote:

> *Dear Mr. and Mrs. Whinstone,*
>
> *I'm so sorry to have worried you about Stephanie. She seems to have turned a corner. While her affect and cadence of speech remains unconventional, she is making an effort to interact and play with the other children.*
>
> *I believe you have a unique daughter. I would encourage you to have her IQ tested; there may be special classes available to her through the school system. She is currently reading at a sixth grade level, and I believe that is a very conservative figure.*
>
> *You have a very special child to be treasured.*
>
> *Sincerely,*
>
> *Abigail Roland*

Perhaps the carrot would work if the stick didn't. If they had Stephanie's IQ tested, other tests might be included and a diagnosis could be made. All Abigail Roland knew was that Stephanie was a gifted, perhaps brilliant child who presented to the world as being very odd.

After graduation, the Whinstone family went out for ice cream sundaes. Stephanie wore her cap and tassel and kept changing it from side to side.

Daddy said, "We are very proud of our big girl."

Mommy held the note from Mrs. Roland. Her eyes were shiny and little beads of tears rolled down her cheeks. She took one of the napkins from the chrome dispenser and dabbed away the tears. "Look, Phillip," she said, handing Daddy the note from Mrs. Roland. "She says our Stephanie is brilliant."

"I told you there was nothing to worry about."

Mommy tucked the note inside her purse. She would put it in Stephanie's Treasure Box of Memories.

When the waiter asked Stephanie for her order, Daddy told her she could have anything she wanted.

She looked directly at the waiter. "I would like to order one scoop of lemon sherbet and one scoop of raspberry sherbet in two separate dishes, please."

Mommy and Daddy looked at each other and, for a moment, fear could be seen in their eyes. Then they recalled Mrs. Roland's letter. With their concerns about Stephanie now replaced with the knowledge that they had a brilliant child, they put away any worries, exchanged relieved looks, and smiled.

❀   ❀   ❀

Stephanie woke up from her nap. *Where am I?* She had to think for a minute. Gayle and Robert's. She breathed a deep sigh of relief. She had a dream about being little and having two little fishies. Mommy was right—they didn't live long. She found them floating on top of the water one morning. But, she didn't feel sad the way Mommy said she would. Should she have?

She could hear Robert bustling around the kitchen. "Cooking lesson time," she said to herself.

❀   ❀   ❀

"Nice nap?" Robert asked cheerily.

"Yes, Robert. I'm ready for my cooking lesson."

"What would you like for dinner?"

She smiled. "Pizza."

Robert scratched his head. That would be six days out of seven this week. "Let's stretch our culinary palate a bit and then have pizza tomorrow."

"I'm used to stretching, Robert. Three days a week at the VA and four days here. May I choose, Robert?"

"Yes, but whatever you choose you have to make."

She liked this game. "Too many choices," she said.

She thought for what seemed like forever. "I choose meat pie! And, I memorized my mother's recipe."

Robert leaned against the black-and-yellow-tiled kitchen counter, a mug of coffee in his hand. As much as he had resisted having Stephanie live with them, he was enjoying her company. Gayle seemed to be gone for longer and longer periods of time, and he was missing her. Requests for speaking engagements were coming in, and she had been approached to create a podcast on aging. His career was showing signs of winding down and hers was picking up. What if they didn't have as much time left as they thought? Would regrets be the last feelings they would share?

Returning from his reverie, he replied, "Is that your heart's desire?"

Stephanie became serious. "I haven't thought about my heart's desire, not for a long time. Do you want to know what it was, when I was a kid?"

"I'd love to."

"I wanted to study ocean life."

"You mean, become an oceanographer?"

"Yes. There's a whole other world in the sea."

"What happened to your dream?"

"Oh, it got lost somewhere. But, I never lost my mother's recipe for meat pie." She grinned.

Her mother's mantra in life was "no fuss, no muss." She wondered how her mother and father were. *I guess I caused her one too many fusses and one too many musses. That must be why she stopped loving me.* She felt something she hadn't felt before. She remembered when they would sit in a circle at the Happy Brook Preschool and talk about their feelings. *Sad*, she thought. *I must be feeling sad.* She wiped a tear away. She whispered inside her head, *Look, HE, real tears.*

Robert handed her a notepad and pen. "Make a list of the ingredients. We'll go to the market and you can show me your shopping *and* cooking skills."

Robert took her to Whole Foods, an organic and natural food market she had heard about from her buddies in the Army, but had never seen. A few people looked at her; she knew they were wondering why someone so young needed a walker. She thought about wearing a sign: "Wounded in Iraq." But then, she thought, maybe their guessing game was fun for them.

They walked up and down the aisles, Robert pushing the cart, Stephanie following right behind him. Robert showed her how to read the labels and insisted on organic-only ingredients. When it came to the meat, only grass-fed organic beef would do.

She found herself squirming from excitement on the way home. *Home*—she had become accustomed to calling it home, although she knew, as she improved, the days of staying with Robert and Gayle became shorter. And soon, she would once again become a drifter.

Robert laid all the ingredients on the butcher-block kitchen island. She liked this time when they would talk as they cooked. Sometimes, Robert would ask her pointed but not nosy questions, and she would enjoy opening up about herself.

"So, Stephanie, tell me, what drew you into the military?"

"Hold your horses! I need to concentrate first on making the dough. Pass the Bisquick, please." She painstakingly followed the printed directions for making biscuits and then rolled the dough into a circle.

"When I was going into eleventh grade, I got a full scholarship to UM. We need to fry the meat and onions, Robert. And lard. My mother always used lard."

Robert almost choked at the thought of lard. "Try this olive oil," he said, handing her the bottle of extra virgin olive oil. "UM?"

"University of Miami, Rosenthal School of Marine and Atmospheric Science, to be specific. Doesn't fit with my personality, does it?" She looked up from her task while a small smile played across her face.

"I'm really smart, Robert. When I was six, I found a book at a garage sale. That was how my mother and I spent our Saturdays. I had a fit because my mother said I was too young to read that book. I still have it, *An Introduction to the Biology of Marine Life* by James L. Sumich," she recited in a childlike, singsong fashion.

"I read the entire book, with a dictionary right next to me. I knew that was what I wanted to do: understand the world of fishies. Surprised? Don't be. I just come off as dumb."

Robert's expression of mingled amusement and admiration suggested he thought anything but.

"When I got the scholarship, my parents said no, I was too young and immature. So, I decided to leave. I packed up a few things in a backpack and ran away. Okay, back to Rachael Rayville. We need to peel the potatoes, boil the suckers and mash 'em up with lots of butter and whole milk."

Robert winced at the thought of whole milk and *lots* of butter. He could just about feel and hear his arteries hardening, his cholesterol levels growing by leaps and bounds. His thoughts quickly returned to the way Stephanie spoke about running away with the same flat inflection as peeling potatoes.

Stephanie continued. "Okay, back to my story. So I kinda bummed around the country doing a lot of odd jobs. A few years ago, it was a really cold day, and I was walking down the street and there's this US Army Recruiting Station. And I walked in, thinking I could get a cup of hot coffee and maybe something to eat. The rest is history. After I got wounded, I thought, maybe I really am dumb. Because if I had waited until I was eighteen I could have gone to UM."

"Don't you have any contact with your parents? After all, that was years ago."

"No, I went to see them after I finished boot camp. I thought they would be proud of me for serving my country and all. My mother said, 'No more, Stephanie. We're done.'"

"I'm sorry to hear that. It's never too late to rediscover your dreams." Robert thought, *That holds true for me, as well.*

"Maybe someday, I'll find a new dream. In the meantime, Robert, it's your job to mash the potatoes when they're soft. I'll brown the onions and hamburger, then we mix it all together and put it right in the middle of the Bisquick dough. Pull the sides up, and as my mother used to say: *Ta-da!* Bake until brown."

❀   ❀   ❀

Robert and Gayle plopped into bed. They had rolled over on their sides, each finding a distant edge in the king-sized bed.

Robert groaned. "Honey, pass an antacid."

Gayle handed him the bottle. "I've gained five pounds! Bobby, we've got to get back to our salads."

"I know, but I seem to be reaching her through cooking."

"You won't be able to reach *around* me soon. Try something else, for God's sake."

"It's what she seems to really enjoy. She wants to move on to desserts."

Gayle groaned.

Robert popped two antacids in his mouth. "I don't know much about it, but do you think she has Asperger's?"

"She may have been diagnosed with that as a child, but I don't think so. It's probably...something else."

"That's rather broad, isn't it?"

"It's better to be uncertain than to mislabel. That's what happens to half the population. Once they're in that box, they're stuck. Honey, I'd roll over to kiss you, but I'm not sure I could roll back over. Good night, Robert."

"Good night, darling."

CHAPTER 16

Stephanie heard the grandfather clock chiming. She counted out loud in a whispery tone: one, two, three, four, five...six. She smiled at the game she played every morning. Six chimes, and she didn't have to be up until seven. That gave her a whole hour to lie in bed and talk to HE. HE could be a brat, but he was still her closest and best friend. She squirmed around on the sheets, letting her arms and legs stretch out straight. She noticed an absence of something, as if a familiar companion had left. Pain—she had no pain. Everyone would be happy to hear that, especially Gayle. She liked Robert, but she *loved* Gayle. Robert was more curious about her, as if he was trying to figure out what made her so odd.

Turning onto her right side, she whispered to the empty pillow and bunched-up blanket: "Good morning, HE, no pain this morning. And, Gayle promised us waffles."

She shifted her weight and sat half up in bed. Suddenly, hit with a shock of pain, she grunted. "Don't worry," she whispered again. "It's only stiff muscles from working so hard. A hot shower and stretching should fix it. Guess what, HE? Gayle bought me a new bathing suit. She said anyone who works this hard should have a new bathing suit.

"Robert's really funny. Were you up when it rained yesterday? He told me, 'April showers bring May flowers.' I can't wait until May...oh, how I love flowers.

"No! I don't want to leave, HE. I like it here, and I'm not all better yet. It's too soon, just too soon."

She swung her legs defiantly over the side of the bed and steadied herself on the walker. "Almost done with you," she said optimistically to the walker.

She would practice walking with a broad-based cane today. "You're making incredible progress," Madeline had told her, giving her one of her majorly huge hugs.

She turned the shower on and, holding onto the grab bars, put her head directly under the cascading water. She loved water. That, her mother had said, was because she was a Pisces. She couldn't wait to be able to swim again...*really* swim.

Madeline had said, "Soon...be patient...maybe five minutes— we'll start with floating, then arms only...it will happen—soon."

She dreamed about water every night. The same dream ever since she could remember. Was that because she was a Pisces?

The dream book said her dream was trying to tell her something really important. She wished she could understand what that was. It wasn't a fun dream and, last night, the dream felt stronger than ever.

She continued to stand in the shower, thinking about the dream and how it had haunted her for her whole life. It always began with her being a teeny, tiny fish, the size of a guppy. Floating—floating in warm water. Free to move, turning, twisting...she was a happy, little fishie. Then, she became a bigger fishie, but there wasn't enough room for her to dance in the water.

Bump. Bump...something kept bumping up against her. The bumps became harder, stronger...*ouch!* Something began to squeeze, taking away her space...she was being pushed and pulled. Horrible pressure, excruciating pain. Then cold...so very cold.

The dream changed, and she was back in the warm water. Now she was a mermaid with colorful scales on a luminescent tail.

She glowed with happiness. She would never go back into that other place, that space where only cold and pain existed.

Stephanie began to whimper, then moan until a deep cry of anguish escaped. The pain in the dream had become real. She had never felt anything so intense, not even after her surgeries. She tried not to scream, but the cries came on their own. Gasping, she lowered herself to the shower floor. In her pain, the cheery pink-and-white tiles seemed to be closing in on her; the warm water now turning icy cold, pummeling against her fragile back. Gasping, long sobs—had she ever cried like this before? She tucked her arms and legs until she became an infant, curled up on the shower floor. "HE," she pleaded, "what's happening? Where are you? HE?"

She heard rapid knocking on the bathroom door.

"Stephanie, it's Gayle, are you okay?"

She had to pull herself together or they would send her away. "Yes, Gayle, I had a bad dream last night," she said, stifling another sob.

HE came alive, twisting her insides, torturing her brain with his gravelly voice. "Shame on you! Keep your mouth shut about your dream. How many times have I told you we've got to leave this place? It's not safe anymore. They're getting too close."

She sobbed, "I don't want to go away. You go away, HE. Go away! I'm happy here."

Robert came rushing into the bedroom. "What the hell is going on? I'm calling 911!"

Gayle's hand was on the bathroom doorknob. "No! Call the VA and cancel Stephanie's pick-up for the rest of the week. Then, call my service and have them reschedule my meetings and my patients. Tell them I'll be back in the office on Tuesday."

Robert mumbled, "Good God, what have you gotten us into?"

Gayle threw him an angry look. "Go, Robert," she said tersely.

Robert left, his head down, blankets of shame covering him.

Gayle regretted her angry statement to Robert. She could understand his frustration and confusion at seeing his home turned topsy-turvy, but there was an underlying venom in his tone that was unlike him. She could not have known taking Stephanie in would lead to this, but it had, and there was nothing they could do but deal with it.

Something had drawn her to this child. *Child,* she thought. From the moment she walked into her hospital room at Landstuhl, she saw her as a child. And why was the only book Gayle had brought with her to Germany a child's book of poetry? She had been filled with a sudden and overwhelming compulsion to get *A Child's Garden of Verses* from her bedroom. She had even made the shuttle wait while she ran back into the house and swept it off the nightstand. Gayle had clutched the book all the way to Germany as if it were her last connection to life. She knew now, it was never meant for her; it was meant for Stephanie.

Gayle's hand remained frozen on the doorknob. Stephanie had cried out, "HE." Gayle had refused to try to diagnose her, but now her mind began to race: multiple personality? Dissociative disorder? She could name half a dozen such conditions. *No,* she instinctively thought, *there is no diagnosis for Stephanie, and I'd be damned if I let her fall into the system.*

Gayle took a deep breath and opened the bathroom door. She spoke softly as she turned off the water. "Stephanie, the water is freezing. I won't be able to lift you up—you need to help me. Can you reach for one of the bars, honey?"

Stephanie grabbed onto one of the bars. She had thought she was strong, but she felt weakened, as weakened as she did in her dream.

"I'm sorry, Gayle," she said, shivering.

Gayle wrapped the oversized towel around her. "There is nothing to be sorry about. It's only to be understood."

Gayle had never seen Stephanie so exposed and fragile. She had a stunned look, as if she had been carried into an unknown universe of nightmares, fears, and pain. For the first time, Gayle saw the extent of her physical injuries. She knew what the nurses had told her at Landstuhl. Bullets ricocheted off her spine and tore her bladder. Scars crisscrossed her back and abdomen. *Scars, inside and out.* "Lucky to be alive," one of the nurses had whispered to her.

Whatever her affliction was, she was not abandoning this child. Wrapping the towel around Stephanie, she brought her closer, until she was safely cradled in Gayle's arms.

Stephanie tried to pull away, a wild look in her eyes. "Let me go, Gayle, please. I need to pack and leave."

"Not a chance. You're not getting off that easy. It's time, Stephanie, for you to tell someone...*me*...what the hell is going on."

Stephanie whispered, "HE will kill me...I took an oath. Upon pain of death. HE will kill me."

"No one is going to kill you. I'm right here. I'm going to help you get dressed, and then we're going to have a long talk. No VA for you and no office for me."

"Please, I can't miss the VA. I was going to practice with a cane today."

Stephanie's eyes kept moving from the bedroom and back to Gayle.

Gayle's eyes followed the same path as Stephanie's. She took in the way the bedding was arranged. A pillow and a blue blanket, not askew the way bedding would look in the morning, but waiting for someone to rest their head and join Stephanie in bed.

Why had she not noticed it before? The way Stephanie spoke, with the cadence of a child. She was a child stuck in time. She had cried out "HE," as if she was speaking to another person. And the twos...everything always in twos.

"Stephanie, two fillings for the cake. Two blankets. So many things you ask for and need in twos." Gayle took a deep breath. "Are there two of you?"

"I took a sacred oath...never to tell." She looked at Gayle, her eyes fixed and staring. "A sacred oath, upon pain of death."

"Listen to me, those are just pretend oaths that children take when they join a secret club. Or something a bully uses to intimidate and frighten the less powerful. Have you ever told anyone that someone else lives inside you?" Gayle asked, flipping on the switch to the overhead heater. "You're freezing."

"I can't stop shaking. My insides are so cold."

"I'll get you some hot chocolate, in just a bit."

Stephanie wiped her tears with the end of the towel. "I told Mommy and Daddy about HE when I was little but, I stopped talking because Mommy and Daddy were so worried. We were afraid they'd send us away."

Gayle had heard of similar cases of adults adrift in time because of an imaginary friend who had never left. But Stephanie's strange affliction was more than that, she thought. Something was tickling her memory. She was reminded of a talk she had years ago with an old friend about pre-birth and birth trauma. *Could it be?* she wondered. *Was it possible this was a pre-birth memory?*

It was Jack Slater who had talked about it, believed in it. She hadn't seen Jack for...it must be at least ten years. Jack was one of her favorite people, but someone who needed to travel a different path. She had heard he still lived locally in Topanga Canyon, a scenic hikers' paradise in western Los Angeles County that blossomed in the 1960s into a haven for creative types, free thinkers, and hippies—and earned unwelcome notoriety as the starting point of the Manson Family's killing spree.

"Stephanie, do you trust me?"

"I love you, Gayle," she said solemnly.

"But do you *trust* me?"

"Yes."

"Good. Then I'm going to see if we can pay a visit to very good friend of mine...a wise man...a person much wiser than I could ever be."

CHAPTER 17

It was a lucky break to find Jack at home. "I've got a lecture and book signing at the Getty Museum at seven tonight," he said on the phone. "Come as soon as you can. You can't miss the house, it's a third of a mile into Stone Canyon."

Gayle drove eastbound, leaving her home and the ocean climate behind them. Stephanie had closed her eyes and nodded off shortly after they got into the car. Occasionally, Gayle would glance at the young woman sleeping next to her. The lines that had etched deeply across her brow had softened; the contours of her face had relaxed. Once again, Gayle saw the face of an innocent. It was only the occasional whimper that hinted of a deep disturbance. *What a torturous way to live. To be constantly haunted by an invisible entity.*

Stephanie stirred. "I fell asleep," she said groggily.

"Do you feel rested?"

"Yes, no bad dreams. Where are we?" Stephanie asked, stretching and yawning.

"We're on the Ventura Freeway right now, heading toward Topanga Canyon. That's where my friend Jack lives. It's a very unusual place, a small community surrounded by a huge state park. The people who live there...let's just say they're cut from a different cloth."

"That's what my parents used to say about me. I think it means odd."

"Odd is an interesting word, used to try to pigeonhole people who think outside the box."

Gayle took the Topanga Canyon exit that led her to a wide boulevard that could have been in Anytown, USA. Strip malls fought with gas stations for the best corner location. Traffic was bumper to bumper until gradually the view changed from apartments and duplexes to 1950s California ranch-style homes built on small lots with only ten feet of separation.

"We'll be heading through the Canyon and, if we kept driving, we would end up at Malibu Beach. I think you're in for a pleasant surprise in about ten minutes."

"I like surprises, Gayle. But not scary ones. This morning was a scary surprise."

Gayle was relieved to hear Stephanie bring the subject up on her own. "Does HE pop up like that?"

"Sometimes. I think when I'm happy, HE gets jealous. I've never talked to anyone about HE, at least not for a long time. When I was little I did, but when it upset everyone so much, I...*we*...stopped."

"It makes me feel very special that you are sharing your story with me."

"I trust you, Gayle. You're my best friend."

❀   ❀   ❀

As they drove farther into the canyon, the four-lane road narrowed into two lanes. The traffic gradually melted away until they became one of a few cars driving on a switchback road that cut through hills covered with sparse wild grass and chaparral.

Stephanie, wide awake now, became alert to new sights. "What's up this road?" she asked, pointing to a directional sign reading INN OF THE SEVENTH RAY.

"That's one of my favorite restaurants. The inn was once a

church, and then, during the hippies' heyday, it became an organic, vegetarian restaurant. Robert and I will take you there sometime. Perhaps for their Sunday brunch."

Stephanie frowned. "Only vegetables?"

"Not any longer. I think you'll find that perfect something. It's a very lovely setting; the tables are set around oak trees and overlook a creek. It's a popular spot for weddings."

Stephanie spoke matter-of-factly. "I don't think I'll ever get married."

"Why not?"

"Realistically? Who would take a chance on me...on *us*?" She wiped her tears away with her hand.

"Someone who has a truly open, loving heart, that's who."

❀ ❀ ❀

A rustic handmade sign pointed to Stone Canyon, a private unpaved road scarred by deep potholes. Every so often, one of the ruts had been filled with gravel in an attempt to win the battle with Mother Nature. As they drove farther into the canyon, the ruts deepened and the scenery changed to outcroppings of stark boulders smattered with occasional wildflowers hanging precariously onto life.

❀ ❀ ❀

Except for a white picket fence covered with roses, Jack's house had remained unchanged over the years. Gayle opened the car door and stood for a minute taking in the sound of the nearby creek, the buzzing of bees, the smell of lavender, and a sense of peacefulness that surrounded the modest clapboard cottage.

"No steps," she warned Stephanie, "but the ground is bumpy and the flagstone walkway was laid in Jack's very personal style."

Stephanie's mouth twisted as she clung to the handles of the walker. "I wanted to use a cane, Gayle, not this dumb walker."

She cautiously navigated the zigzagged walkway, anger oozing out with every step.

Tears before, now anger. Ah, Gayle thought, *the power of feelings rising to the surface.*

A blackboard hung outside the French door bearing a hastily scrawled message: *Welcome, Gayle and Stephanie. Come right in. Coffee is brewing, back in five.*

"That is so Jack," Gayle muttered. Back in five what? Five minutes, five hours, or five years?

Gayle and Jack first met in 1972 during their orientation as social workers for Los Angeles's Children Protective Services. They made an immediate connection, both of them bent on an idealistic path, certain they could make a difference.

Little by little, their idealism had shifted from healing the world to putting out fires in an overwhelmed, underfunded system. They were both burned-out. Gayle had thought of returning to school to become a psychoanalyst, and Jack had unique dreams of his own.

They were called into an emergency staff meeting after two children had been severely abused after being returned home. "Lost in the Labyrinth of a Bureaucratic System" was the title of the story broadcast on every local news station. There was a public outcry at the incompetency of the system and staff. Someone would be made the scapegoat.

During the meeting, fingers were being pointed in every direction until Jack had finally burst out with, "Have we forgotten what the fuck happened? Two kids in our care are now in the hospital. And that, my friends, should be the focus of this fucking meeting."

Jack passed a note to Gayle: *I need to decompress. Lunch after this fiasco?*

She nodded.

❀   ❀   ❀

They walked the seven uphill blocks to Grand Central Market, a downtown landmark filled with food vendors representing the diverse cultures in Los Angeles. They crossed the street to the neighborhood park, carrying plastic bags filled with soft tacos, beans and rice, and tall cups of iced coffee.

Gayle motioned toward a nearby bench. She handed Jack his lunch; he handed Gayle her coffee.

He opened his Styrofoam package. "Damn, this smells good."

"I'm done for the day," said Gayle, sighing with relief. "I'll finish my paperwork and phone calls at home. As my favorite heroine, Scarlett O'Hara, would say, 'After all, tomorrow is another day.'"

"I'm done, too."

"Good for you, Jack. You've been pushing yourself too hard."

"No, when I say I'm done, I mean I've resigned. Handed it in today. When I return—"

"Return from where?" said Gayle with a puzzled look.

"I got accepted to study with the Fulton Group in London."

"Pre- and post-birth memories?"

"Yes, that's been a long-standing interest of mine."

"It's such an unproven field."

"Ah, my pragmatic friend. Near-death experiences have been reported for many years and investigated. More and more people, including academicians, are accepting that something does happen after death. What that something is, however, has yet to be proven or agreed upon. Why, then, should we scoff at pre-birth experiences? It's not a quantum leap—it's about the circle of life."

Gayle raised an eyebrow playfully. "You, ahem, believe in reincarnation, then?"

"I'm not quite ready to go *there*...yet. But there's some measurable proof to pre-birth memories. We are alive in the womb, and we are having experiences. Why would they not be stored in our brains and perhaps impact us after birth? We know that the fetus can hear the mother's voice and other ambient sounds. And we know the fetal heartbeat and movements change with the sound of music."

Jack took a sip of his drink. "It's my belief that pre-birth experiences are stored somewhere in the brain, or perhaps even in body tissues, and may have long-lasting ramifications on the personality."

"That reminds me. I read an article about tissue memory recently." Gayle paused to recollect the gist. "An assault victim's healed bruises momentarily returned during an intense therapy session. Afterward, they faded away, as did many of his fears. Did you read it, too, Jack?"

"In a way. I wrote it."

Gayle guffawed. "Oh, I'm so embarrassed! I didn't notice the byline. It's fascinating stuff, Jack, and you present a good theory—one you must follow."

"And you, my dear Scarlett, will make a wonderful psychoanalyst. How much longer before you follow your dream?"

"I've got the names of several institutes."

"Fill out those applications and go for it."

"They're on my desk. Who will I talk to now about all this—" she waved her hand around vaguely "—hocus-pocus? Damn, I'm going to miss you."

"We'll reconnect. I won't be gone that long."

They spent the rest of the hour saying their good-byes...talking about the good times when they were able to make a difference in the life of a child, a family. And the sad times, the all too many sad times, when the system failed.

Jack stood up and, leaning over, kissed Gayle on the forehead. "See you in five," he whispered.

He walked away, his hands in his pockets, whistling the theme from the romantic fantasy movie *Somewhere in Time* starring Christopher Reeve and Jane Seymour. Gayle watched until he faded from sight, and she could no longer hear his whistle.

She heard from Jack in five, all right...five years.

He had moved to Topanga Canyon when there were few building codes and small cabins and houses expressed the creativity of the owner. Jack referred to his home as "Helter Shelter," a wry nod to one of the notorious Manson Family's favorite slogans. He would stay in his beveled siding clapboard cottage for a few months, and then drift around the world, always seeking answers to his ever-expanding questions about pre-birth and traumatic birth memories. From time to time, Gayle would get a postcard from India, South America, and Africa, always with the same closing line: *See you in five.*

Gayle and Stephanie entered the all-purpose room that served as Jack's sitting area, dining room, and office. They had to navigate through a maze of books scattered around the room like precarious stacks of Jenga blocks. The bookcases lining the walls fairly groaned from books, books, and more books taxing the narrow shelves. A wicker couch and chairs were huddled into a small space facing out toward the patio.

Stephanie and Gayle settled into the two white wicker chairs.

Stephanie whispered, "He must like to read."

Gayle agreed with a broad smile, when she heard a familiar tune. She stood up just as the door opened, and Jack put down the bags of groceries to hold out his arms. The years had thickened his middle and thinned his hair, but his eyes remained the same—as black as a deep lagoon, and as wide as a child's discovering the wonderment of the world for the first time.

Gayle thought, *We all change, day by day. And it goes unnoticed. Fifteen years have flown by...I was thirty pounds thinner then, with no gray in my hair. Is he as surprised as I?*

They embraced.

Jack looked at Gayle with a penetrating but thoughtful gaze. "It's our eyes that don't change."

"Ever the mind reader, Jack. But *your* eyes are even deeper, more soulful. Have you discovered the answers to your questions?"

"A few, only a few," he said with a sigh. "It seems that for every answer, there are a dozen more questions."

"Another thing we share. Thank you for seeing us."

"For you, Gayle, anything. It must be kismet. I only returned yesterday for tonight's lecture." He turned toward Stephanie and held out his hand. "And this must be Stephanie."

Stephanie leaned on her walker as their hands met. She sniffled, "I was supposed to graduate to a cane today, but Gayle thought I should come here instead."

"I'm glad you did. Did Gayle tell you anything about me?"

"She said you were a wise man and have traveled the world and maybe could help me." She added a whispered, "To get HE to leave."

Their gaze met, and Jack looked into honey-colored eyes filled with pain and a plea for help.

"Perhaps we can begin with a journey in understanding. Gayle told me you have had a most unusual dream for many years and that you are quite bothered by someone who lives inside you. Will you sit down and tell me your story?"

"You won't laugh at me or think I'm crazy?"

Jack crossed his heart. "I promise."

"Okay then, here goes."

"Is HE with you now?" asked Jack.

"HE is quiet now," Stephanie said pensively. "Sometimes, HE has been quiet for years. When I joined the Army, he left. He told me he didn't like it. But after I was wounded, HE came back. And now that I'm getting better, HE's stronger and angry."

Jack nodded. "Did you like being in the Army?"

"Yes. But at the very beginning, no one thought I could do it...pass the physical tests and endure those long marches. *Whew!* I get kinda winded just thinking about them. I'm thin but really strong. And then, they accepted me. I had friends there for the first time, and they liked that I knew a lot of things."

"What kind of things?"

"Facts...I'm a fact collector—a trivia nut. We used to play a game called Stump Stephanie, and no one could. That was the happiest time of my life, until now. But after I got shot, HE came back. At first, he was really sweet. He would tell me I could do things when I thought I couldn't. I had four big operations and each time...you have to act brave in the Army even if you don't feel it. HE would take some of the pain for me. But now he's become stronger, and HE is so mad at me."

"Do you understand why HE is so angry?"

"HE wants to kill me because I broke my oath never to tell. Everywhere I go, HE follows me. It's just like in the poem that Gayle gave me. HE is my shadow."

Gayle interrupted, "It's the Robert Louis Stevenson poem, 'My Shadow.'"

Stephanie said, "Gayle brought me a book of poetry when I was in the hospital in Germany. And when I read that poem, I thought, that's HE." Stephanie shifted her eyes, looking around the room. "I've never told anyone about who is inside me. And now I can't stop talking, but if I don't stop, HE'll kill me. I'm afraid to go to sleep. What if he kills me while I'm sleeping?"

Jack leaned toward Stephanie, resting his hand on hers. "We'll make sure that doesn't happen."

Stephanie turned her eyes toward the patio door, where a mid-sized black-and-white dog with a wide grin and a pink-and-black long tongue was making her presence known by pawing at the door. Her tail, though docked by a previous owner, caused her back end to wag in an affectionate sort of way.

"What kind of dog is that?" asked Stephanie.

Jack grinned. "Ah, she is a most interesting breed. I had a DNA test done, just out of curiosity, mind you. She's a combination of golden retriever, Border collie, and Australian Shepherd. If you look at her, you can see her face screams out golden retriever, but her color is from her Border collie side."

"And her Australian shepherd part?" asked Stephanie.

"That's the part that loves to play ball and Frisbee."

"I used to like to do those things," Stephanie mumbled.

"Would you like to play with Sitara? Gayle and I will have a visit and then we can all have lunch on the patio."

Suddenly distracted from her fears, Stephanie said, "Is there a ball I can throw?"

"If you throw the Frisbee, she'll jump and catch it in her mouth."

"I love dogs. What does her name mean?"

"It is Hindi for morning star."

❀   ❀   ❀

"Gayle, what made you think of me?" Jack said, rubbing his domed forehead out of long habit.

"I never forgot the presentation you made about the little girl who kept wrapping cords around her neck."

"Yes, it was understanding her behavior that led me on my path to investigate the impact of pre-birth experiences. My encounter with her was quite serendipitous. Want to hear the whole story?"

"Yes, I do."

"I was attending one of those horribly boring fundraising dinners. I happened to be seated at the same table as her parents. We made the usual introductions, and when they heard I was a therapist they began to tell me what I thought was a very strange story about their five-year-old daughter. The problem began when she was just a toddler. She had a habit of wrapping drapery cords around her neck. They did what any good parents would do: They removed any access to the cords."

"But that didn't stop the behavior."

"Sadly, no. She began to use her hands and self-choke. They saw every specialist, from psychiatrists to neurologists. Finally, at the age of four, she was diagnosed as being psychotic with suicidal ideation and eventually, the doctors recommended long-term placement.

"They pleaded with me to see her. I told them that my experience was limited, but they insisted. They observed through the one-way mirror as I interacted with the child."

Gayle sat quietly, entranced by Jack's story.

"She seemed quite alert and even engaging. Then, suddenly, as if some uncontrollable urge got triggered, she began to tighten her hands around her neck until she choked. This was way beyond my scope at the time, and I told her parents I didn't think I could help, but was interested in seeing her medical records."

"Two days later, I received a box filled with copies of the child's medical records, beginning with her mother's pregnancy. Every doctor, every psychologist, even details of dietary changes had been documented. Quite frankly, I was stumped."

Jack pointed to a dust-covered box in the corner of the room. "There they are. I was consumed by the mystery. As a last ditch effort, I decided to go all the way back to her mother's pregnancy and her birth. And there it was. She was born with the cord wrapped around her neck and needed to be resuscitated. Almost didn't make it. I believed she was trying to tell us how she had suffered by reenacting her original trauma."

"What did you do?"

"I found a referral for a play therapist that would not laugh at my theory. The child made a full recovery after a year of treatment." Jack's hand strayed again to his high, wrinkled forehead. "I have to ask you again, Gayle, what made you think of me?"

"I immediately associated Stephanie's dream to your case. Can you tell me what you think so far?"

"I do believe it is a pre-birth dream. The beginning of her dream is the way a young child might conceptualize herself in

utero and the birth experience. At seven weeks, the fetus is unde-
fined; sometimes people see it as looking like a fish. I've never had
a case that went that far back in development. I've had several
cases of children dreaming of being squeezed and forced out of
the only world they have known. There is an unusual complexity
to her dream, and that is where she becomes a mermaid. My opin-
ion: it appears to be a wish to return to the safety of the womb."

"What about HE?"

"Many children have imaginary friends, and for the most part
they're benign. Protective at times, even fun to be with, especially
for a lonely child. HE disappeared while Stephanie was in the
Army. That was a time of acceptance for her. HE reappeared after
her injury, when she needed him again. A second trauma. I think
she is ready to stand on her own two feet in more than one way,
but HE is not willing to let go."

Gayle shuddered. "Are you saying HE is a real entity?"

"No, not at all. HE is part of her but only in some fragmented,
ghost-like way. Her conflict is not with HE, but with her need for HE."

Gayle said, "What do I do?"

"There's no easy answer," he sighed, glancing toward the patio. "Look outside at her, playing with Sitara."

They watched as Stephanie held onto the walker with one
hand and threw the Frisbee with the other. Sitara jumped in the
air, ran back, dropped the Frisbee at Stephanie's feet and sat,
wiggling and waiting for the next throw.

Jack said, "Tell me, is Robert still the gourmet cook that he always was?"

"Is that a hint for a meal?"

"It's a hint for several meals. By the way, I leave for India in a
few weeks. There's a child who is able to remember her past life
to an incredible degree, and I must go there. I can't take Sitara
with me. How would you feel about Stephanie taking her home
and keeping her until I return?"

"I don't think Robert would mind, and Sitara and Stephanie
certainly seem to have hit it off."

"It might be just what she needs. Someone for her to connect to, and Sitara is a very special dog."

"Special in what way?"

"There are those of us who believe that humans aren't the only ones with souls. If you look into Sitara's eyes, you'll understand. In the meantime, I'd like to visit once a week, to talk to Stephanie—and, of course, to get some of Robert's home cooking."

"It's a wonderful plan." Gayle's eyes became misty. "Thank you. I was feeling so out of my depth. And Robert has been struggling, I think, with something." She held Jack's hand. "I really needed your help."

"Then it's decided. I'll focus on Stephanie and you—" he looked at Gayle with compassion "—my very dear friend, focus on Robert."

He looked at his watch. "Almost one. Hungry?"

"Why, yes, I do believe I am."

Jack packed all of Sitara's belongings, including her Service Dog vest. He leaned over and whispered to Stephanie, "You can take her everywhere you go. Sitara is your new shadow."

They took Topanga Canyon toward the freeway. The sun was beginning to fall behind the hills and the sky was changing to twilight hues.

"It's quite beautiful, isn't it, Stephanie?" said Gayle. She glanced through the rearview mirror to see Stephanie's eyes closed, her head resting against the back of the seat in repose, her hand resting gently on Sitara's head. She slept as if it was the first peaceful sleep of her life.

What a day, Gayle thought as she pulled into their driveway. *Was it still the same day?* This morning seemed a lifetime ago.

Stephanie, half asleep, stumbled out of the car. Gayle pointed her finger toward the back of the house. "Bed for you two. I'll unpack."

No argument, she thought as she watched Sitara follow Stephanie to the bedroom. *They've bonded.* Satisfied, she began to unload the car.

She finished unpacking and left Robert a long message on his phone. She peeked into Stephanie's bedroom. Stephanie was snoring softly, and Sitara was lying on top of the blue blanket previously reserved for HE.

Gayle settled into bed, sighing as her body relaxed into the familiar mattress. She said her nightly prayer, "Thank you, God, for this bed."

Her mother had taught her early on to be grateful for everything she had, and the small prayers came automatically throughout the day. Sometimes, she questioned if the God of her mother had ever existed, or if being here on earth was simply a fluke of nature. It had crossed her mind that this life was some kind of a grand joke. The cruelty she had seen in her life, how could a loving God allow it?

Yet, her mother had such unshakeable faith. "It's God's will," she would say to a young Gayle. In spite of her questions, the habit remained, and throughout the day she found herself thanking a God she could only hope was listening in.

She wondered how Robert would take to their new addition: a dog. Not just any dog as Jack hinted, but a dog with the deepest soul and the power to heal.

She was irritated...no, angry, with Robert for the comment he had made this morning: "What have you gotten us into?" That was completely out of character, or was this a Robert she really didn't know?

She tried to read a wonderful book on a shame-based culture, but found the lines were moving around like ants marching across a kitchen counter. She put the book down. Her heart was beating rapidly; she could feel her face flush and her nightgown dampen. *A hot flash. The perfect end to a perfect day.*

She heard the front door open and Robert moving down the hallway. He opened the door quietly.

"I'm up," Gayle said tersely.

"The meeting went on longer than I expected. I didn't want to wake you."

"I'll bet you didn't," she said, sitting up.

CHAPTER 18

Claire had one of her more brilliant ideas to combine steps one and two: finding the lucky sperm donor and getting ready physically and emotionally.

"Why not multitask?" she had said, after a particularly interesting exploration of *The Kama Sutra for Us*. Practicing her newest persona of better living through maturity, she observed, "Most of our steps can be combined, and with our newfound means of communicating through I-statements, I do believe we can move smoothly through our steps. We've already conquered one of our major issues. I think we did splendidly in sharing the ice cream...and popcorn, too."

Kathleen, still in that blissful twilight zone of post-lovemaking, couldn't disagree and nodded as she sneak peeked ahead to position number twenty-five.

They decided to go to the beach to work on steps one and two. They brought their yoga mats and music, packed a picnic lunch—made by Helen—and, at the last minute, thought they would throw in a hike for good measure.

Kathleen used her new backpack to carry their lunch and water. Her iPod with a portable speaker fit perfectly into one of the side pockets. The yoga mats were slung over her shoulders. Left at home was *The Kama Sutra for Us.*

Claire was weighted down with a portable file-storage box, complete with handle and lid. Kathleen saw it being packed this morning: files, pens, scissors, stapler, and a folder filled with papers of unknown origin. She cringed at the thought of what might be hidden in that mysterious stack of documents, scrupulously fastened together by the largest rubber band she had ever seen.

Kathleen was so tense she wondered if she would be able to swallow one bite of Helen's homemade potato salad, freshly roasted turkey breast (on homemade bread), fresh fruit, and oatmeal cookies for dessert.

Claire said, "We better take advantage of this food...we are in major food trouble after your birthday, and this month is tick-tocking away."

Kathleen stiffened at the use of the forbidden tick-tock word. Claire smiled, her ever-present dimples deepening.

They walked to a grassy knoll overlooking the sand and sea. It was going to be a beach-perfect day. The sun was out, the breeze was gentle, and the picnic area was filling up quickly.

"I'm grabbing that empty table," said Kathleen as she quickened her steps and took off her backpack. *That little jaunt was exercise enough,* she thought, flopping down with a sigh.

Claire asked, "Eat first or do step one first?"

"Yoga first. Can't do yoga on a full stomach. And we can count that as step two."

Kathleen unpacked her iPod and portable speaker, and they began a routine that was familiar to both of them.

Kathleen thought, *I never was that much into yoga. Just not my thing. I'd rather be running on the sand, flying a kite.* She glanced at Claire; she appeared to be in a hypnotic trance and was following the routine as if it had entered at a cellular level. *Damn, she's good. But, she can be such a spoiled brat. I wonder if she'll spoil our baby.*

She flashed on a scene. It would be Christmas and the presents would take over the sunroom. The baby would be overwhelmed and have a full-blown Claire tantrum.

Claire tried to concentrate on the New Age music for yoga CD they'd brought along, but baby-centric songs kept running through her mind: "There's a Brand New Baby at Our House," "I'm Having Your Baby..."

She kept telling herself, *Oh, Kath and I will be the best moms,* but negative thoughts reared their ugly heads. *Of course, Kath can be a bit on the rigid side. I hope she doesn't squelch our baby's creativity. And at Christmas, I'll bet she'll want to limit the number of gifts.* She could see their little girl or boy, its eyes filled with disappointment at the two boring, practical presents lying under the tree. *I'll have to make up for it on Hanukah—a present a day for eight days!*

The music ended; they shared a smile and sat down at the picnic table.

"I see a dim food future," said Claire. "Can you see us doing something like this?"

Kathleen's mouth drooped at the corners. "Damn, Helen and Sam delivered a low blow when they said we'd have to go cold turkey—pardon the pun—and fix our own vittles. Guess this is Helen's last hurrah as our personal chef, huh? Pass the homemade potato salad, please."

"Helen would have never been this cruel on her own."

Kathleen nodded, her mouth full of scrumptious food. She swallowed and followed with a swig of bottled water. "Yeah! And here I thought Sam was my best friend."

"At least we have a common enemy."

They finished their lunch after remarking that they had done a superb job of sharing.

Claire heaved the plastic file box onto the table. "See how Dr. Friend's magic has worked so far? We're taking care of two steps today and haven't bickered once. I think Dr. Friend would be proud of us."

Kathleen gulped. "So far."

Claire ignored Kathleen's comment and began to spread the contents of the box onto the picnic table. "I think you'll be impressed with my organizational skills," she said with a twinkle in her eye. "I have everything we'll need to begin the process of finding the sperm donor—except for the initial registration fee, which just happens to be one hundred dollars."

"One hundred dollars!" Kathleen repeated, benumbed.

"I filled out the registration form, and I've got the donor catalog. Now to save time, I checked off the donors that most resemble you."

Claire handed a copy of the paperwork to Kathleen.

"So you've done everything," said Kathleen, opening the file.

"Just sign here on the dotted line," said Claire, handing Kathleen a pen.

"Not so fast, Sherlock. I may want to see an attorney first," Kathleen said with an edge to her voice. She reviewed the document. "Hmm...Applicants' Status: Available soon." Kathleen glared. "That's us, right? Uh, aren't you rushing this a bit? Guess you conveniently forgot our three-month agreement."

"Well, I think I found the perfect donor, and we don't want him to go to 'sold out' status."

"You're kidding me...sold out?"

"Consider his background: English, French, and Irish. Eyes and hair: dark brown. Height: six feet, two inches. Weight: one hundred eighty-five pounds. IQ: one hundred forty. Very athletic."

Kathleen's voice began to rise. "What about freckles? Did you include my freckles in your search?"

"Make your I-statement, Kath."

"I think—"

"No, it has to be I feel—"

"I feel this is *bullshit*! What are the fees?"

Claire mumbled.

Kathleen persisted, biting off the words: "I asked: What. Are. The. *Fees*?"

"Here's the fee menu," Claire said, reluctantly handing Kathleen a glossy trifold brochure, complete with illustrations of happy couples and happy babies. "The fee depends on the motility of the sperm."

"I knew I shouldn't have eaten. So roughly, what's the cost, with shipping? Bottom line, Claire."

Claire mumbled.

"I'm making an I-statement: I can't hear you."

"Top of the line, with baby picture, educational history...shipping and handling included: one thousand dollars. That's per frozen straw."

"Per straw..."

"If we start with four, the shipping fees are the same as one."

"Four..."

"We save on shipping fees."

"So roughly..."

"Four thousand, plus shipping and handling."

"I can only imagine what the handling is," said Kathleen, scowling. "And where exactly do we get the four grand?"

"I have a plan. Actually, two," said Claire. "But I thought we could start with a garage sale."

CHAPTER 19

Stephanie rolled over in bed, reaching for Sitara, who had, for the last month, slept next to her. She rubbed Sitara behind her ears and was rewarded with a sloppy kiss and a whine.

"Okay, girl. I know you have to go potty."

Stephanie let her legs dangle...*always dangle first,* Madeline had told her. *Get your equilibrium going before you touch the floor.* She reached for the quad cane, putting her weight gingerly on one foot and then the other.

Good, she thought. *Only a little pain.* She found her balance and called to Sitara.

"Let's go girl, potty first, then breakfast, and then out for our walk. Two miles today—and don't whine! Jack will be over tonight, and you can give him a big, sloppy kiss. It's his last night here before he goes bye-bye to India, so be extra good and show off your new trick."

Sitara wiggled her tailless tail and made her way to the kitchen and the patio door. Stephanie poured her coffee and stepped outside onto the patio. She looked around the garden. Robert wasn't kidding when he told her April showers bring May flowers. The yard was bursting in color—marigolds, pansies, snapdragons—

they were all her favorites, but she thought pansies were her most special favorite of all. It was their faces that were intriguing and made her think. When she looked deeply at a pansy wearing a purple hat, she thought its brow was furrowed in thought, just as hers had been these past few weeks.

Last week, Jack had suggested, "You might want to think about volunteering at the Veterans Long-Term Care Facility. So many lonely people there; a beautiful young woman and a very talented dog would make them heart-happy."

She didn't want to tell Jack that she would be leaving soon. She'd be throwing away her cane and returning to her life as a drifter.

Sitara came over and nudged Stephanie's leg. It was her way of saying, "I'm ready for breakfast." Stephanie petted Sitara, thinking how much she would miss her. The road was no place for anyone, but especially not for a dog with a deep soul. She felt a lump rising in her throat.

She would miss Gayle and Robert; she wiped away her tears with the hanky Gayle had given her. "We used these all the time when I was growing up. Perfect for wiping your brow on a hot day, or dabbing away tears."

She put Sitara's food in her bowl and got another sloppy kiss before Sitara dived in lustily. Stephanie sat at the kitchen table drinking her coffee and enjoying the quiet of the house. She had lived so much of her life inside that sometimes it was hard to stay outside for very long.

Robert and Gayle had gone to the Farmer's Market to get a few things. Robert was barbequing, and there was one stand where a fabled marinade was sold, its recipe only known by its creator. She knew that Gayle would buy rosemary garlic bread and a surprise dessert.

Stephanie had now gained ten pounds since living with Gayle and Robert. Her angular features had softened, and there was the slightest hint of curves replacing what had been a bony figure. Gayle was sure it was the extra calories, but Stephanie was just as sure it was because she was happy, except when she thought about leaving.

❀   ❀   ❀

Jack came over every Friday for dinner, and after dinner, he and Stephanie would walk with Sitara and talk. Tonight would be Jack's last night before leaving for "the exotic subcontinent India," as he facetiously called it, and he thought it would be a good idea if they sat in the den. It was a cozy room with a real fireplace, and even though it wasn't that cold, Robert would pretend it was and build a fire.

"The dinner was magnificent, Robert," Jack said, wiping his mouth with the paper napkin. "It's perfect out here on the patio. So beautiful, and the marinade on the chicken—scrumptious!"

"I can't take credit for that one. God knows I've tried to duplicate it. But something is missing."

Jack fingered his lofty dome. "Ah, the missing ingredient. Sometimes we have to rely on someone else's creativity or skill."

"So I've discovered. A bit late in life, perhaps. When do you leave for the—what was it—the exotic subcontinent of India?"

"Tomorrow at noon. Ah, the chaos at LAX—I'd better be up by five."

"I have to hand it to you; one adventure after another. You'll visit us again, when you return?"

"Of course."

Robert nodded. "There seems to be a bit of a chill in the air. I'll start the fire in the den."

Gayle said, "Robert doesn't do well with failure. I'll bet he'll be up all night trying to discover that missing ingredient."

"Sometimes," Jack observed, "all you have to do is ask."

"What a concept," laughed Gayle. "I'm going to clear the dishes. You two relax. I think we need a break before our surprise dessert. I discovered an incredible baker at the Farmer's Market."

Jack and Stephanie leaned back on the forest-green recliners, their legs comfortably lifted by the footrest.

"I love a fire," said Jack.

"Me, too, and so does Sitara. I like the way she lies in front of the fireplace, with her head down and deep in thought. Jack, how did you get Sitara?"

"Actually, she found me. It was late at night, and I was returning home after visiting some friends. It was a cloudy, moonless night, and you can imagine how dark it was in the canyon. She ran right in front of me. I slammed on the brakes, opened the passenger door, and she jumped in. I never found her owner. Didn't try very hard, I have to admit."

"I like that story."

"It's difficult for me to keep her full-time, I travel so often. Sitara loves it here with you, Stephanie." Jack became thoughtful. "Perhaps I have just been a foster parent, and she was meant to be yours. Any thoughts about keeping her?"

"I can't. You see, I'm not permanent. Not here, not anywhere."

"Why is that?"

"I drift. Except for the Army, I've been drifting ever since I was sixteen."

"It sounds as if you are searching for something."

"Like you, Jack?"

"Maybe," he said, smiling. "Stephanie, we've talked about your dream. Was it always the same dream?"

Stephanie looked surprised. "I think so."

"I've told you about my thoughts on pre-birth dreams, and the first part of your dream seems to fit. However, I just don't understand the segment of the dream where you become a mermaid."

Stephanie lowered the back of the recliner to a supine position. She felt so relaxed. The fire, the way Jack spoke in such a soothing tone. She closed her eyes.

"*The Little Mermaid* by Hans Christian Andersen," she recited sleepily. "My daddy used to read that story to me all the time."

"What about the story intrigued you?" he prompted.

"She was a mermaid princess. A happy, underwater princess living in a beautiful world. And then, one day, she fell in love with a human. I can't remember it all, except to become human meant she would be in pain, horrible pain."

Stephanie began to cry.

"Look, Jack...real tears. Mermaids can't shed tears...maybe I'm human, after all."

PART THREE

A Mad Tea Party

There was a table set out under a tree in front of the house, and the March Hare and the Hatter were having tea at it: a Dormouse was sitting between them, fast asleep, and the other two were using it as a cushion, resting their elbows on it, and talking over its head.

"Very uncomfortable for the Dormouse," thought Alice; "only, as it's asleep, I suppose it doesn't mind."

The table was a large one, but the three were all crowded together at one corner of it: "No room! No room!" they cried out when they saw Alice coming. "There's plenty of room!" said Alice indignantly, and she sat down in a large armchair at one end of the table.

—Lewis Carroll, *Alice's Adventures in Wonderland*

CHAPTER 20

$\mathcal{T}$he overcast skies, common to Southern California in June, joined the gloom that had been cast over Gayle and Robert's relationship since Robert's beyond-the-pale comment about Stephanie.

Gayle and Robert had their usual weekend breakfast of bagels, cream cheese, and hand-squeezed orange juice. Two polite strangers eating breakfast together, avoiding eye contact as they became engrossed in their respective newspapers. Gayle turned the pages of the *Los Angeles Times*, glancing at the plethora of advertisements without interest. Robert's eyes stayed fixed on one article in the *Wall Street Journal* speculating on the United States Supreme Court ruling on the constitutionality of the Defense of Marriage Act.

The sun had struggled to break through the gloom, but failed. Robert stood to turn on the overhead light and ceiling fan. The light brightened the room and the fan began to move at its slowest speed, barely stirring the stagnant air.

Gayle shivered and, without looking up, said, "Shut the fan off, Robert. It's chilly enough in here."

Silently, Robert turned off the fan and tried to return to the article on DOMA.

They had always thought of this as a time to share some news that piqued their interest and drew them closer. Instead, they sat silently, unable to break through the comment that had redefined their relationship. *What have you gotten us into?* A single sentence that hurt Gayle, and shamed Robert.

Their eyes remained fixed on their papers, with an occasional glancing up to reach for a piece of toast or the ancient crazed coffee mugs with their first names written in a childish script, a gift from one of their nephews more than twenty years ago.

Sounds of Sitara's barking and Stephanie's shouts of, "Go get it, girl!" drifted from the backyard into the house. So commonplace now, they went unnoticed for the most part.

"More coffee?" Robert asked quietly.

"Yes, please," Gayle replied without looking up.

Robert cleared his throat. "Quite a busy scene going on out there," he said as he glanced out the door to the patio.

"Hmm, they've been at it for almost an hour."

"Sitara's made quite a change in Stephanie." He returned the coffeepot to the stove. "Look, Gayle. How long is this cold shoulder going to go on?"

"Until you tell me what the hell is going on."

He hung his head. "I owe you an apology for the comment I made."

"Well, then, let's hear it."

"I was completely out of line. And I just want to say, I'm sorry."

"That was very out of character for you and hurtful to me. Look at her. She is not the same person who straggled in here a few months ago. And for the most part, you've been terrific with her. But that comment, 'What did you get us into?' Where did that come from?"

Before Robert could answer, Stephanie burst into the kitchen, completely out of breath. "*Whew!* I really wore Sitara out."

Gayle smiled. "Looks like Sitara did the same to you, dear."

Stephanie went to the cupboard, took out a box of Captain Crunch, and filled a large bowl, topping it off with milk until it nearly overflowed.

"Starving," she said as she pulled a chair up to the table.

Sitara sat next to Robert, her mouth open, and her eyes staring.

Gayle said in a scolding tone, "Robert, have you been feeding her table scraps again?"

"Who, me?" he said, slipping a bit of bacon into his hand.

"When do we leave for Kathleen's party?" asked Stephanie.

"Ten sounds about right." Gayle watched Stephanie chowing down on the cereal. "That should get us there right around one. Robert, would you make some sandwiches?"

"Will six do?"

Gayle couldn't hold back a smile. "Just about."

"I should pack," said Stephanie, "for me and Sitara. I got her a new outfit." She gulped down the glass of freshly squeezed orange juice, cleared her plate, and walked briskly toward her room.

Gayle laughed. "Don't tell anyone, but she forgot to take her cane."

"I noticed," said Robert. "She's just got a bit of a limp now. Amazing." He cleared his throat. "Uh, Gayle, there's something I want to tell you that I haven't told you before. It's about the comment I made."

"I'm listening."

"I told you years ago about my sister, Myra."

"Why, yes, she had Down syndrome."

"That was a very long time ago. But, some memories are harder to put away than others. I was three when she was born and six when she died. They didn't have the medical procedures or the understanding about Down syndrome that they have today. I remember being in kindergarten and the kids teasing me about my sister. My mother waited for me across the street, holding Myra. She never met me at the gate, and I'm sure she was trying to save me from being embarrassed. How she loved Myra, and I know she loved me too. It was just a tough deal all around.

"I've thought a lot about the comment I made. I think the way I felt as a kid...well, I just couldn't understand why all of my mother's time had to go to Myra. Something got triggered, and

I'm ashamed to say this, I think I've been feeling jealous about all your time going to others. I only wish, now, that I could take back what I said."

Gayle went over to Robert and cradled his head against her chest. "I love you more now than I ever have. That's all I ever want from you, dearest— the truth."

Stephanie and Sitara walked into the kitchen. "Forgot my cane." She looked at Robert and Gayle. "Whoops! Excuse me! Am I interrupting a tender moment?"

Gayle and Robert looked at each other, shook their heads, and smiled before their lips met in a gentle kiss.

CHAPTER 21

"Happy birthday, Kath!" Claire said, taking a running start and bouncing on the bed.

"Yuk. Has the day finally arrived?"

"That good, huh? Guess it's up to me to cheer the birthday girl up. I've got good news!"

"I sure hope so. I got the bad news from Robert last night. We're in the red again. I may have to go back to working in the ER. How can I even think about starting a family?"

Kathleen fluffed the pillows and leaned against the headboard.

"You have to learn to trust me. Wasn't I right about the head-board?" Claire said, burrowing into Kathleen's neck.

"Yes, but making a headboard from *stuff* found at a yard sale is not the same as having a baby."

Claire took Kathleen's hand. "I think we need to get a wee-bit more financially creative, and admit it, you do tend to be just a tad on the stubborn side. Let me ask my bubba for some help. She loves us both, and she keeps telling me, 'So what's my money for?'"

Kathleen shook her head. "No, Robert says he can fund us for another six months. He thinks we'll turn the corner. Practicing medicine is changing. We've got the number of patients; it's the overhead and low insurance payments that's killing us. Sometimes, I'll do a procedure that costs five dollars and get back half. The other part is this house. The windows need to be replaced; the heat goes out faster than it comes in. And then there's the kitchen that I can't stand. Shit!" Kathleen exclaimed, punching the pillows.

"Do you want to work on a primal scream?"

Kathleen leaned back, laughing. "You can, Claire-bear, but I think I'll pass."

Claire reached into the nightstand drawer and took out a small box covered in gold foil. "Maybe this will help. Last birthday present for this year."

"Where are you getting the money for all these gifts?"

Claire became serious. "Remember the antique shop that I frequent on a weekly basis?"

"The one on Main Street? Forever Young?"

"That's the one. I traded some website design work for these. Now put away your guilt and open it up."

Kathleen reached inside the box, lifting the square of cotton to reveal a pair of pearl stud earrings.

"Oh, I love them. Thank you, my love." She reached up to bring Claire closer. "This is so much better than a primal scream," she said, kissing her softly.

"For once, I agree. Now, put them on! They're Akoya pearl earrings. Classic pearls for a classic woman."

Sighing now, Kathleen put them on, then opened her arms. Claire snuggled in. "Thank you."

"Seriously, Kath, I can find part-time work. Forever Young wants me to design a web store for them."

"You're already running the front office. No, let's table that for now. I don't want the next two days taken up with anything but having fun. Tell me your good news, babe," she said as she began to move her hands from Claire's shoulders to her breasts.

"Hmm. Am I supposed to answer that while you are doing what you are doing?"

"Try."

"We made four hundred dollars from our garage sale."

"Ten percent of the cost of the sperm," Kathleen spoke dreamily. "Close, but no cigar."

"Well, I *do* have another idea."

"Not now, no more ideas. There is something I do want: another birthday gift," she said seductively.

"Oh, Kath, I love to buy you presents."

"You won't have to buy this one. I've been thinking about *The Kama Sutra for Us*. Great book, wouldn't you say?"

"Well, duh! Best book ever written. Right up there with the Bible."

"Do you think, just for my birthday, I could skip ahead?"

"Have you been sneak-peeking?"

"On occasion."

"Anything in particular you had in mind?" Claire said huskily.

Kathleen's eyes smoldered. "Just this..."

CHAPTER 22

$\mathcal{H}$elen glanced at Claire and Kathleen as they opened the kitchen door.

"Good morning! You two certainly slept in," said Helen with a wink.

"Turn away, Sam," said Claire. "I don't want to embarrass you."

"Oh, I'll do better than that. I'm heading outside to arrange the tables and chairs."

"Come here, you." Claire motioned to Kathleen. "Sam's gone and Helen could give a damn."

Claire held Kathleen until any space between them disappeared. "I'm so in love with you," she murmured. "I think your idea of skipping ahead was brilliant."

Helen turned away from the stove. "Ah, love in bloom. And those are awesome earrings you're wearing, Dr. Moore. Okay, down to business. Birthday girl, you are exempt from all work for the weekend. Claire, you are assigned to do the work of two."

Oscar sidled in, rubbing his body against Helen's leg. "Oh, here's the beggar. He knows I'm fixing tonight's dinner, chicken tacos."

Kathleen laughed. "Hey, have you noticed Oscar has put on a few?"

"*Shhh,*" said Claire. "He's very sensitive about his figure."

Oscar sashayed up and down the kitchen floor before returning to Helen and the morsel of chicken the kindly hairless ape—as Oscar regarded all humans—held in her hand. *Putting on a few? Muscle all muscle.*

Helen turned around, the spatula becoming a baton in the hands of the maestro.

"We have three hours before everyone starts to arrive. So pay attention," she barked like a drill sergeant. "Linc is coming early to help Sam with the barbeque. He's also in charge of bartending. Devon and gang are bringing tomorrow's lunch—and I suspect a few pies, just in case there isn't enough food."

"I ordered the cake," said Claire. "Believe me, no one will want pie after they see this creation. It should be delivered by noon."

Helen continued. "Gayle and the gang are bringing the green salads and fruit salads. Now listen closely: It might get a little misty in the afternoon, and I thought that we'd hang out in the solarium after lunch. Claire, did you get the games organized?"

"Board games, computer games for the kids, and pin the tail on the donkey. Prizes included."

Helen said, "Okay, on to sleeping arrangements. Devon and gang are bringing sleeping bags; they'll hunker down in the sunroom. Robert and Gayle will stay with Sam and me. And Stephanie and Sitara will use the guest room."

Claire's face fell.

"What about it, Claire?" said Helen accusingly "Is it ready?"

"Oh, there's a thing or two left to do."

"Humph!" said Helen. "You forgot all about it."

"I'm on it, Helen—promise!" *I need bags to carry everything up to the attic.* "By the way, who's this Sitara?" Claire asked, munching on her last bite of toast.

"Stephanie's dog."

Oscar let out a howl. He arched his back and flexed his claws.

Claire scooped up the privileged kitty. "A d-o-g? This should be interesting. Come on, baby, let mommy rock you. Bye, you guys, we're off to clean the guest room."

Kathleen hugged Helen. "Thanks for all of this. This is really my first birthday party."

Helen put down the spatula, changing from the matriarchal figure that could be the boss of everyone, to the empathetic mother hen that understood the deepest of pain and disappointment.

"I remember your sharing that story of your birthday party with me." She held Kathleen's hands. "Now, you listen to me, Dr. Moore," she said rather sternly. "You are no longer that child. You have friends and family who love you very much. As for Claire, I might give her a hard time now and again, but you'll never find anyone with a more generous heart than that lovable kook. Don't sabotage what you have just because you think you are that child that deserves nothing. *Capeesh*?"

Kathleen nodded. "I can't wait to play pin the tail on the donkey. Don't tell anyone, but I've been practicing," she whispered.

CHAPTER 23

$\mathcal{K}$athleen and Devon took the path that led from Canfield House to the hillside brick patio. They stood at the rim, taking in the vista of trees and the storybook town below.

Devon said, "Canfield looks so tiny from here."

"Look over there." She pointed to a stand of dogwood tree. "Now let your eyes move a bit to the right of the town. Tell me what you see."

"Wow, the ocean. Quite a view. You did well for yourself, big sister."

"You, too, baby bro. A pie maker with his own bakery, three kids and an incredible wife. I'd say that makes you pretty darn successful."

"Remember the first time I came here?"

"Remember it?" She held his hand. "It was the best Christmas present I ever got. You stood at the door, and when I saw you, I knew."

"It's the red hair that's the dead giveaway. Even though I have to admit it's a lot thinner."

Kathleen reached up to rumple Devon's hair. "As thick as ever," she said, leaning over to plant an affectionate kiss on her brother's cheek.

"If you had been bald I would have known you. It's your green eyes. They're the same color as Mom's, and the shape of our hands..." She held out her hands. "Look. Same long fingers."

Devon said, "I knew you too, as soon as I saw you. Same broad grin when you saw me and those freckles; couldn't ever forget them!"

Dev cast his eyes downward taking in the pattern of the brick patio. He felt a lump rising in his throat. "Just the thought that I found you—kinda tearing up here. This is the first time I've taken a couple of days off in years, but there was no way I was going to miss my big sister's birthday...we've missed so many."

Kathleen squeezed his hand. "We won't miss anymore, I promise. I get the deal about no time off, and I have to admit, right now it's feeling great. Two days with nothing to do but hang out with family and friends. What could be better?"

She placed her glass of wine on the mosaic table between the two chaise lounges. "What a glorious day," she said, easing onto one of the loungers.

A puff of air lifted their party napkins upward, toying with them until they fell to the ground.

"Sometimes I think I landed in heaven," Kathleen sighed, leaning over to pick up the errant napkins.

"Who's filling in for you?" Devon asked, using a small rock to keep the napkins in place.

"Dr. Grant, next town over. Dr. *Cary* Grant." She giggled.

Devon shook his head. "I don't know why parents do that to their kids."

"He's learned to live with it. His mother was in love with Cary Grant and apparently his father didn't argue the point. Doc Grant has been around forever. He has a wealth of experience. Younger docs rely so much on tests; he's got wisdom and a bedside manner to die for."

"Not the best choice of words, sis."

"Ha-ha, smartass!" Kathleen shot back good-naturedly. "We sometimes forget how important touch is, not just in diagnosing, but in healing the patient, as well. Mrs. Roth taught me that. I'd give anything to have her here today, to know—to know I'm okay. Dev, do you remember when we were really little? When Da and Mom were happy?"

"Not much, just a memory or two. I remember Mom baking Irish soda bread and singing while she baked. Maybe that's why I became a baker. Mostly, I remember you, Kat. The way I would climb in bed with you to keep warm. You really took care of me. Hell, you kept me alive," he added plaintively, "Do you remember all the stuff Mom carried around in her shopping bag?"

"Some of it. What did you ever do with it?"

"Amy got on my case—she kept talking about closure. Finally I caved and we sorted through everything. We tossed most of it, just worthless scraps of paper and old grocery store receipts. It was hard to make any sense out of it. Have to admit, I did cry; a lifetime of memories reduced to a single nine-by-twelve-inch envelope."

"So sad, Dev...so very sad. Now you've got me tearing up." Kathleen wiped her eyes with one of the paper napkins decorated with "Happy Birthday" and colorful balloons. "What did you end up with?"

"A few photos and recipes. I made her chicken potpies for to-morrow's lunch," Devon said shyly.

"Amy insisted on bringing the envelope with us. She got the idea that you and I should go through everything together...said it's part of the grieving process."

"And where exactly did she get that idea?"

"From the one and only Claire Hollander. They've become thicker than thieves. Ready for this one, sis? They are calling each other sisters in arms."

Kathleen shook her head. "That sounds downright dangerous."

Dev patted Kathleen's hand. "The 'sisters' have decided that the envelope should be left here. Maybe someday, you might want to look through it."

Kathleen shook her head. "I don't know if I'll ever be ready. It was such a mixture of feelings for me. I was happy that you found me and yet, it was one of the saddest times in my life. To see Mom after all those years and to know she was dying. I only hope she knew I was sitting next to her."

"I think she did. Somehow, she knew." Smiling, he raised his glass of wine, "In honor of Mom! May she have found peace."

"I'll drink to that," Kathleen said as they clinked their glasses.

"Now, tell me about you and Claire. Any progress on the baby-making adventure?"

"We're struggling. I want to give Claire everything she wants, and right now it's a baby. It was one hundred dollars just for the application fee and money isn't coming easily right now."

"Application fee?"

"You forget I can't *give* her a baby. It's to purchase sperm."

"Seriously? You mean there's a market for jism?"

Kathleen made a face at her crude brother. "A market? It's a huge moneymaking industry. It's costing us four thousand smackers to get started."

Devon shook his head. "Quite a brave new world we live in."

Kathleen grew reflective. "What's it like, Dev? Being a parent. You have three kids. Aren't you afraid sometimes—afraid of what the future holds, I mean?"

"Afraid? Hell, yes. But, I can't let that get in the way. I get up at two a.m., seven days a week, and work twelve-hour shifts at my bakery. I know the kids will need braces, and I'd like to give them things we didn't have. Amy's taking some classes over the Internet, and when Baby Kat is a little older, she wants to become a teacher. I'm just so damn proud of her—of all of them.

"Just wait until you hold your baby in your arms. Kat, it's the biggest miracle there is. Your whole world will be turned upside down, forever. And for at least the first eighteen years, you'll wonder if there is a floor underneath all the mess. But I wouldn't trade one minute of it for anything."

Devon glanced up. "Look, here comes Helen. Damned if she doesn't look like mean old Miss Gulch from *The Wizard of Oz*."

Kathleen gently slapped Devon's arm. "Helen's on task, and

when's she's on task, watch out! Cyclones have been known to spring up out of nowhere, ya know."

Helen panted. "That hill gets a bit steeper every week." She used a dishtowel to wipe her brow. "Status report: Sam and Linc are firing up the grill, which means they will be exchanging "war" stories all morning. Linc told us he has a detailed record of Canfield's criminal history—started by the previous sheriff, Steamroller Cruz, that goes back more than one hundred years. Every crime ever committed here, and Dr. Moore, don't think there wasn't a murder or two. Not such an innocent town after all."

"I wouldn't mind getting a peek at those records. Helen, whatever you do, don't breathe a word of it to Claire. She'll be dressing up like Sherlock Holmes, breaking into his office and pilfering the "evidence."

"Oh, got that covered. I told Linc if he whispers one more word, he's never getting another one of my famous cappuccino cheesecakes. The guy paled. Okay, back to logistics: Gayle called to say they should be here in about twenty. Kathleen, you need to greet your guests, and Dev, you better take charge of the kids. So far, Baby Kat has attacked the birthday cake, Brandon is claiming he can fly, and Jennifer has decided that Sam is her one and only."

Helen scouted the immediate area. "By the way, where are the conjoined beloveds?" she asked, referring to Claire and Amy.

Kathleen said, "Last time I saw them, they were walking to the meditation garden."

Helen shook her head. "Did it ever occur to either of you that you fell in love with the same woman?" She laughed. "Just when I thought I had Claire under some control...double trouble!"

Peals of laughter floated up to the patio as Helen took the path back to the house. Dev chuckled, "Helen's got a good point about our beloveds. So much for our days off with nothing to do. We better head back before Brandon decides to jump off a roof, Jennifer announces her engagement to Sam, and your namesake eats the rest of the cake."

"Can we talk as we walk? I need your advice."

My big sis asking me for advice. "Of course," he said.

"The other kids—I've talked to them, and I want to meet them, but I'm worried. Will they be angry with me? Accept me?"

"Angry with you for what? Accept you as what? Kat, it could be a mixed bag. When I first talked to them, I just told them I found you, and that you're a doc, had served in Iraq...that kind of thing. The kids were so young, they barely remember anything. Evie told me the only memory she has is of being cold and someone covering her in old blankets, but she doesn't remember it was you. She said her adoptive parents told her everything they knew, which wasn't much. She knew there were brothers and sisters out there, but thought she should leave well enough alone. Evie has her own family now, a husband and kids. And her adopted parents are *her* parents. End of story."

"When I spoke with Evie, she seemed closed off," said Kathleen. "As if she really didn't want to talk or meet me. I left her my number. I got the feeling she never wrote it down."

"What more can you do? Evie sounds happy. I think we should be grateful for that. Frankie and Liam didn't have it so easy. They were placed in foster care and were shifted around. They were lucky in one way: they had each other."

Kathleen stopped before taking the path to the back garden, where everyone was gathering.

"Frank and Liam seemed more curious about me—asked a bunch of questions about being a doc and what it was like in Iraq. Said they did real well working as plumbers. But then, Frank said, 'Not everyone got the chance to go to school and become someone. I guess you lucked out.' He sounded bitter. Part of me feels like I let them down. If only I could have fed them..."

"Stop right there, Kat. That's a child talking—an innocent, wide-eyed kid that thought she had the power to save the family."

"Why can't we find Rose and Charlie?" Kat wiped her tears away with one hand. "I don't feel complete without knowing."

Devon took her by the shoulders and turned her around. "Sometimes, all we can do is let go of our guilt and live our lives. I tracked them as far as the Catholic Adoption Agency, and that was where the trail ended. I left letters in their adoption files to let them know there was family trying to find them. The only ones who can unseal the records and find us are Rose and Charlie."

CHAPTER 24

$\mathcal{K}$athleen followed the path that led away from the front of the house toward the driveway. It was a gravel lane that began at Thornberry Drive and curved its way through a thickly planted wood-like area. She would wait for Gayle, Robert, and Stephanie in the adjacent rose garden and, if she sat perfectly still, she might see an unsuspecting doe, or hear the squirrels chattering noisily as they foraged for food. She rested on one of the stone benches, surrounded by rose bushes in full bloom, and enjoyed the few moments of solitude. She watched the black-capped chickadees splashing in the birdbath. Maybe they were the lucky ones, not overthinking life but simply functioning on instincts.

She thought about her talk with Dev. He had his fears, too, but it didn't stop him from taking risks and having his family. She could remember word for word what Dr. Friend had told her when they had talked about her fear of returning to the ER:

"Just because you reacted one way does not mean you have to run from that situation. That's rather limiting, don't you think? Instead, you have to create an arsenal of positive alternatives. It should be looked at as a challenge, not something to fear."

She saw Robert and Gayle's car slow down and park at the end of the driveway. She put her thoughts aside and stood to wave. The back door opened and a dog bounded out and ran toward Kathleen.

"She never does that," said Stephanie as she walked toward Kathleen. "She must know you from a past life."

Kathleen smiled and held out her hand. "I'm Kathleen and you must be—"

"Stephanie, and this is Sitara. I want to thank you for inviting us to your birthday party."

"Why, you're more than welcome. We were almost room-mates at Landstuhl, I understand. I'm so glad you're here."

Stephanie whispered, "Wait, I have something for you."

She handed Kathleen a box wrapped in happy face birthday paper. She thought a five-gallon aquarium would be the perfect gift for Kathleen. And if Kathleen wanted, she could set it up for her. No fishies yet, but she had a gift card from the aquarium store in Santa Barbara and an "all about fishies" book.

"It's an aquarium," said Stephanie excitedly. "If you like, I can set it up for you."

Kathleen was struck by Stephanie giving away the secret of the gift, something a young child would do. "Well, I guess I don't even have to open it now, do I?" she deadpanned.

Stephanie was alarmed. "No, no, you have to open it!"

"I was just kidding," Kathleen reassured her. "It's very thoughtful of you. I've always wanted an aquarium, but I never had one."

Stephanie clapped her hands in delight. "So, you love fishies, too?"

"Uh, yeah. I love fishies."

Gayle had told her that Stephanie was a bit unusual, but she found her childlike manner to be quite charming.

"Gayle and Robert, may I steal Stephanie away for a few minutes?" Kathleen asked. "I'll send Dev down to help you unload the car."

Gayle said, "Have fun, you two."

She turned to Stephanie. "Follow me. My office will be the perfect place for it."

"You mean, you're gonna open it now?"

"Right now. Not even gonna wait for the party."

"Cool," said Stephanie. "Dibs on setting it up!"

It was the kind of day that wrapped around conversation and nonstop food. It started off with a barbeque of hot dogs, hamburgers, and chicken—Robert had finally asked for the secret ingredient.

The buffet table, placed underneath the second-story balconies, groaned from the weight of early summer ears of golden corn—steamed to perfection—vegetable and fruit salads from Gayle and Robert's garden, and loaves of freshly baked Irish soda bread.

Linc was in his glory, playing bartender, carding everyone—including Baby Kat—serving wine and beer to some adults and making smoothies for all.

The partygoers had just finished eating, compliments on the food were flying around, while groans of "I ate too much," could be heard from time to time. The ocean breeze came in right on schedule, and as Helen had predicted, gifted them with scattered showers that sent them scurrying into the solarium for shelter.

During the workday hours, the solarium was used as a waiting room for patients. Filled with toys to inspire the imaginations of children, magazines to hold the varied interests of adults, and soft music playing in the background, it served to calm the most anxious of patients.

Now, the solarium was filled with friends and family gathering to celebrate Kathleen's birthday.

The floor was covered with Legos, and the play table with finger paints and Play-Doh. Kathleen understood what Devon had said: "Lucky to see the floor for eighteen years." She thought, *I could live with this.*

Sitara, who was wearing her new patriotic tri-pack vest designed for service dogs, complete with the American flag and
three gold stars, took the commotion in stride and lay with her
head on the floor next to Stephanie.

Oscar was nowhere to be found. Claire heard a faint "meow"
coming from the back of the hallway closet. "It seems as if one of
us is always in one closet or another," she jokingly said to Kathleen. "He'll come out when he smells the cake."

Claire handed out birthday hats, confetti, and party horns. They
played some games first, with Claire declaring: "No birthday party
is a party without pin the tail on the donkey." She tied a kerchief
around Kathleen's eyes. Kathleen won, hands down. She wore her
gold crown with a wide grin and handed out loot bags to all.

Oscar came out from hiding; there was no way he was going to
miss getting a loot bag or begging for a no-no; a piece of cake.

The cake was designed as a road map of Kathleen's life. In
spite of Baby Kat's quick grab—they all knew she would grow up
to be a magician—everyone snapped pictures, oohed and aahed
and sang a very loud rendition of "Happy Birthday to You."

The cake, chocolate on chocolate, was much larger than needed for thirteen people, but perfectly sized to show Kathleen's major life events: her birth in Boston, attending medical school in
Los Angeles, a map of Iraq, and a sign by Christmas River that
said END OF THE ROAD. An icing replica of Kathleen's 1975
Dodge truck was parked alongside Christmas River. No one else
would know what that truck meant, but when Kathleen saw it she
smiled, and Claire knew she got it.

A three-dimensional sculpture of Canfield House had been
created out of cake and fondant icing. If someone looked carefully, they would see that the baker had drawn a small baby carriage
next to Canfield House.

Eagle-eyed Kathleen noticed it, pulled Claire next to her, and
whispered, "You are the love of my life. I'm on board a hundred
percent. I'll make this happen. Somehow, I'll figure out how to
get the money."

Claire rested her head on Kathleen's shoulder. "I want only you, for now and forever."

Sam said, "With all this mushy stuff going on, who's going to cut the cake?"

"Gayle, would you mind?" asked Kathleen.

"My pleasure. I'll cut if Robert delivers."

"No portion control, Gayle," quipped Sam.

"Could I have the piece with the truck on it?" asked Stephanie.

"Like old trucks, do you?" asked Linc.

"I've always liked those old trucks, just never learned how to drive."

"Well, that's a pity. Know what? I picked out Kathleen's Dodge truck. Knew it fit her from the moment I met her. And I got Claire her VW bug. A talent of mine," he whispered.

Linc became pensive and everyone in the room, except for Stephanie, knew exactly where this conversation was going. Linc sat down on one of the folding chairs, took a bite of cake and said, "Best damn cake I've tasted in a long time." He reached under his windbreaker and loosened his belt buckle. *I sure hope no one noticed that. Damn, if I don't get rid of this corset, they'll be calling 911.*

"It so happens, little lady, that my son owns a 1957 Chevy half-ton shortbed pickup. Nice shade of baby blue, almost fully restored. Asked me to sell it for him just the other day. Coincidently, it comes with a full set of driving lessons."

Stephanie sat up straight and alert. Sitara's ears perked up, too.

"Let me tell you a little about this sweet baby," said Linc.

Stephanie closed her eyes for a moment. Opening them, she recited, "Production: 198,538. Weight: 3,127 pounds. The V-8 model had 160hp—"

"Whoa, little lady!" Linc exclaimed. "How did you come to know all these specs? I thought you didn't even *drive*."

"I don't. I saw the stats once in Hemmings Motor News. When you're in the Army, you have to read what's hanging around," she said apologetically. "And I guess I've got sort of a photographic memory."

Claire and Amy exchanged looks and raised eyebrows.

Claire said, "Tell me Stephanie, how computer savvy are you?"

"Just so-so, I guess."

"What does so-so mean?" pushed Claire.

"I had a nickname in the Army: Geek Girl."

"Claire, where are you going with this?" Kathleen asked suspiciously.

"Now that you bring it up, Amy and I, as sisters in arms, were talking today. About a few things, actually. May I speak freely, Sister Amy?"

Amy, who had been smiling so lovingly at Baby Kat, handed her to Devon and removed her horn-rimmed glasses. Her eyes, as black as the rims, glowed. "Yes, it's time for all to be revealed. Right, Sister Claire?"

Sister Amy...Sister Claire? Good lord, What's next?

"Very well," Claire began. "Among this intimate group of family—after all, good friends *are* family..." Claire paused for effect. "Amy and I were talking about the elephant in the living room. Following the research of Dr. Imajean Friend, the secret—or perhaps I should say *mystery*—that is keeping Kathleen and, according to Amy, Devon, from having a life complete and free from angst, is the mystery of the missing babies."

Helen said, "I can hardly wait to hear this one."

Claire rummaged around in her sloppy plastic carryall—found at the Under A Buck Store—filled with all the critical essentials that might be required to solve any mystery. She put on her Sherlock Holmes deerstalker cap and handed Amy a guaranteed genuine replica of Dr. Watson's black bowler hat.

"I'm calling this meeting to order. Sherlock Holmes had his Baker Street Irregulars, and we have a Baker's Dozen—that's thirteen to you lay people. With the combined intellects gathered together in this room, we shall solve the mystery before us in a trice: What happened to Charlie and Rose?"

Sam leaned toward Helen and whispered, "A trice, my ass. We're in for a *looooong* night."

CHAPTER 25

Linc swung off Canfield House's gravel driveway onto Thorn-berry Drive. It had been years since Linc had stayed up past 2:00 a.m. without any sense of being tired. In fact, quite the opposite, he felt invigorated.

He pulled over, unbuttoned his shirt, took off his corset, and sucked in the cold night air. *First decent breath I've had all day. Damn, I'm going to have to face this getup one way or another. And this corny wig—my scalp itched like a sonofabitch for the entire party.*

The election for sheriff of Canfield would be coming up in two years and there were wannabe candidates already jockeying for his job. Hotshot kids with visions of a new Canfield. *Out with the old and in with the new. The same old shopworn slogans, only now delivered via social media—whatever the hell that was.*

Then he had the issue of having to take and pass his upcoming annual physical. He always went over to the next town. Doc Grant had known him for years and was one of the few who ever saw him without his disguise. If anyone scratched deep enough, his secret was bound to come out and his career would end in humiliation.

Claire and Amy had opened a can of worms and the Baker's Dozen had stayed up most of the night talking about Charlie and

Rose. Devon had gone over, in great detail, the information he had gathered since he began looking for his brothers and sisters.

"Trying to get through the Catholic Adoption Agency's red tape was like getting a private audience with the Pope. All they would tell me is they were adopted and the records are sealed. I was allowed to put letters in their files in case they come searching. At this point, it has to be up to Charlie and Rose. They have to want to find their family; it's all there for them...waiting."

Linc thought about Claire. Boy, she was on a roll tonight. Kept going on about how crucial it was not to have secrets and unsolved mysteries hanging over their heads. Claire must have fallen under the spell of this Doctor Imajean Friend. *Probably some kind of New Age screwball,* he mused. He'd have to do a background check on that one.

He thought about the publicity that could come from finding Charlie and Rose. Maybe this idea of Claire and Amy's wasn't as crazy as it seemed. Maybe it was doable, and he would be the one to do it. Hadn't he been studying for this moment all his life? Rather than slinking off in shame, he could retire in glory. He could picture the headline: LINCOLN ABRAHAM HATHAWAY, SHERIFF OF CANFIELD, REUNITES FAMILY.

CHAPTER 26

Claire came out of the bathroom wearing a pink nightshirt embroidered with "Woman of Mystery or Just Plain *Mashugana?*"

Kathleen looked up. "New nightshirt, I see. Is that your way of apologizing for tonight's bomb? That was a surprise ending to a perfect birthday."

"It *was* a perfect party, if I do say so. I guess up until the end. Amy and I might have overstepped a teeny-weeny bit of a boundary." In a faint voice she asked, "Are you mad at me?"

"Claire, if I got mad at everything you pulled, I would be in a perpetual state of rage. Come here," said Kathleen, patting the bed. "I want to talk, and no wiggling out of it by being so damn cute."

"No *Kama Sutra for Us?*"

"Not with Stephanie and Sitara sleeping across the hall."

"Oscar's with them. I think he has a major crush on Sitara." She shook her head as she settled into Kathleen's waiting arms. "That's one screwed-up cat."

"Did you hear what I said tonight?" asked Kathleen, ignoring one of Claire's all too common attempts at diverting a conversation. "I'm on board a hundred percent, and I want us to have a

baby. I want you to put this whole idea of finding Rose and Charlie to rest. It's time for us—for me—to let go and move on."

"Well, Kath...truth be told..." She snuggled deeper into Kathleen's arms. "That was only idea number one."

Kathleen's cell phone rang. "It's Dev," she said.

"Jesus, Dev, it's three in the morning. Is everything okay?
They *what?*" She bolted up in bed. "Stop laughing. You think it's
funny? Well, I don't. Coffee? Now? No, there's someone I have to
strangle."

Claire rolled over on her side, mumbling, "Gee, I didn't realize
it was three a.m. Night, Kath. Sleep tight, don't let the bedbugs
bite."

Kathleen tapped her on the shoulder. "This one is way over
the top. Even for you."

"It was really Amy's idea."

"Yeah, well your *sister in arms* said it was your idea."

"What did Devon say?"

"He was laughing so hard, I couldn't hear him."

"Oh, come on, Kath."

"I just can't believe it. Dev actually thinks it's a great idea!"

Claire sat up, her curls bouncing, her dimples deepening. "And
what do *you* think of the idea?"

"My brother, the father of our child? His children and our
child, brothers and sisters?"

Claire said, "This family is so screwy as it is, I can't see that being anything but normal to them. Think of it this way: No cost...no
application fee...and he's as close as we can get to your DNA."

"I'm putting a couple of conditions on it."

"Anything you say, Doc."

"Okay. One, we go to an obstetrician for the insemination. No
making the baby at home. This is not *If These Walls Could Talk.*
And no baster."

"You knew about the basters?"

"Claire, you ordered a case of them."

"Oh, yeah."

"Two, you see the OB/GYN for all your checkups and no home delivery."

"But I want you to deliver our baby."

Kathleen relaxed. "Darling, I want to be at your side holding your hand while you blame me for getting you into this mess. And I want you to get the best of care. Even if you are a certifiable nutcase—that's my medical diagnosis."

"Oh, Kath, I'm sorry, I don't really know why I do half the nutty things I do. I do have one condition of my own."

"Okay, what is it?"

"That we don't know the sex of the baby until it's born."

"Deal."

"Deal," said Claire, "sealed with a kiss."

PART FOUR

Hush-a-by baby
On the tree top,
When the wind blows,
The cradle will rock.
When the bough breaks,
The cradle will fall,
And down will fall baby
Cradle and all.

— *Mother Goose's Melody*
(London, c. 1765)

CHAPTER 27

"You look beautiful, mommy-to-be," said Kathleen, admiring Claire's off-white maternity shirtdress.

"I feel beautiful, mom-to-be. It's my first 'I'm having a baby' outfit and I want the world to know. Feel how big my tummy is getting."

Kathleen rested her hands on Claire's tiny baby bump. "That's our baby," Kathleen murmured, her eyes suddenly filling with tears. "Tell me how you're feeling about today? It's our first ultrasound."

"I'm just happy you'll be there...as my partner in life, not as my doc. Only one thing, though."

"Only one?"

"God, I have to pee."

Claire and Kathleen sat in adjoining chrome-framed chairs, holding hands. Across from them, sitting on a matching couch, were two men and a very pregnant woman.

One of the men leaned over and spoke to Claire. "Your first?"

Claire smiled and nodded.

"This is our second. My mom is watching our son, James. I'm Steven; this is Jeffrey, the other dad, and our baby's mom, Marne. We're having a girl," he beamed. "You'll love Dr. Bonnie; she's quite a hoot. And the delivery room, well...it's almost like a party."

Marne gave Steven a friendly shove. "Ha! A party for the two of you, you mean."

With a sigh and a great deal of effort, Marne shifted her position on the couch. "Don't you worry, honey. I'm sure your delivery will be much more civilized than our first one. Steven, here, panted and pushed as if he was having the baby, and Jeffrey..."

Jeffrey looked up from his magazine and smiled congenially.

"Jeffrey always has his nose in a book," Marne went on. "He sat reading until the second James was born. Then he bolted up and announced, 'I get to cut the cord!' I wouldn't change a thing. And don't you let people scare you because your family is out of the ordinary."

Marne took out a photo. "This is James, he's three years old."

Kathleen and Claire admired the photo of a sturdy looking three-year-old poised to go down the playground slide, a wide grin crossing his face.

"I'm not just a surrogate," Marne said. "I'm in his life, and how can it be wrong to have so many people love a child?"

Steven asked, "You two have family support?"

Kathleen winked at Claire. "Why, yes we do. A very wonderful extended family. In fact, if it wasn't for them we wouldn't be sitting here today."

"Jeffrey's family lives in the mid-west so they don't get to see James all that often." Steven lowered his voice. "They bought all the baby furniture. Out of guilt, I think. What about your family? Anyone volunteer?"

Jeffrey piped in, "Steven, there you go again with your boundary violations." He tsked. "And out of our six steps you had to break number one."

Claire's eyes widened at the mention of Dr. Friend's six-step program.

Kathleen said, "Gayle and Robert, my mom and dad, are buying the furniture. The baby's aunts and uncles are buying all—" she began to stammer nervously "—th-th-the extra things." Beads of sweat began to form on Kathleen's forehead. "Is it warm in here?" she croaked.

Jeffrey shook his head.

"Ah," said Steven. "All the accoutrements." He handed Kathleen a business card for Steven and Jeffrey's Baby Finery. "Keep us in mind. Twenty percent discount to Dr. Bonnie's patients."

"Th-thank you," said Kathleen, feeling the card dampen from her sweaty palms.

"Now that we've told you all about us, what do you two do?" Steven pried.

Jeffrey said, "Oh, leave the poor girls alone. Kathleen, do you need some water?"

Kathleen shook her head. *No, I could use a Valium. I don't know why I'm so nervous. After all, it's Claire that's doing all the heavy lifting, so to speak. I guess I'm just realizing how much I love the nut. And should anything go wrong—no, I don't want to think about it.*

Dr. Bonnie's nurse, Dotty, opened the door and called their names. "Kathleen and Claire, please come this way."

She motioned them into the second exam room and closed the door.

"I called you in a little early. I thought you could use some rescuing. They're a wonderful trio, but Steven does tend to go on."

Dotty looked at Claire's chart. "Second visit for you, Claire, and an exciting one. Don't forget Dr. Bonnie's rule number one: No more bottoms up for you. From now on it's bottoms off." She handed Claire a drape sheet. "Dr. Bonnie will be right in."

"I'm glad this office has a sense of humor," said Claire.

Kathleen sat on the chair next to the exam table. "Humor and skill—a great combination. You're sure you don't want to see the ultrasound?"

"Are you positively certain, beyond any reasonable doubt, that I won't be able to see the baby's sex?"

Kathleen raised her right hand, "I do, your honor. How about if Bonnie looks first, and if she says we can't see the gender, we look."

"Done deal."

A quick rap on the door, the door opened, and Dr. Bonnie strode in, smiling.

"Hey, you two. Still debating about seeing the ultrasound? Highly unlikely at this stage we could tell if it's a goose or a gander. Of course, I can always do the needle and thread test."

"Finally, a doctor who believes in some of the tried and true ways," quipped Claire.

Dr. Bonnie took Claire's blood pressure and temperature. She looked at Claire's chart, bobbing her head at the encouraging data. "All the blood work came back normal. Pap smear: excellent. Lookin' really good. Let's get a look-see at this little one so you can pee. And don't forget, we need a specimen."

Kathleen stood to hold Claire's hand.

"Okay, Claire, lie back and try to relax. What I'm going to do is put some gel on your belly." She did so.

"Man, that's cold!" Claire exclaimed.

"Ain't it, though?" said Bonnie. "Kinda makes you really want to pee, doesn't it? Now I'm going to be moving this thingamajig around your tummy and see what we can pick up. It's a bit early, but we might get some cooperation from your little one and hear the heartbeat."

Bonnie began moving the transducer over Claire's belly. "Well, lookie here." She continued to focus on one area. "Hear the heartbeat? Nice and strong, and within normal range."

Kathleen and Claire smiled at each other and squeezed each other's hands.

Dr. Bonnie said, "As I expected when you came in last week, you're about eight weeks into your pregnancy. Everything looks very normal. I'll just be moving the transducer around a bit."

Kathleen could feel the beads of sweat running down her cheeks. *She keeps going back to that same spot*, she thought. *Is she just being thorough or has she spotted an abnormality?*

Bonnie broke the silence. "Say, guys, I really think you might want to look at the screen."

Kathleen said, "Bonnie, is there anything wrong?"

"Heavens, no! I'm moving the screen so you can both see. You won't be able to identify the sex, I promise you that."

Dr. Bonnie pointed to a half-inch spot. "Okay, right here...a little bit hard to see this early into your pregnancy, but I'm looking at eyelids, ears, and a tiny tip of a nose. Arms and legs just where they should be. Good, strong heartbeat. Now watch. As I move the probe...lookie right here, another sac, another strong heartbeat, arms, legs—the whole kit and caboodle. Looks to me like you won the jackpot: you're having twins. Congratulations!"

Claire shrieked, "Oh my God! It's what I've always wanted—twins! Oh, Kath, it's meant to be."

"Twins?" said Kathleen, suddenly turning pale and gripping the exam table. Bonnie guided her back to the chair. "Sit down and put your head between your legs. This happens all the time with stressed-out co-moms."

"I'm okay, really, Bonnie," Kathleen said sluggishly. "It's just a bit of a surprise. Twins," she said dreamily. "That means two, right?"

"Yes," Bonnie said. "Last time I checked, in the Annals of Obstetrics and Gynecology, that's exactly what it meant."

CHAPTER 28

"Ta-da!" exclaimed Stephanie, bounding off the VA van toward a waiting Gayle and Robert. "Graduation time. No cane and no limp. Madeline said I'm good to go."

Gayle gave Stephanie a hug and a whispered, "I'm so proud of you."

"Congratulations," Robert said. "Let's go in the kitchen and have a bit of a celebration. Remember the first day you came here?"

"I'll never forget that day."

"I made another scrumptious chocolate cake, but I wasn't sure if you wanted the same fillings."

"One, Robert—I only need one filling. Could we make it strawberry?"

Gayle had determined years ago that the most life-altering changes occurred while sitting around the kitchen table. She wondered if that's why she couldn't lose those pounds that had crept up on her over the years. *How convenient*, she thought, *to project the blame outside of herself.*

230

Everyone remarked on how delicious the cake was. They went through the motions, but the bites were small and infrequent.

Stephanie's lips trembled. "I can't thank the two of you enough. You took me in, a perfect stranger. And helped me beyond belief. And now...now, it's time for me to see where the road will take me. I can't take Sitara. Her feet will wear out, and it's dirty out there—and what if I can't buy her food?"

Gayle was reminded of the first time they had met at BAMC when Stephanie's mouth had twisted from the physical pain. *Now it's emotional pain, but pain just the same.*

"Robert...Gayle...will you keep Sitara for me?" she pleaded.

"No, Stephanie," Gayle said sharply. "Robert and I have talked it over and Sitara is your responsibility."

"I don't know what to do," she said, wiping tears with the back of her hand.

"Maybe it's time for you to stop running and figure out the whys." Again, the sharp tone.

"Are you mad at me, Gayle?"

"Damn right I am! Maybe I can understand your parents now. My, how they must have worried about you after you ran away. Perhaps when you told your mother you had joined the Army, she just couldn't take another night of worry."

Gayle began to cry softly into her hanky.

Robert patted her shoulder. "I think what Gayle is trying to say is, you have been loved—maybe not in a perfect way, but loved nevertheless. It's fine to search. I think we are destined to do it throughout our lives, but to search aimlessly or to run away without any sense of knowing why is futile. It's time for you to figure this one out, don't you think?"

"What do I do then? Can you see me serving hamburgers at a take-out stand?"

"Hardly. That's not how I see you at all." Gayle handed Stephanie a tissue.

Robert said, "Gayle and I had an idea, and it's been discussed with everyone at Canfield House. Claire won't be able to work much longer. She's getting bigger by the second and someone has to help Helen in the office. What would you think about spending some time in Canfield learning Claire's job? It would help them *and* give you time to think about what you want to do."

"Where would I stay? The spare room is for the babies."

"There's a small cottage on the grounds," said Robert. "Originally, it was used as the playhouse for Otis Canfield's children. If you don't mind tiny, it should be just about perfect for you. You could have your privacy and a chance to decide what you want to do with your life."

"They would let me keep Sitara?"

Gayle replied, "Of course. Claire told me Oscar has a major crush on her. And the real bonus is, you can earn enough to buy that truck off Linc—and he's throwing in driving lessons, to boot."

❀   ❀   ❀

Linc had not been idle since Kathleen's birthday party. Something dormant had been stirred to life inside of him. Something that had been missing for many years: Now he had a purpose.

He remembered all those afternoons he spent with Steamroller and the detective magazines. Maybe he had watched one too many episodes of *The Andy Griffith Show*. He had tried to model himself somewhat after Sheriff Andy Taylor—easygoing, affable; a simple man blessed with uncommon horse sense; a friend of the people. Barney Fife, the well-meaning but overzealous and incompetent deputy, had taught him what a law enforcement officer should *not* be.

But this wasn't Mayberry. This was a real case: two children were missing. They knew the search stopped at the Catholic Adoption Agency, but what they didn't know was what had transpired between the time Rose and Charlie were taken from their home and the time of their adoption. He would work backwards, looking for clues that would let him move around the closed files and the law.

He couldn't do it alone, he wasn't that computer savvy. But Stephanie was.

A fair trade, he mused. *His son's truck for Geek Girl's expertise.*

CHAPTER 29

Claire and Stephanie ambled along the gravel path from Canfield House toward the playhouse.

"The playhouse is a hop, skip, and a jump from the main house," said Claire. "Stay straight on this path, and *bam*, you're there."

They came to a split on the path. "If you turn here, to the right, you'll end up in the meditation garden. To the left there's a pond. It's empty right now, but we thought one day we'd fix it up and stock it with koi."

Stephanie's eyes widened. "Could I help? I know a lot about fishies."

"You will be in charge. I hereby proclaim you Stephanie: Supervisor of the Fishies." Claire suddenly doubled over. "Ugh!"

"Are you okay, Claire?"

"Fine," she said, out of breath. "The babies are awake and doing their thing. Put your hand right here." She took Stephanie's hand. "Can you feel it? This is Baby A. It dances like Michael Jackson doing the moonwalk."

"Wow, I feel it kicking!"

"Now, put your hand here. What do you feel?"

"Nothing. Am I doing it wrong?"

"No, just wait a minute."

Stephanie looked wide-eyed. "I think I just felt a foot or a hand!"

"That's Baby B. It stretches more than it kicks."

"Do you have names besides A and B?"

"We've got our top secret ten. We thought we'd wait until after they're born to see what fits. Names are really important. Do you know what your name means?"

"I never thought about it. My mother said I looked like a Stephanie when I was born. What does it mean, Claire?"

"It means crowned in victory."

"Really? That's a lot to live up to."

Claire smiled wisely. "I think you already have."

The gravel trail ended at a white picket fence.

"Here it is," said Claire, opening the gate and pointing to a Victorian-style playhouse. "Do you like the colors? I liked the idea of just a hint of yellow on the shingles and the shutters trimmed in forest green."

Stephanie nodded. "I love it," she said, adding dreamily, "it looks like an illustration from *A Child's Garden of Verses*."

Kathleen had told Claire how charming she found Stephanie's childlike outlook on life. Claire liked it, too.

"Helen said she'd help you plant the front," Claire said. "We cleared out all the weeds. You can choose whatever you like. I'll show you what we've done, so far. We took out the pretend kitchen and put in a kitchenette. Kath and I were hoping you'd take your main meals with us."

"That sounds like fun."

"Do you like to cook?" Claire asked casually.

Stephanie nodded. "Robert taught me a lot about cooking *and* baking. He said I'm almost good enough to take over for him."

Claire's mouth watered as she gave Stephanie one of her most captivating smiles. *Wait until I tell Kath. We may have stumbled onto the answer to step six and our food dilemma.*

"What Kathleen and I have been doing for the past couple of months is taking turns. Rotating the cooking and the cleaning. It's drudgery, and neither one of us is any good at it." *And we almost needed another visit to Dr. Friend.*

Stephanie shrugged. "Heck I don't mind KP...it relaxes my mind."

I have reached Nirvana! Claire smiled sweetly. "There's enough room on the porch for a chair or two."

Stephanie stopped, suddenly struck by the hand-painted sign dangling over the front porch threshold: STEPHANIE'S COTTAGE.

She wiped the tears streaming down her face. "Oh, the front porch is so cozy. One chair and plenty of room for Sitara, too," she said with a catch in her voice.

"Open the front door," Claire urged.

Stephanie looked around at the compact but well-utilized space.

"It's pretty bare-boned right now. I wanted you to decide how to decorate the place. Come, let me show you around," said Claire, taking hold of Stephanie's hand.

"This is the main room, right off the porch. I thought you could furnish this as an all/everything room or, if you feel adventurous, you could use the loft for sleeping. And this alcove—" she pointed to the right "—faces the woods—perfect for a breakfast nook or for working on your computer. I think we'll need to get some electrical work done, installing more outlets and things like that."

"My dad was an electrician, so I know all about that."

"Think it will work for you, then?"

"It's perfect! I've never had a real place of my own."

"Fantastic. Now, what kind of furniture do you like?"

Furniture I like? Her mother had picked out everything in the house, of course, and the Army barracks and rooms that she rented in other people's homes were already furnished. "I don't know," she mumbled.

"Pick a color, your favorite color."

Mom always picked out my clothes, and then it was the Army's turn. She looked at Sitara. "These colors," she said, pointing to Sitara's service dog vest.

Claire said, "We are going to have fun with this place. Patriotic colors—red, white, and blue—with a splash of gold."

❀   ❀   ❀

For the next couple of weeks, Stephanie stayed in the spare room across from Kathleen and Claire with Oscar and Sitara cuddled up next to her. She thought it was the most interesting and unusual time of her life.

Claire gave her simple things to do: filing and learning to meet and greet the patients.

"That's the most important part of this job." Claire had told her. "People are scared when they come in to see a doctor." She whispered, "Sometimes their blood pressure goes through the ceiling. Smile when you see them and always tell them how adorable their kids are. And, if they whip out photo albums of their pets, remember *they* are their children, too."

The filing was easy, but learning to meet and greet was an intimidating challenge for Stephanie. Sitara had no problem in smiling, and everyone made a fuss over her. Stephanie discovered that once Sitara had broken the ice, she could smile, too.

After work, Claire, Stephanie, and Kathleen would go into the kitchen and make dinner. Stephanie thought it was funny, seeing the two of them trying to cook and ending up with inedible food and the messiest kitchen she had ever seen.

She liked watching Claire's belly get bigger; it seemed to grow every day. Kathleen would stop what she was doing, put her hands on Claire's belly, and bend down to talk to the babies. She never knew two people could be so much in love. She saw it in their eyes, even if they were bickering about something silly, like trying to follow a recipe in Helen's cookbook.

She didn't mind volunteering for KP duty. The lovebirds didn't seem to care, and they never said anything when she slipped some scraps to Oscar and Sitara. Sometimes, after KP, she would stay and watch a movie with Kathleen and Claire. *My, how they loved their popcorn.* Claire said she was on a no-salt, no-butter diet, so they drew an invisible line down the middle of the bowl. Plain on Claire's side and heavy on the butter and salt on Kathleen's side.

She thought a lot about the couples she had met since staying with Gayle and Robert. Each so different, but they all shared their love for one another. She had to admit, she wished she had what they had.

It was usually dark by the time she said good night. She would walk the path to her home with a large flashlight in hand and Sitara by her side. She was never scared; she pretended she was in a forest in England, filled with fairies. In the disappointing absence of any real fairies, she fancied the fireflies flitting about in the trees were enchanted beings, painting the night with their dancing lights. When she got to Stephanie's Cottage, the automatic lights would go on and she knew she was home. She called it her teeny, tiny castle and wished she could stay there forever and ever.

It was the first time she had lived alone. But not completely alone; even though HE was gone, Sitara was there. Sitara was outside *and* inside of her. HE had never been on the outside. Gayle had told her that HE might not be completely gone, and during times of stress HE might return.

But probably less and less, Gayle had thought. *And maybe one day she would not need him at all, and HE would be gone forever.*

❀   ❀   ❀

Stephanie liked the idea of helping Linc find the lost children. She wasn't sure about his plan, though. It was a bit like *Where's Waldo*. A big picture with two babies to find. Two little babies—twins—side by side, just like Claire's babies. She began by scouring the online archived newspapers in the Boston area, looking for anything that might hint at seven children being placed into foster care. Nothing. *Not important enough*, she thought. *Seven kids without a home; just not news.*

Late at night she would sit at the computer, sometimes just thinking and asking questions to herself. How could two children disappear without a clue?

After she moved into her cottage, Claire came in for a final inspection. "It's looking really good. I love the way you accented the wall colors. The alcove looks perfect in blue, and the red kitchen is a wow! White walls for the great room and gold for the bathroom. It's a knockout. Stephanie."

"Thanks, Claire. That's a real compliment, coming from you."

"Flattery will get you everywhere. How are your driving lessons going?"

"Linc says I'm a natural at mastering four on the floor."

"Glad to hear it, 'cause this weekend, we're taking Kathleen's truck to find furniture. You drive. We're going curbside shopping."

"Curbside shopping?"

"The most fun and cheapest kind of shopping there is. Someone else's trash will become our treasure."

Stephanie learned something new, something valuable every day. She had trudged the roads all around the country and saw a lot of abandoned furniture. Claire had shown her how something that wasn't of value to one person could be priceless to another.

She wondered if that was true of people, as well.

CHAPTER 30

Claire was lying on the couch in Kathleen's office, a green floral couch with tones of mauve. Claire had insisted on throw pillows in red and purple. "I love red and purple," she had said.

"Doesn't it clash?"

"Kath, it's like us. We're so different, but do *we* clash?"

Kathleen smiled. "Only 67.5 percent of the time."

"See? Red and purple it is."

The red and purple pillows propped Claire into a half-sitting position with her feet on Kathleen.

"Rub my feet, Kath," she said. "It's the only part of me that feels normal."

Kathleen picked up the bottle of Badger's Vanilla Orchid Body Oil. She cupped her hand while squirting the oil with the other. She took one of Claire's feet in her hands, moving gently from her feet to her calves.

"Oh, Kath, I feel like such a whale."

Kathleen lifted her foot, kissing it gently.

"I know, babe. Soon, you'll be back to normal."

They exchanged winks and laughter at the use of the word *normal*.

Kathleen said, "I hope Stephanie sticks around after the babies are born. I think she's a perfect fit with our family, *and* she likes to cook."

"Would you believe our luck? She not only cooks, but she cleans up, too. I kinda feel like we're taking advantage of the kid."

"But not enough to make her stop, right?"

Claire grinned. "Right! By the way, what's Aunt Bee making tonight?"

"She said it would be a surprise. I hope not another one of her mother's recipes. The last one was a doozy: tuna casserole with potato chips and creamed soup. She chowed it down like there was no tomorrow."

"I know. The babies and I were up all night."

"Stephanie asked if she could look at the envelope with your mother's recipes. I think she wants to surprise you. I hope you don't mind."

Kathleen, engrossed in rubbing Claire's feet, said absentmindedly, "It's fine."

"Say, you haven't looked through that stuff, have you?"

"Maybe one day. Right now I want to enjoy us—the four of us."

"I never thought I could stretch this much." Claire's lips quivered. "I'm scared, Kath."

"Baby, I'll be there, every minute. Just call me Coach Kath."

"It's not about that. What if I'm not a good mother? Did we do the right thing?"

"*Now* you ask."

"Baby alert!" Claire bellowed. "Quick, put your hand on my belly. They're doing the cha-cha."

"Good lord. It feels more like a bullfight dance."

"I can just picture them in their cute little matador outfits."

Stephanie knocked lightly on the door. "Hi, guys. Supper's almost ready. Helen told me to always serve salad first. Then, Kathleen, from your mother's own recipe—drum roll, please—Garden Patty-Go-Round."

"I remember that," said Kathleen, sitting up attentively. "It's one of my favorites!"

I hope I don't die tonight. "What's in it?" asked Claire.

"Ground beef, white rice with bacon bits, and canned peas."

Hold on, babies, I think we're in for a rough night.

Stephanie had set the dining room table. "Since it was your mom's special recipe, I thought we'd eat in here instead of the kitchen."

Kathleen smiled at Stephanie. "That was very thoughtful of you." She admired the platter sitting in the middle of the table. "It looks exactly the way I remember it. Oh, my how I loved this dish. It was Mom's Saturday night special and you've arranged it perfectly."

"There was a clipping from a magazine with the recipe and a photo. Hamburger patties go around the rim. Then the rice, and last of all the canned peas sit right in the middle."

Kathleen ate three helpings. "This is even better than I remember it. Hey, Stephanie, you relax. Claire and I will do the dishes."

Claire fumed. *Claire and I? Speak for yourself, Dr. Moore. I'm calling this one, Operation Solo!*

"No, you guys chill. I'll tidy up and lock up before I leave."

Stephanie finished the dishes and cleaned up the kitchen "nice and tidy," as her mother always said.

She hung the damp dish towel on the kitchen hook, feeling a sense of pride at the "nice and tidy" kitchen. Only one thing left to do before going home: return the recipe to where it belonged, with the rest of Mrs. Moore's few possessions.

She suddenly felt overwhelmed with a sense of sadness. Everything left from Mrs. Moore's life fit neatly into a manila envelope. A woman, a drifter like herself, with only a few papers to show for her life. Would she end up the same way? A guest in someone's house, a night in a shelter, and a life of wandering the streets looking for what she had lost or never had?

She wondered if her mother had kept Stephanie's Treasure Box of Memories with the photo of her graduation from preschool, the letter Mrs. Roland wrote to her parents, and all of her report cards. Maybe some drawings she made when she was little. One time, she had tried to draw HE and her mother got upset and threw it away.

She entered Kathleen's office and smiled when she saw the aquarium filled with four happy fishies poking around for food. Kathleen told her it was one of the best birthday gifts she had ever received.

She took the envelope off the bookshelf, opened it and was about to slip the recipe in, when she had a sudden impulse to look inside. She hadn't looked before; just pulled the Garden Patty-Go-Round recipe from the top of the stack. Maybe what she was about to do was wrong, but something inside was pushing her...was it HE?

The contents slid out easily. Reverently, she began to look at the items, one at a time, carefully keeping everything in the same order.

Underneath the recipes were a few crinkled photos. She lifted the first one; on the badly foxed back, neatly printed in pencil, were the names Mommy, Kathleen (4) and Devon (6 months). She turned it over and gazed at the faded color photo.

Mrs. Moore was a beautiful woman, she thought, with copper-red hair and a happy smile. Kathleen leaned against her mother, her fingers hooked around her mother's arm, a wide grin spreading across her face. Devon slept, his chubby legs dangling from an open blanket.

The next photo showed five children clustered around Mrs. Moore. The same house in the background, but now it looked rundown and in disrepair. There were no smiles this time and no writing on the back of the picture. Kathleen looked around nine, serious now, as if she carried the weight of the world on her shoulders. Five sad-looking children and a woman with a swollen belly, looking older than her years.

More recipes, a few more photos. Stephanie turned over the last photo to find a small envelope taped to the back of the photo. She peeked inside to see two dried miniature roses and a note card with the inscription: *Charlie and Rose, I will never stop looking for you, Mommy.* She turned the card over. Scribbled on the back, in faded pencil, was an address.

She copied the address on a scrap of paper before placing the envelope back on the bottom bookshelf, where it belonged...behind a stack of childhood books.

She hesitated. Linc would want this information, but what if finding Rose and Charlie only brought more pain to Kathleen and Devon?

No, this would be her quest. She was meant to follow the lead and see where it took her.

She scribbled a hasty note and left it on the kitchen counter:

Sorry, everyone, I have to leave, but I'll be back. Something urgent came up.
Don't worry.
Stephanie

CHAPTER 31

Stephanie walked hastily to her cottage, packed some clothes and blankets, and food and water for her and Sitara. Grabbing her computer, she turned off her cell phone, got into the truck, and took off into the night.

She stopped at a gas station with an ATM and convenience store. She filled the truck's tank, took two hundred dollars out of her checking account and bought two large cups of coffee, a bag of cookies, and dog biscuits. She settled back into the truck and set her GPS: Los Angeles to Grand Junction, Colorado.

She rubbed Sitara's head and started the engine. "Okay, girl, we are on night maneuvers."

Do your stuff, four on the floor, she thought as the Chevy peeled away from the traffic light and down the highway.

If anything, the drive could only be described as boring. She rolled the windows down, turned the radio up, and sang along with every song that came on—whether she knew the words or not—praying all the while she wouldn't fall asleep at the wheel.

She got to the outskirts of Grand Junction at sunrise. Motels began to appear, and she stopped at the first one that gave any sign of being clean and that welcomed dogs.

She fell into a deep sleep and dreamed the same dream, except at the end she didn't turn into a mermaid. She couldn't return to where it was warm and safe: she had no choice but to be born into a cold and alien world.

She woke to see the sun setting. She took a quick shower, fed Sitara and took her outside for a short walk. They were facing another long drive, but if she timed it right, she would arrive at her destination in time for breakfast.

❀   ❀   ❀

She stood on the porch for a moment, taking in the fragrance of breakfast being cooked. She closed her eyes: coffee, bacon, and eggs and toast. She felt her stomach grumble.

She knocked using the brass doorknocker in the shape of a lion's head.

A woman peeked through the side window before opening the door.

"Hello, Mommy," she said.

"Hello, Stephanie. Welcome home."

CHAPTER 32

*D*addy settled into his well-worn, overstuffed chair. It was the same chair he had used as far back as she could remember; back to when she was three and she would climb on his lap for a bedtime story. He didn't mind that she wanted him to read *The Little Mermaid* over and over again.

All of the furniture remained unchanged, except, like her parents, it appeared worn and faded. It had been years since she had last seen her daddy. He had lost weight, and his bony structure was outlined beneath his short-sleeved shirt. He gripped his Kansas City Chiefs mug of coffee, took a sip, and then walked over to the small liquor cabinet. He put a shot of bourbon in the mug, ignoring the irritated look from his wife.

Mommy sat at one end of the couch, Stephanie at the other. *A small couch, but a very big space between us. It was always there,* she mused.

Mommy said, "Dogs belong outside, not inside the house."

Stephanie felt her eyes harden and her voice become firm. "Mommy, Sitara's a service dog and by law, she's allowed everywhere. She stays with me."

Stephanie put her head against Sitara's and whispered, "I

know you aren't really a dog, but let's not tell them."

Mommy went into the kitchen and took a Sara Lee pecan coffee cake from the freezer and popped it into the microwave. It was something she always served whenever they had company.

"We never thought we'd see you again," said Mommy, handing her the first piece of cake. "What brings you back here, now?"

Stephanie wanted to ask, *Why didn't you come to the hospital after I was wounded?* Instead, she blurted out, "I'm not your little girl, am I?"

Her mother brought a piece of cake to her daddy. "How did you find out?" she said with a sigh.

"It's a long, complicated story."

"No doubt," her mother said with an edge of sarcasm. "I tried to make you my little girl just as much as if I had you myself."

Her mother dabbed her eyes with one of the floral hankies she always carried in the pocket of her apron: white trimmed in lavender with bursts of flowers along the edges.

"Why didn't you ever tell me?"

"We meant to, but then the years went by and you had so many problems. The right time never seemed to come. We did what we thought was best."

She saw her father go back to the cabinet and pour another shot of bourbon into his mug.

"Your daddy and I weren't blessed with children. I wanted an infant, and I wanted a daughter. I wanted to raise a little girl to do all the things mothers and daughters do: lunching at a nice tearoom, attending plays, shopping for clothes. We were on a waiting list with Catholic Charities. There weren't a lot of babies available for adoption at that time. At least, not the kind I...we wanted."

"The kind you wanted?"

"Why, yes, someone like Daddy and me—white, from a Catholic family. We had just about given up when I got a call from one of the sisters at St. Joseph's Hospital. She told me a most unusual story about seven brothers and sisters all placed in foster care. She said there were twin infants. She knew how much we wanted a baby...a daughter. Would we consider taking a boy and a girl?

"It was thirty years ago, Stephanie. We didn't think we could handle two. They told us you both might have long-term learning disabilities and emotional problems. You were malnourished and so terribly thin. I fell in love with you as soon as I saw you, and when you were released from the hospital, you became ours."

Her father stood up, his face turning red. "Lois, I told you not to separate those children. For God's sake, they were in the same womb for nine months." He turned to Stephanie. "I want you to know, pumpkin, I would have taken your brother."

"We agreed, Phillip," her mother said angrily. "We agreed to take one. Don't throw this on me. We agreed," she sobbed.

Stephanie smiled at her daddy. "Daddy, I have never forgotten the fishies you got me for Christmas. I knew it wasn't Santa."

"I loved you then, and I love you now." Daddy dabbed his eyes with his napkin.

"Everyone wants to make me the bad one. I refuse to wear that mantle," her mother said tersely. "You began to have nightmares. Every night. Screaming bloody murder. I couldn't soothe you. I walked the floors with you night after night. And then, when you were about two, you started talking to someone who wasn't even there. I did my best, and that's all any mother can do.

"When you ran away, God help me, I thought, it's so peaceful now. Sixteen years of worrying and trying. And when you came back, all puffed up in your Army uniform, I thought I couldn't go through it again. I couldn't face another night, another day of worrying."

"My brother, Charlie—do you know what happened to him?"

"Up to a point. I have letters from the social worker who was as-signed to him. They stopped for a while after he was adopted, but after a year, they began again. They were heartbreaking, but I thought someday you would want to know." She went to the rolltop desk. "Here, Stephanie, are the letters from the social worker." She handed Stephanie a packet of letters, stacked and tied neatly with a blue ribbon.

"You think I was this horrid parent? You think you had it so bad? Well, let me tell you, you had it a lot better than your brother

Charlie. He wasn't as lucky as you. I know you blame me, but after he was adopted he became much like you. His adoptive parents couldn't handle it and returned him. His name was never changed back to Charlie Moore. It's Charles Joseph Sterling."

Her mother breathed a sigh of relief. "I hope we've swept the cobwebs away. Would you consider spending a few days with us? I'd like us to go through your memory box. I think you'll see there were many times I was proud of you."

It was strange sleeping in the tiny twin bed that HE and SHE had shared for so many years. Her mother had tried to meet her halfway, and she thought that's all anyone can ever hope for.

Stephanie left the letters as she had received them. Devon and Kathleen should read them first. Devon, because he had searched for all his siblings, and Kathleen because she had a hole in her heart that needed to be mended.

Her mother filled a cooler with food for her trip home.

"Thank you, Mommy," she said, hugging her mother with a closeness she had not experienced before.

Her father handed her a thermos of coffee. "Be careful on the road. The news is predicting heavy storms heading for California. Stay safe, my girl."

"I will, Daddy."

Stephanie started the truck, leaned over and kissed the top of her daddy's head.

Sitara sat up straight in the passenger seat of the truck.

Her daddy said, "That's a mighty fine dog you've got there."

"Yes, she is."

She watched as her parents stood next to each other, waving good-bye.

She put the truck into gear. "What do think, Sitara? No more running and no more searching. Let's go...*home*."

CHAPTER 33

"How's the temp working out?" Kathleen asked.
"Not too bad," said Claire. "She's not much fun, though. Works her hours, leaves, and doesn't cook our dinner. We're down to the frozen food Bubba sent."

"Don't worry, sweetheart, I'll order in."

Kathleen put her arms around Claire. "Do you realize how close and how far apart we are at the same time?" She smiled, letting her hand drift to Claire's belly. "It's ginormous," Kathleen said, using the word they thought best described Claire's size and shape.

"I'm going to explode at any minute." Claire became serious. "Kath, what do you think happened to Stephanie? It just doesn't fit with who she is. Do you think she was kidnapped? Maybe she's being held for ransom! Has anyone received any strange phone calls or tried to trace her cell phone?"

"You're forgetting she left us a note. And remember, she thinks of herself as a drifter." Kathleen put Claire's head against her shoulder. "Here, baby."

"I'm worried. And I really miss her...and not just because she does KP."

"I know, I know. I talked to Gayle and Linc. Gayle's worried, too. She thinks Stephanie's becoming so close to all of us might have overwhelmed her. Linc wanted to put out an all points bulletin for a missing person, but I convinced him to hold off. All we need is to have Stephanie pulled over for driving a truck not registered in her name *and* no driver's license."

"You don't think it was the KP duty, do you?"

"Are you feeling guilty?"

"We did take advantage of her."

"I don't think that was it. I think she felt important taking care of us, being able to do something we obviously suck at."

Kathleen turned her head at the sound of the windows rattling. "Be right back," she said. She scurried around the room checking the locks and fastening the bolts at the bottom of the wooden windows.

"It's starting to rain."

"We need it; it's been a dry year."

"I'm not liking this at all. The weather nerds on TV and the radio say we may be in for some nasty weather. I want us to go into Santa Barbara early."

"Oh, Kath. Don't be alarmed. I'm not due for a while, and first babies *always* come late."

"Claire, you've read everything there is on having twins—and they're usually early, not late."

Claire reached out her arms. "Need a hug?"

Kathleen glided into her open arms.

Claire cooed, "My sweet angel is such a worry wart. You shouldn't fret so; I do have a doc on hand," she added lightheartedly.

"Yes, you do. And this doc is taking charge. We're leaving for Santa Barbara first thing in the morning. I'll commute, and you can have all the room service you want. End of argument."

CHAPTER 34

$\mathcal{K}$athleen woke to the sound of the wind howling and the rain splattering against ancient windows. She stared at the clock, 3:30 a.m.

Claire was lying on her back in a deep, soundless sleep, her legs sprawled across the bed—the only position she found comfortable in these last few weeks of her pregnancy. Kathleen felt the damp morning air sneaking into the room and covered her with an extra quilt. Shivering, she began to move methodically around their bedroom, placing old towels around the drafty windowsills.

She took the stairs toward the kitchen, glimpsing every now and again at Oscar's shadow on the staircase wall. She filled his food and water bowl and bent down to rub his head and pet his back.

"We're in for something nasty," she whispered to the feline that seemed unruffled by the increasingly threatening sounds of rain and wind. He took his first dainty bite from the bowl. *Breakfast first, worry later. That's my motto.*

She moved from room to room, checking the windows for leaks. A queasy feeling began in her gut at the sight of the rain pelting against the eastern side of the house. *Sweet Jesus. This is no ordinary rainstorm.*

Kathleen returned to the kitchen, without so much as a glance at the hideous orange and green linoleum she so detested. She started a pot of coffee and turned on the Christmas gift from Linc, an emergency weather radio.

Linc had pointed out, "This portable baby is the Swiss Army knife of radios. It's got multiple radio bands, an LED flashlight, and it comes with emergency weather alerts. You'll get a tone alarm before broadcasting. Oh, yeah, and it's got a battery backup."

Claire had quipped, "So far the weather here has been: possibility of slight showers; morning fog with sunshine in the afternoon. Wear your sunscreen."

Having been raised on the east coast, both Claire and Kathleen had smiled at the possibility of any kind of California weather coming close to New York City or Boston's.

"You two can make all the fun you want. But I've seen it before. We have a few dry years, fires leave the hills denuded, and then we have a wet year. The rain won't stop for a week and *then* the mudslides take over."

Linc had turned to Helen and Sam. "I want you to stock up with two weeks of food. I know these two," he said, motioning to Kathleen and Claire. "They'll starve after the ice cream melts."

The lights began to flicker, turn back on, only to begin flickering again before failing altogether. Kathleen froze until she heard the standby propane emergency generator kicking in and saw the lights holding a steady glow. They would have power on the first floor. The rest of the house was now cast in darkness. Kathleen grabbed the flashlight hanging next to the kitchen door. She would wait a while before waking Claire, Sam, and Helen. *No need to panic,* she kept telling herself.

She opened the door to the reception room to find the office phone lit up with static-filled messages from the night before. *Sorry, Doc, canceling our appointment... We're hunkering down, expecting mudslides... Sorry for the last-minute cancellation. Hope you're all safe.*

The phone lights dimmed and then darkened. She picked up the landline, hoping for a dial tone, only to be greeted by complete silence.

She glanced at her watch. A little after 4:00 a.m. Her body was trying to tell her something. She knew the signals: butterflies in her stomach and a feeling of foreboding. She was moving into a state of vigilance and preparedness.

She picked up her mug and walked back to the kitchen for a refill. Why had she been so upset about the way the kitchen looked? The stove worked, the fridge worked; they laughed and fought and even made love in the kitchen. How many times had they sat at the scarred table sharing a pint of ice cream? *Dozens,* she thought, *dozens.*

She heard the warning tone coming from the weather radio. It was time for her to take as much control of the situation as possible.

She knew exactly what she had to do. She made her way to the trauma room.

She breathed a sigh of relief and felt a sense of control at the sight of the familiar surroundings. She was home. The trauma room was small and certainly not intended to replace an emergency room, but a doc in a more rural area had to be prepared to treat crises.

This was the room where she first saw Claire, lying on the EMT gurney and mumbling about her beloved 501 Levi's. "Originals," she kept saying. She thought if it weren't for having this room, she would have never met Claire. She had lost so much of her faith over the years, but she had to wonder, was all of this just happenstance? Or was there, in fact, a God with a divine plan?

She had to shift away from those thoughts and return to her role of physician. She surveyed the room, looking at the equipment she had purchased over the past few years: a standard hospital bed, exam table, ultrasound scanner, digital X-ray equipment, warming cabinet, crash cart, and a compact lab.

Robert had told her, only the other night, that one of the reasons she was in the red was that she kept adding more equipment.

"You're not running an ER," he said crisply.

"We're an hour away from the nearest hospital. Copters can't always fly in because of the weather. I want that golden hour."

"I get that, and I would think less of you if you didn't place the lives of the patients over everything else. But right now, you're thousands in debt because of that room."

"What price for a life, Robert?"

"I don't have an answer to that. You wanted to know why you're in the red and that's one of the reasons: a big one. Keep it in mind."

Keep it in mind? One night in Iraq would never leave her mind.

She and Sam were called to the home of a woman in the late stages of labor. They were transported under heavy guard, sitting in the back of an armored personnel truck, hanging onto their obstetric delivery kit—everything that would be needed for a normal delivery. It wasn't enough. The baby was breech, and the mother had labored too long, with only the assistance of her mother-in-law. She would never forget that night. The feeling of failure on her part, the family's pain at the death of the infant, followed by gratitude that she and Sam had saved the mother.

It was so very different for the pregnant women in Canfield.

Some chose to use the local midwife, Sally Fuentes; others went to St. Mona's Birthing Center.

Kathleen had met Sally at one of the continuing education seminars at St. Mona's. It was difficult to guess Sally's age. Her face was lined from the sun and her hair was gray, but her eyes were mirthful and she had a quick smile.

"We've lived in Canfield for more than thirty years," Sally had told her. "My husband Chip and I wanted to raise our children away from the city. Funny, when they grew up, they all wanted the city life. Go figure," she chuckled.

Kathleen thought of her as the living embodiment of an earth mother. She nurtured the earth through her gardening and nurtured the stray animals that found their way to her home. Most of all, she cared for women throughout their pregnancy and childbirth.

There was another side to Sally, and that was the experience and skill she had as a midwife. "After twenty years," Sally said, "you think you've seen it all. Then another surprise comes along. It's never boring, and each time you hear a baby cry for the first time, you are witnessing a miracle."

Kathleen had attended a couple of home births with Sally, not because she was needed, but because she was still pained by her experience in Iraq and wanted to learn. She never wanted to look in the eyes of a mother and father whose child had died because of a lack of equipment or facilities. She hadn't shared her dream, not with Robert and not even with Claire, to someday build a birthing center on their precious ten acres of prime property.

She opened the double doors to the cabinet labeled OBSTETRIC SUPPLIES, taking a mental inventory.

Top shelf: delivery packs. They included everything needed for a normal delivery: baby blankets, bulb syringes for clearing the infant's throat and mouth, placenta basins, and everything in between.

She picked up the package of infant caps knitted in genderless colors of pink, blue, yellow, and green.

Sally had told her she only used the caps on babies who were premature, low birth weight, or born in a room that lacked heat. "When I put the baby on the mother's chest, I cover the baby's backside with a blanket, but sometimes the moms want the caps because they are so darn cute. A warm room and skin to skin contact is really all most of them need."

Next shelf: instruments for clamping and cutting the cord, episiotomy scissors, suturing kit, and forceps.

Now she moved to the medication cabinet, taking a mental inventory of what she might need: anti-hemorrhagic meds, saline solution, and oxytocin to stimulate contractions.

She closed the cabinet doors and leaned against the wall. She prayed, "Please God, don't test me...not again."

CHAPTER 35

They huddled in the reception room, listening to the emergency radio. The rain and wind had joined forces, causing the old windows to shudder in their frames. Sam thought it was the safest room to ride out the storm, as the bank of windows were situated high on the wall and covered with heavy wooded shutters.

They were in the full thrust of what was predicted to be one of the worst storms in California history.

Claire lay on the sofa, shaking. Helen had covered her with quilts. "Honey, you're just scared. I'll make you some chamomile tea."

The babies were quiet, moving occasionally, but not doing their usual cha-cha dance. *Oh, God...I have been such a shit all my life. Now I've got two babies inside me. What if they aren't okay?*

The front door rattled, then banged.

"Is that the wind?" Claire asked, her voice trembling.

Kathleen knelt down next to Claire. "I'll check," she whispered soothingly.

Linc stood on the front porch, his southwestern hat dripping.

"I'm on my way to the back hills. Wanted to see if you're all okay."

"Linc, is there any way out?"

Linc spoke rapidly. "Doc, we're going to be slogging through this weather for another couple of days. It's a low-pressure system out of the Pacific. They're calling it a Pineapple Express. We're in for it. Canfield's locked in and no one is getting in *or* out. Christmas River has risen to the top of its banks, and we've had some mudslides in the back hills. The Farleys barely got out. Lost most of their llamas."

"Are they okay?"

"Yes, got out by the skin of their teeth."

Linc looked down bashfully at his mud-covered rain boots. "Listen, Doc, I get your situation with Claire and the impending twins. Don't even think of trying to leave the house. Our EMTs are on call. How's Claire?"

"Scared to death and very quiet. I'm getting everything in place, just in case."

"The landlines are gone, but so far, the cell phones are still working. Call me if you need me. If we get a break in the weather, we can try to helicopter Claire out."

Kathleen shook her head. "It doesn't look as if there's going to be a break, and I'm not risking others' lives. If it comes down to it, Sam and I have delivered babies in worse conditions than this."

Linc impulsively hugged Kathleen. "It's different when it's your own."

"Yes it is, Linc...it is."

Claire stood in the doorway of the trauma room. Kathleen seemed lost inside and hadn't noticed her. I met Kath in this very room. She seemed so aloof; I didn't think she liked me. God, she's beautiful. I don't tell her often enough how much she means to me.

She gazed at the woman who had become her lover, her partner in life. She smiled, thinking of how shy Kathleen was that day at Christmas River, when they sat in the truck and kissed for the first time. *She's not so shy now.*

Kathleen looked up and smiled. "Hi, darling. Did you have a good nap?"

Claire trembled. "Kath," she said, looking down at the growing puddle on the floor. "I'm really scared. My water just broke."

CHAPTER 36

$\mathcal{H}$ow strange it all seemed. She always wanted to be the center of attention, but not like this.

Helen helped her into a hospital gown and Sam inserted a heparin lock.

Sam said calmly, "You might not need an IV at all, but if you do, we'll be ready. And the good thing about this is you won't be tethered to an IV pole. Once we get you set, you can walk around, get all the back rubs you want, and blame Kathleen for everything." He tacked on a whispered, "If you want to scream, go right ahead. Better out than in."

"I don't have to be brave?"

"You are one of the bravest people I have ever known; you don't have to prove it. After all, you've put up with me, haven't you?"

Kathleen rolled the ultrasound scanner next to the hospital bed.

"Remember the first time Dr. Bonnie did your ultrasound?" She did a convincing impersonation of their beloved baby doc: "Let me move this thingamajig over your belly. Now, lookie here...two really strong heartbeats and both babies are in a perfect position for delivery." She became serious. "How long have you been having contractions?"

"I didn't want to worry you."

"How long, Claire?" Kathleen insisted.

"On and off since I woke up. I was hoping it was something I ate."

Kathleen kissed her ever so softly, whispering, "Now listen to me, Claire. I have to be your doc. I'm going to examine you, and we're going to get these babies delivered. Years from now, you'll be telling them the story of how they were born in the middle of the Pineapple Express."

Claire had never noticed that the trauma room was windowless. How could she not have been aware? Day and night now fused into timelessness.

She gasped the first time the fluorescent lights flickered off, casting the room in complete darkness. They blinked on and off before returning to a steady light.

Sam patted her arm and said, "It's the generator. It'll do that every once in a while. Don't worry, we've got you covered."

Kathleen said to Sam, "Let's get the procedure light in place."

"All charged up and good for more than four hours," Sam said as he rolled the portable light to where Kathleen was sitting.

She nodded. "Let's keep it charging for now." *Next time someone tells me I've spent too much on equipment, I'll tell them this story.*

The contractions became closer, stronger. It wasn't so bad at first—*no worse than menstrual cramps*, Claire thought. She walked around and leaned against Kathleen, groaning when the first hard one came.

Helen kept rubbing her back, helping her to change positions and coaching her on her breathing. "Claire, you're panic-breathing with every contraction. Remember how you breathe when you're meditating? Keep the in-breath the same length as the out-breath. Concentrate on the breath."

Groans changed to cries of anguish. Helen wiped her brow. "I know these contractions are really painful, but with each one, just remind yourself your little one is making its way down."

Kathleen examined Claire. "These babies mean business. You're fully dilated. When you feel the urge, start pushing."

"God, Kath, I've been wanting to push for hours. Can I say our routine first? Just like we rehearsed?"

"Go for it."

"Whose idea was this, anyway?"

"Mine, babe...all mine."

"Another one's coming," Claire said, grabbing Helen's hand.

Helen was seemingly as cool as a cucumber. "Steady breaths, now. You can do this, Claire."

Claire groaned and then screamed. "Goddammit it, Helen, *you* try it!"

Kathleen said, "Babe, you're doing great. The top of the head is out. I want the baby's face to come out slower. Start panting on the next contraction, no pushing. That's it...I can see two perfect little ears. One more like that and the face will be delivered."

Claire panted through the next contraction.

"The full face is out to the chin," said Kathleen. "And Baby A is turning exactly in the right position."

Helen said, "Let's try a cleansing breath between your contractions. In through your nose and out through your mouth."

Claire watched as Helen drew in a giant breath and exhaled noisily, looking and sounding exactly like a balloon a child had blown up and let fly. Claire half-groaned. "If I wasn't so pissed off and in pain, I'd be laughing my ass off."

"Anything to distract you, dear."

Kathleen said, "Next contraction, return to pushing. We need to get those shoulders out. Push, push, push...I can see the shoulders. Two more pushes, and we'll have our baby. Next contraction, push as hard as you can. Let's get this baby delivered! The shoulder's out. One more, babe...one more like that!"

Claire gathered her strength and bore down.

Kathleen let out a whoop. "Sam, suction please!"

A loud cry echoed throughout the windowless room.

"Time of birth," announced Sam, "4:35 a.m. Nothing wrong with those lungs," he added.

"Boy or girl? Boy or girl?" Claire chanted.

Kathleen's voice trembled as she lifted the baby into Claire's view. "How would you feel about having a daughter?"

Claire's eyes streamed. "I'd feel...blessed."

Kathleen said, "Sam, I'd like to hold Claire's hand right now. Will you take it from here and please do us the honor of cutting and clamping the cord?"

"You sure grow 'em sturdy, Claire—and feisty," said Sam, responding to the baby's cries. "She's already giving me an argument."

Sam laid the baby on Claire's chest, covering her gently with a warm blanket. Claire motioned to Kathleen to come closer and whispered softly in her ear.

A brief smile, mingled with tears, crossed Kathleen's face. She turned to face Helen and Sam.

Kathleen cleared her throat and announced, "Sam and Helen, meet Annie Hollander-Moore. Claire and I were hoping you would be Annie's godparents."

Helen turned away, covering her eyes with her hand. "I'd be honored."

Sam said, with a catch in his voice, "She'll be a challenge, but I'm up for the job."

Claire gushed. "She's so beautiful. And look how smart she is! She's already latched on. Oh, Kath...it really wasn't so bad," said Claire, feeling Annie suckling. "I think the little angel's starving."

"Well, she certainly has the Moore figure," quipped Helen, trying to regain her composure.

Kathleen stroked Claire's forehead, "I'm so proud of you."

Claire cringed. "Quick, someone take Annie. It's starting again!"

Kathleen said, "Helen, take care of Annie. Sam, let's get a second ultrasound and see what Baby B is up to."

"Doc," said Sam, "Baby B has spun around into a frank position."

"What does that mean?" asked Claire between contractions.

Kathleen looked at the ultrasound. "It means we have a breech birth. Baby B is coming out bottom first."

Kathleen broke out in a sweat. *Not again.* She exchanged troubled looks with Sam.

"Too late in the game to try to turn the baby—it's in the pelvis," Kathleen said. "I'm going to break the membrane to help things along. B is getting delivered exactly the way it was meant to."

Kathleen had spent one late night and early morning with the midwife, Sally Fuentes. It was a similar situation, a surprise breech birth. She remembered how calm Sally had remained. "Breech births are just as natural as head first; it's just a variation. With a bit of luck and a technique or two, we'll just let the little one slip out on its own. Step by step, Kathleen. Step by step."

Step by step, she thought, before kicking into action and taking control.

"Helen, get some blankets and towels out of the warmer. Sam, turn the heater up and remove the footboard. Claire, we're moving you all the way to the end of the bed so Baby B can have some dangle room."

"I'll fall off!" she cried.

Kathleen spoke calmly. "No, you won't. Breech babies need to have some dangle space, and I need room to change Baby B's position if I have to. Sam and Helen are going to be holding your legs, so you won't fall. I promise you that."

Kathleen looked at the clock. Ten minutes had passed since Annie's birth.

"I want you to focus on pushing now, just the way you pushed with Annie. Big push on your next contraction. *Push, push, push!*"

CHAPTER 37

She was being torn apart by pain when suddenly she began to float away. Was she dying? It wasn't the way Claire thought death would be. There was no tunnel and there was no light. She was moving through time and space. *This is way cool,* she thought. She passed the moon; she passed the planets and floated beyond the stars.

She fell into a wormhole, down, down, down, until *whomp!* She landed softly on a bunny on a carousel menagerie. It didn't look like Alice's White Rabbit, wearing his nifty waistcoat with the outsized watch tucked in the pocket, and it certainly didn't look like Mr. Fluffy, her Passover bunny with his button eyes and cottony tail. It was a pink rabbit with a gold saddle, trimmed in blue and wearing a necklace of bells around his neck that jingle-jangled with the movement of the carousel. The carousel was turning slowly, its music playing in half-time rhythm. *Everything in this world was in slow motion,* she mused.

She remembered there was a before world. She had a baby, a daughter, in that world. And someone she loved, who loved her back. She couldn't remember her name, but she could see her face. Oh, she looked so sad when she last saw her; her eyes filled with the deepest pain she had ever seen. She tried to hold on to that other world, but it was going...going...gone.

She looked up. The woman with the sad eyes was straddling the carousel horse in front of her. A ferocious animal, with nostrils flared as if he was ready to go into battle. She remembered her name: *Kath*. Why did it hurt so much to think of her name? She called out to her, but she looked straight ahead. *That is so Kath,* she thought, *always on task.*

The carousel stopped, and Kath's horse strode off the platform and began trotting away.

Her bunny became animated and followed the horse from a distance. *I'm in Kath's old dream.* She was surrounded by the devastation of war, and she felt her heart shatter. *This is what war looks like. This is what Kath and all the others saw. Why couldn't I understand before?*

Bodies were strewn everywhere: men and women in uniforms, civilians and children. She felt her heart break. *Oh, the children— the poor babies.*

She heard a faint memory of a voice: Kath's voice.

"Push, Claire...*push, push, push.*"

She heard a scream. It belonged to her.

Where am I? Where's Sam...where's Helen...where are my babies?

She heard Helen's voice. "Doc, Claire's BP is dropping...dropping...dropping..."

Why were the sounds so far away?

"Helen, start the saline drip."

The sounds and memories faded.

They left the horrors of war and crossed a bright-green meadow filled with flowers in rainbow colors. *So beautiful,* she thought. *I could stay here forever.* Her bunny continued to follow the horse, past the meadow to a riverbank. Claire watched as Kath's horse began to swim across, its proud head held high, clouds of steam spurting from its flaring nostrils.

Claire's bunny planted its paws firmly on the ground.

"Giddy-up, giddy-up! Follow that horse!" she commanded.

Bunny turned to the right. "Silly, I can't cross the river," he said haughtily.

"Holy smoke, a talking bunny!" she said out loud.

"This is as far as I can go," said Bunny. "Dismount, please."

"Where am I?"

"Dismount, please."

Claire slid off. Great. Stuck in the middle of nowhere without a compass. She glanced down. *Oh, thank God! I've got my pre-pregnancy figure back.*

A mantle of fog rose from the river. "You called?" said the Fog.

"Huh?"

"You said 'thank God,' so I came."

"Um, you're God? I thought you'd be really old with a long white beard and white hair—more like a fluffy cloud, not fog."

"I come in all shapes and sizes. You've met me before, but you didn't recognize me then, either."

"Was that when I was in Ireland?"

God chuckled. "Could be. Come, follow me."

"I'm glad one of us can see some humor in this."

Presently they came to an animated meadow. The emerald-green grass swayed to the sounds of fat little chipmunks playing "Tubby the Tuba" on hollowed-out pinecones that served as oca-rinas and oboes, while the trees picked up their roots and danced to the happy tune.

Two children were on swings hanging between the trees. Oh, they went so high. Claire shouted, "Be careful!"

They turned and smiled at her. *Sweet smiles*, she thought. The girl had red hair and freckles; the boy had the darkest black hair and the deepest blue eyes she had ever seen.

God said, "Don't worry, Claire. The children will be fine. Come join us at the picnic table."

Four women were sitting at a round redwood table playing cards. "Claire, I'd like you to meet Mohammed, Jesus, Buddha, and Moses."

Claire looked at him quizzically. "But, they were all men."

"I recycle everyone in different forms."

"Can I play, too? Bridge or canasta?"

God laughed with a deafening roar. Claire held her hands over her ears.

"We're playing the cards of life. This is where we deal out people's dreams and talents. I must say, we've been a bit disappointed in you. We gave you so much to share with others."

"But, God...should I call you Sir God or Madam God?"

"No, just plain God is fine."

"I have used all my talents," she insisted. "I dance, I sing, I make people laugh."

"Those were minor talents that we threw in at the last minute. Perhaps that's where we made our mistake. We gave you the gift to heal and you ignored it; that is why your hands no longer get warm."

"I'm sorry, God. I didn't know."

"No use in crying over spilt milk—that is, unless you are Oscar Tilquist the Third. Right now, time is of the essence, and we have to get down to business. You can't stay too long, lest you get stuck here before your time."

"God, may I make a request before I have to leave?"

"Request away, but quickly now."

"This is a big one, and it's been on my mind for a long time. Could Kath and I live to be very old and die at the same moment?"

"You are both destined to live to a very old age, but no two people can die exactly at the same time."

"And why is that?"

"Why? Because I said so, impudent whippersnapper! You see, one of you must feel the grief...the loss of the other. I built that into all my creations; the ability to grieve is paramount to being human. That is why I made it the Rule."

God thought for what seemed an eternity to Claire, but in God's time it was only a second.

"I'll tell you what I'll do: I will let you choose. Who will die first? And who will be left to feel the pain? You or Kathleen?"

"I don't want Kath to suffer."

"I can make it short...shall we say, one second?"

"Take Kathleen first, I don't want her to feel any more pain."

"I must say, Claire, you always were one of my favorites. We are running out of time—tick-tock, tick-tock. Before I send you back, hold out your hands."

"My hands?"

"Yes. I am giving you a second chance. But, this time you may use your gift only once. Do you understand? Only once...use it wisely..."

❀   ❀   ❀

Helen said, "Doc, she's coming back. BP 110 over 65. Pulse: 59."

"Only once," mumbled Claire. "Only once." Her eyes fluttered, then opened. "I've been gone a long time," she muttered.

"About two minutes," answered Helen, wiping Claire's brow with a damp cloth.

"Kath...Baby B?"

"Not yet, darling."

Claire reached out. "Give me your hands, Kath."

Kathleen glanced at Claire; there was a look about her, one that she had never seen before. She pulled off her gloves and put her hands in Claire's. She felt the urge to pull away from the intense heat, but Claire drew her closer. *I'm using it wisely. I'm giving it to the one who can save our baby.*

Kathleen closed her eyes; she felt Sally Fuentes standing next to her, smiling, putting one hand on her shoulder. *Don't let fear control you. Follow your instincts. I'll be by your side through every step.*

Kathleen put on a fresh pair of gloves and returned to the stool at the foot of the bed.

She heard Sally's voice echoing through her mind: *So far so good. You've got Claire in the correct position, buttocks at the edge of the bed and legs elevated. Remember, Claire's fully dilated. A breech is much safer if it's the second twin. Trust your instincts.*

❀   ❀   ❀

Claire's contractions were stronger, closer together.

Kathleen felt Sally's words reverberating. *Trust your instincts...trust your instincts...*

"I can see the buttocks," she announced.

Claire moaned. "Here comes another one."

She flashed to when she would climb the hill behind the house to meditate. Her mind drifted back to those mornings, when she would face east to greet the new day. She moaned when the contraction came—she bore down with the strength of a mother determined to save her child.

"Push, Claire. I need more of the buttocks to be delivered."

Claire groaned, "I'm going to be holding this over you for the rest of our lives."

"I'll remind you if you forget. Excellent! The back of the knees are out, and I'm going to give the rest of the legs a bit of an assist." Kathleen pushed on the inner part of the knees—first one, then the other—sweeping them out of the vagina and into the world.

Sally's hand rested on her shoulder. *You're doing fine, Kathleen. You've learned well.*

"Boy or girl? Boy or girl?" Claire asked dizzily.

"One hundred percent boy, I guarantee it. I'm wrapping a blanket around the parts of Baby B that have been delivered. We don't want him shocked into breathing before he's fully here."

"Oh, God, can't you just yank him out?"

"Don't worry, Claire-bear, we're almost there. I'm supporting him while he dangles. You push, I support. It's the Rule, Claire."

"You and my bubba and God with your rules. *Arghhh!*" she shrieked.

"The shoulders are coming out. I can see the scapulae."

What's next? whispered Sally.

Kathleen knew: *Take him by the hip and rotate 90 degrees.* "Here we go, little guy, gentle turns." *Now, I reach up, hooking onto one elbow, and sweep the arm out. Rotate 180 degrees and repeat.* "Arms are out."

"I have to push."

"I can see the nape of the neck. Don't push—pant through this one. I'm going to ease the head out."

"Promise, last one?"

"Yes, guaranteed, and here he is!"

"I can't hear him."

"Give him a minute. I'm cutting and clamping the cord. Sam, I want you to deliver the afterbirth. Helen, keep watch on Claire's vitals. Let me know stat if there are any changes."

A tacit nod was all that was needed from the three who now worked as a body of one.

Kathleen carried the slack infant to a side table. "His heartbeat is strong," she announced after placing the stethoscope to his chest. She put one of the infant hats on Baby B to keep the heat from leaving through his head, and began to rub him vigorously with a towel. She urged, "Come on, Baby B. Take a breath for Mom. Checking the airway and suctioning."

She urged, "Come on, little B. Breathe, baby, breathe."

She rubbed him again vigorously with a towel, flicked the bottom of his feet and flicked again.

Sally whispered, *Give him the gift of life with your breath.*

Kathleen leaned over and puffed ever so gently into his mouth. A whimper, a breath, a lusty cry.

Sam glanced at the clock. "Time of birth: exactly 5:00 a.m."

Helen thought how close they had come to having death visit them. How many times can we die in this one lifetime? Every

time we tell a lie, every time we keep the truth from someone we
love, death pays us a visit and steals a piece of our heart, a piece of
our soul.

She went to Sam and put her hand on his shoulder. He turned
around and went into her open arms.

"Helen, I've kept something from you." Sam's lips trembled.

"So have I. Remember when we first met, and I told you there
was something I would never talk about?"

"Yes."

"I want to talk about it. I don't want anything between us."

"Yes," he said hoarsely.

"Claire's settled and comfortable, I don't think we're needed
right now. Let's leave them alone for a while. Call Linc and see if
he can get Dr. Bonnie and a pediatrician helicoptered in. I'm going to make some coffee and see if there's any real food in the
house. Sam, I'm going to start cooking again."

"I'll help," he said tearfully.

❀   ❀   ❀

"Look at them," Claire said, balancing the two babies on her
chest.

"You did most of the work; you get to choose Baby B's name,"
Kathleen said softly.

Claire spoke in a whisper. "His name is David."

"That wasn't on our top ten," said Kathleen, surprised.

"They don't look anything alike, do they?" Claire said, ignoring Kathleen's comment about the name. "Annie's so long and
thin, like your side of the family. But David..." She looked at their
son, plump rolls showing on his thighs; a thick patch of black hair,
olive skin, and deep-blue eyes.

Kathleen said, "You weren't making up the story about there
being gypsies in your family?"

"Of course not! All my stories are true."

"Even the one about the leprechaun?"

"Especially that one. I know you think I passed out because of my blood pressure dropping, and I don't suppose you'll believe this story any more than you've believed the rest of them. But I was with God, and I was inside your dream. I know, Kath, I know what you saw, and I know what you felt."

Claire cried. "I always thought my gift in life was to make people laugh. And then...and then, when I was there, wherever there was, God gave me a second chance. He told me—I could use the power to heal only once. And I knew when I saw you struggling to deliver David that I had to pass that gift on to you to save our baby. Before I came back, God whispered to me, 'His name shall be David.' It means beloved."

Kathleen said, "After I touched your hands, I had the oddest experience while David was being born. I was so very frightened I might lose you both. I don't know if I can explain it, but I was being guided."

She took David in her arms. "David Hollander-Moore, welcome to this imperfect world."

As Kathleen held David, his fingers wrapped around hers. "His hands are warm, unusually warm." She felt his forehead. "The rest of him is perfectly cool."

"My pragmatic darling," said Claire. "I'll make a believer of you, after all."

"Perhaps not so pragmatic any longer."

"Look, the lights have stopped flickering and the power is back on."

"I think the storm may be passing."

Claire smiled wearily. "Yes, so do I."

PART FIVE

Then came the healing time, hearts started to shine, soul felt so fine, oh what a freeing time it was.

—Aberjhani,
Christmas When Music Almost Killed the World

CHAPTER 38

The drive from Kansas to California proved to be anything but boring. Stephanie stopped the first night at the same hotel in Grand Junction and purchased two steak dinners to go from the nearby steakhouse.

"You've earned this, girl," she said as she cut the second steak into small pieces and hand-fed Sitara.

She flicked on the TV and began surfing; every channel was reporting the west coast devastation caused by the Pineapple Express.

She felt like *The Wizard of Oz's* Dorothy. How would she get back to Canfield? No red slippers with magic heels to click. She would have to rely on herself and the things she had learned from Linc during her driving lessons, when he took her through the little known roads that wove in and out of the back hills. His words echoed in her mind: *I don't tell many folks about these roads—it's too easy for them to get lost. But, since you are my assistant on finding the lost children, I'll gladly show 'em to you.*

She would make it back, no matter what. She had friends waiting and family. She muffled a sob. *I have a family waiting for me: Kathleen, Dev, Claire...nieces and nephews. And so many friends.*

They had accepted Stephanie, but would they accept Rose?

❀   ❀   ❀

Stephanie used her key to unlock the front door and stood at the foot of the stairs. She had never felt so awkward. The first floor seemed so empty of life. No need for THE OFFICE IS CLOSED sign.

Oscar appeared from nowhere, sidling his way next to Sitara until he could nuzzle his head against hers. A muffled sound of infants crying floated from the second story and reverberated throughout the vacant rooms.

Should she go upstairs? Did she belong *here*? Maybe she really didn't belong anywhere.

Kathleen stared at her from the top of the stairs.

"Stephanie? Where the hell have you been?"

"I'm sorry. I know I should have called. Hey, who's making all that racket?"

"We had our babies, two days ago." Kathleen looked so tired.

"Oh, wow, congratulations! I don't want to be underfoot—I'll just go back to the cottage."

"You'll be up to your knees in mud. How the hell did you get here?"

"Some of the back roads were open enough for the truck."

"Come upstairs," Kathleen beckoned. "Claire's been worried about you. Shit, who am I kidding—we've all been worried sick."

"You're not mad?" Stephanie asked after meeting Kathleen on the landing.

Kathleen had never noticed that they were the same height or that Stephanie had a light sprinkling of freckles. "Maybe just a little," she said with a sweet smile.

Claire was in bed with the babies resting in her arms.

"They're beautiful," said Stephanie, a catch in her voice. "Boy and girl," she said, noting the pink and blue blankets.

"Yes," said Kathleen. "Annie and David."

"Where were you, Stephanie?" asked Claire.

"I was in Kansas. I'm sorry I didn't call. I didn't know what to do. So I did what I thought was right."

She handed the letters to Kathleen. "I found the lost babies."

CHAPTER 39

Bubba sat at her desk chair, her short legs dangling a good six inches from the floor, her smart phone connected to her headset.

"American Airlines? I need a direct flight from New York to Santa Barbara. It's a family emergency... No, not a death. A birth... Yes, a birth. Twins. Great grandchildren... Yes, I agree it does sound like a bit of a crisis... No, I don't care how much the ticket costs... Tomorrow morning at seven thirty? Seven hours and thirty-four minutes? One stopover at Phoenix? I'll take it."

Stephanie claimed her spot at the Santa Barbara Airport baggage claim area, waiting for Bubba Hollander to arrive. Claire had given her a photo of Bubba before she left for the airport.

"She'll be the shortest one there," she advised. "Probably wearing a red baseball cap and hiking boots. She's never hiked, but she likes the look. One last thing: Do not, under any condition, let her talk you into driving your truck."

Claire was right. Bubba was wearing hiking boots and a red

baseball cap, and she was the shortest passenger in sight, not counting the kids under twelve. Stephanie thought the old lady was irresistibly cute—rather like a Cabbage Patch kid brought to life—and wanted to pinch her chubby cheeks, but didn't dare.

"I used to be the tallest girl in my class," said Bubba, craning her neck to meet Stephanie in the eye. "I stopped growing when I was eleven. What a shock! My, but you look a lot like your sister. You and Kathleen have the same shape face and figure."

"I'll take that as a compliment," Stephanie said.

Bubba took Stephanie's hands in hers. "Same hands, too. You can't hide your genes."

"My truck's parked in the south lot," said Stephanie, helping Bubba with her antique luggage.

"Hey, nice truck!" Bubba said with an appreciative whistle. "I'd ask you to let me take her for a spin but my legs won't reach the pedals."

That's a relief! Stephanie thought.

"So tell me, Stephanie," Bubba said, settling into the Chevy truck's bench seat, "has anyone slept since the babies arrived?"

"Well, Mrs. Hollander..."

"Call me Bubba."

"Bubba, it's absolute chaos. Annie wants to nurse all the time, non-stop. If one starts to cry, they both cry. There are at least one thousand diapers." She lowered her voice. "Claire is only using cloth diapers, and Kathleen looks like she's ready to fall over. If you want any peace and quiet, Bubba, you can stay with me in my cottage."

Bubba said, "Thanks for the offer, but I wouldn't miss all the fun for the world. On our way, stop at a drugstore, if you wouldn't mind. That granddaughter of mine is *mashugana*. The first thing we'll do is switch to disposable diapers. If there's one thing I know about, it's diapers."

CHAPTER 40

*I*t had been thirty days since the Pineapple Express had devastated the coast of California.

The post-storm issue of Canfield's local newspaper, *Town Occurrences*, carried a full front-page spread on the heroism of their beloved sheriff, Lincoln Abraham Hathaway. The dramatic headline read: SHERIFF LINCOLN ABRAHAM HATHAWAY SAVES CANFIELD FROM CATASTROPHE. Linc had purchased ten copies of the issue for posterity, not out of vanity, and no one could blame him.

Because of his evacuation and disaster preparedness program, Linc was raised to the exalted position of demigod, a position he publicly denied, but privately basked in its glory.

❀   ❀   ❀

It was still dark when Linc reached for the month-old copy of *Town Occurrences* that had immortalized him. He read it every night before he fell asleep and every morning when he woke up. He switched on the lamp and rested his head against the walnut headboard, thinking about how his life had changed since the Pineapple Express had visited Canfield.

He hadn't jumped over any cliffs or dived deep into Christmas River to rescue anyone, as some of the town's more creative raconteurs were now claiming. He knew that stories would be told and retold during social gatherings, at the Mountain View Diner, and during Canfield's Weekend in Scotland. As true memories faded, this piece of history would be embellished until fact and fiction were indistinguishable from one another.

It wasn't like that at all. Disaster had been averted simply due to his methodical preplanning. He had known the day would come when a disaster would strike: an earthquake or mudslides or fires, and he had planned and trained volunteers for that day. He thought about how Kathleen and Claire had giggled when he gave them the emergency radio. He didn't mind; he loved them and he had taken care of them. After all, the safety of Canfield's citizens rested on his shoulders.

He began to change the night of Kathleen's birthday party when he thought about finding the missing children. It had started out as a selfish thought, a desire to be a hero and save his job by finding two lost babies.

He knew what Steamroller would have said and done. He would have put his hand on Linc's pudgy arm and recited one of his favorite passages from the Bible: "Do nothing from selfish ambition or conceit, but in humility count others more significant than yourselves. Philippians 2:3"

There is always a Steamroller lesson to be remembered, Linc thought.

He chuckled at the way Stephanie had found herself and became the family hero. She had driven the truck back to Linc's and handed him the keys.

"I had it detailed. Man, you should have seen it before—it was an eyesore from all my travels."

"Looks bran-new, Stephanie, but the truck belongs—"

"Linc, I didn't hold up my part of the bargain," she said with a newfound sense of maturity. "I didn't give you the contact information for Charlie; I gave it to Kathleen and Devon."

He put the keys back in her hand. "You did the right thing. Besides, you and this truck were meant for each other."

Finding the lost babies and saving his job didn't happen the way he thought it would, but then maybe that was for the best. Life rarely follows your plan. It's as if life has its own strategy, and you are only fooled into thinking you have control.

Steamroller would have said, "Don't beat yourself up; learn from your mistakes," and he did. Today was the day he would put his career and his standing in the community on the line.

He felt his belly grumble. God, it hurt, but it wasn't as big, and it wasn't as flabby. He had made a life-altering decision thirty days ago, and today was the day of his unveiling.

He threw the covers off and stood naked in front of the full-length mirror. *Not too bad*, he thought. He had set up a gym in the den and had not missed a day of exercising. He could see the change—slow, he had to admit, but muscle was beginning to replace fat.

He walked into the kitchen, knowing that breakfast would consist of egg whites, toast with sugar-free jam, and fruit.

He chose a full-bodied coffee from Uganda. He opened the vacuum-sealed bag, inhaling the fragrance that promised to be reminiscent of sun-dried tomatoes. No matter what else changed, his morning joe would always remain an adventure.

He showered and shaved and put on his red-plaid blanket bathrobe. *Now*, he thought, *take a deep breath*. He reached for his corset and wigs, walked to the garage, opened the trashcans, and breathed a sigh of relief when he heard them mingle with a week's worth of odorous trash.

He rolled the cans to the curb. Today was not only a day of liberation and celebration; it was also trash day.

CHAPTER 41

Gayle and Robert stood in the three-car garage, surrounded by bags and boxes. *There's barely enough room for one car now,* Robert thought, scratching his head.

"All this?" he asked, looking at the mound waiting to be loaded into the car.

Gayle put down three shopping bags filled with groceries. "Robert, don't forget to leave room for the frozen food."

"I thought this shindig was being catered."

"It is. I bought steaks and roasts and a few essentials for their freezer. I am so excited. I haven't seen the babies for a week—imagine, a whole week without holding the precious darlings. Did you see how fat David is? And those eyes...they're staying blue. And I swear Annie was trying to say nana."

"What's in these boxes?" Robert pointed to three large boxes. "Bodies?"

"Clothes."

"Clothes?"

"Why, yes. One box for David, one for Annie, and one for Claire."

"For Claire, too?"

"Why, of course, dear. It takes time to get back your figure. I consulted with Helen, and together we came up with splendid in-between outfits."

"So, nothing for Kathleen?" he said dryly.

"Helen and I prearranged that. Helen has Kathleen's new out-fit. We found the most beautiful tailored suit in silk...beige. Simple but elegant, perfect for Kathleen's style and the occasion." She sighed. "The babies' formal introduction to the world. Did you remember to pack a suit?"

"A suit...you think I need a suit?"

"You *are* David's godfather. At least a sport jacket. Oooh, I can't wait to see them again! Helen said Annie's grown a foot and little David has put on at least five pounds! We won't recognize them."

"They'll be the ones in the cribs."

"Are you making fun of me? What is it, Robert? You seem re-moved...more distant lately."

Robert stared at the surrounding mess and shook his head. "I don't know, Gayle. Just trying to figure out how to fit a truckload into a four-door sedan."

Gayle put her hand on Robert's arm. "It's more than that—come clean, please."

"When does this stop?" He motioned to the boxes. "I get your excitement—I'm just as excited to have grandchildren as you are. Gayle, I want off this merry-go-round. There are two of us living in this big house and my practice is slowing down. I want to scale back...not fill up with more and more things. I've been thinking lately. It might come as a shock, but I want to sell the house. Re-member how it was when we were young? We had time for each other. Now, our lives are filled with one project after another."

"I had no idea you felt that way. I thought you were so at-tached to the house, your garden. All your projects."

"I know it seems that way. And I haven't been forthright with you. I'm worried that our time together is going to be taken away from us by these never-ending projects. We both do it and once, just once, I want to wake up in the morning with nothing planned and you by my side."

Gayle took him in her arms. "Bobby, I had similar thoughts a while ago, but I thought you were so attached to this house."

"I think we've both been running away from instead of toward each other." Robert sobbed on her shoulder. "It's not things I want. It's you I want."

Gayle cried. "Oh, Bobby, it will take us a while to make this happen. I'll have to scale back my practice, but I would love to move closer to the children. Maybe a smaller home in Santa Barbara with a guest room for the kids?"

"It sounds doable," he said, wiping his tears away. "Can we talk more about it on the way to Canfield? It's a two-hour drive."

"It'll be a beginning...a fresh beginning."

CHAPTER 42

Sam watched as the sunlight began to sneak through the bedroom drapes, slowly increasing in brightness and intensity. *It will be a beautiful day*, he thought. *Ideal for the gathering of friends and family.*

The birth of Annie and David had been as fearful and meaningful as any experience he had ever had. Life and death were once again staring him in the face.

He had been in the military for more than twenty years. He had held the hands of wounded troops; he had heard their screams and watched as they took their final breaths. He had hardened his heart. How else could he have continued on? How else could he have survived? His heart had been so closed he could not let his own son in.

After the storm had subsided, he and Helen had held each other and cried as they talked about the pain that had kept them from being fully available to each other.

He looked at Helen, sleeping soundly on her side. It was impossible to conceive of her as a jilted bride. How could anyone not have loved Helen, the same way he loved and wanted her?

He had told her about Thomas and showed her his letter.

Helen had said, "We won't turn our back on him. He needs a chance. Oh, Sam, everyone deserves a second chance."

He had exchanged letters with Thomas, and soon he and Helen would visit him in prison.

He put his hand on Helen's shoulder. "Dearest, don't we have to get out of bed? Today's a big day. Don't we have cooking to do...or something?"

Helen rolled over. "I've turned over a new leaf. Parties are now being catered. Didn't I tell you?"

He opened his arms for Helen. "I must not have been listening. I might have been on diaper duty. What's on the menu?" he asked lazily.

"It's a baby-naming ceremony, so I've got traditional deli food coming in. Claire gave me the menu. Corned beef, roast beef, cheeses, rye bread, bagels, smoked salmon... Do you want the rest of the menu?"

"There's more?"

"Seriously more. The caterers should be arriving any minute. They have the keys to the kingdom. All we have to do is show up."

"Brilliant move on your part. Does that mean we have time...for us?"

"Umm, time for us and no one else. Unless...have you checked Bubba's baby schedule?"

Sam looked at the eighteen-by-twenty-four-inch schedule hanging on the wall. "We're on for baths in an hour."

Helen yawned. "Oh, we won't have to do that."

"Why not?"

"Did you forget Gayle and Robert are driving up? In fact..." She looked at the clock and laughed. "It's eight a.m. I'll bet they'll be here in a few. They're taking over the bathing and the dressing for the ceremony. Gayle can't wait."

"Ha, ha. Wait until David squirts them."

"Ha, ha, yourself. You got it right in the face when you changed his diaper."

"The boy's got good aim all right."

She reached for Sam's hand. "We do have some time before we get dressed."

"Only *some* time?"

"An hour. That enough time for you, Captain Hughes?"

"Sounds perfect, simply perfect."

CHAPTER 43

$\mathcal{K}$athleen gazed into the crib. Annie and David were lying side by side, together, just as they had been for almost nine months.

Things had calmed down since Bubba's arrival almost a month ago. Bubba walked in, hugged Claire, and whispered something in her ear. Claire nodded, and suddenly the disposable diapers were in place. Bubba gave everyone a diaper-changing lesson and had Stephanie post a duty schedule.

"Just like in the Army," Stephanie said.

Bubba made Kathleen bunk on the couch in her office, four hours a night.

"I can't leave Claire and the babies, Bubba," she said tearfully.

"Look at you—you're a zombie!" Bubba said bluntly. "I wouldn't want to be your patient. Now go! I won't leave Claire alone."

"You'll let me know if anything...anything at all happens?"

"If there's a poop, I'll come get you."

"Uh, Bubba, I kinda check their temperatures with a thermometer wand every hour." Kathleen hung her head.

Bubba patted Kathleen's cheek. "Dr. Moore, I have a tried and true way to check temperatures. Like this." Bubba stood on her toes to kiss Kathleen on her cheek.

"Now go, *tatala*."

"Thank you, Bubba." Kathleen threw her arms around their bubba. "I'm so glad you're here."

Claire was changing. Today would be the babies' naming ceremony, the giving of their Hebrew names. She actually had asked Kathleen beforehand and had not thrown a tantrum to get her way. "Do you mind, Kath? It would mean a lot to my bubba."

"I like the idea," said Kathleen. "I'd like to invite my family and our close friends."

"We should invite Dr. Friend."

"Seriously?"

"She is our friend, after all."

Claire came out of the bathroom. "They're still sleeping?"

"Don't breathe too hard. I think Annie finally got topped off," Kathleen said, moving closer. "You look stunning."

"It's my post-pregnancy basic black dress. I've dressed it up with a scarf."

They both laughed, remembering Dr. Friend and her fondness for scarves.

"This is to go with it," Kathleen said, handing Claire a stained-glass jewelry box.

Claire opened the box to find a pair of diamond earrings. "They're beautiful."

She placed her hand on Kathleen's face.

"Picked them out myself," Kathleen said shyly.

Claire took her hand. "Look at our babies. Now tell me, Dr. Moore, in all your years of medical experience have you ever seen two such beautiful and smart children?"

"Never."

EPILOGUE

Kathleen greeted their friends and relatives as they began to gather in the solarium for the baby-naming ceremony,

She walked over to Dev. "Did you give Charlie the directions?"

Dev hugged his big sister. "For the tenth time, yes. Via email, phone calls, and text. He said he might be late, and not to wait for him. It's over, Kat—we both got our wish."

"I'm complete now, Dev. If it wasn't for you..." She began to cry. "They're all fine in their own way. It's what I needed to know."

Claire was nursing Annie. Kathleen had to smile at the thought of always-famished Annie. She would be tall and slender like Kathleen's family. Her hair was going to be the same copper color as her grandmother's. Her eyes filled when she thought of her mother and the pain that must have resided in her heart.

David was rounder with thick, pitch-black hair and deep-blue eyes; his beautiful skin the color of a light walnut shell. Their son who came so close to death, and whose hands sometimes became unusually warm, was thriving. *Thank the unseen spirit that guided me. Thank God.*

Dr. Friend was in a deep discussion with Linc. *Looks more like pretty heavy flirtation,* Kathleen thought. *Mighty brave of Linc to finally show up without his disguise.* She chuckled to herself. *We think we have a secret and the whole world knows. Not unlike when I thought no one in Canfield knew I was gay. Big joke on me and on Linc.*

After a few feigned looks, and secret winks exchanged among the guests, everyone told Linc how great he looked. Underneath it all, he was still Linc.

Kathleen had invited her other siblings, explaining about the ceremony. She had come out to them at the same time. They declined. They had moved on with their lives, and she had moved on with hers.

When she and Dev had called Charlie, he seemed excited to have made contact with his family. He told them he had always felt there was a part of him that was missing. Now he knew what it was: He was a twin.

Rabbi Jacobs nodded to Claire and Kathleen, a signal that she wished to begin the ceremony. Kathleen held David and Claire held Annie as they took their places on either side of the rabbi.

"Good afternoon, my name is Joan Jacobs," she addressed the gathering. "It's an honor to be here. As I look around the room, I see friends and family gathered to greet Annie and David as they receive their Hebrew names.

"The very concept of family has changed. I see two loving parents...both women. I see godparents, Robert, Gayle, Sam, and Helen, who are not related through blood, but through love. And I see a special blessing that the matriarch of this family, and the infants' great-grandmother, Anna Hollander, is here today."

She turned toward Claire and Annie.

"Annie, I see your eyes are wide open and taking in the world as they should. Your mom and mommy have chosen the name Hannah Deborah. The meaning of the name Hannah is grace. The name Deborah represents the only woman in the Bible to become a judge or tribal ruler. She is known for her great wisdom and fearlessness in battle. Annie, may you walk through life with grace, wisdom, and strength of judgment."

She then faced Kathleen and David.

"David, like your sister, Annie, you are wide awake and resting in the arms of one of your mothers. In the presence of loved ones, we give you the name of David Michael. The name David means beloved and the meaning of Michael is actually a rhetorical question: Who is like God?

"David was the second and greatest king of Israel. As a young boy, he went against all odds and slew a giant. I see you as not fearing to go into battle against those who may seem bigger than life. I suspect that you will grow up to be loved by many while asking the most difficult of questions: questions without answers.

"Annie and David, let your names be honored and respected for wisdom and good deeds. May you walk the path of goodness, beauty, and truth. May God's blessing rest on you now and always. And with this, may we all say: Amen and *mazel tov.*"

Everyone repeated, "Amen and *mazel tov,*" and applauded.

The doorbell rang. Stephanie went to answer with Sitara shadowing her. A man her age stood at the door; a wide grin crossed his face. He held out his hand.

"Hello," he said. "My name is Charles Joseph Sterling. Some people know me better as just plain old Charlie Moore. And you are?"

"S-Stephanie W-whinstone," she stammered. "I'm Rose...Rose Alena Moore."

SHE held out her hand, HE swept her up in an embrace.

Appendix

My Shadow

I have a little shadow that goes in and out with me,
And what can be the use of him is more than I can see.
He is very, very like me from the heels up to the head;
And I see him jump before me, when I jump into my bed.

The funniest thing about him is the way he likes to grow—
Not at all like proper children, which is always very slow;
For he sometimes shoots up taller like an india-rubber ball,
And he sometimes gets so little that there's none of him at all.

He hasn't got a notion of how children ought to play,
And can only make a fool of me in every sort of way.
He stays so close beside me, he's a coward you can see;
I'd think shame to stick to nursie as that shadow sticks to me!

One morning, very early, before the sun was up,
I rose and found the shining dew on every buttercup;
But my lazy little shadow, like an arrant sleepy-head,
Had stayed at home behind me and was fast asleep in bed.

—Robert Louis Stevenson

A DEAD ROSE

O Rose! who dares to name thee?
No longer roseate now, nor soft, nor sweet;
But pale, and hard, and dry, as stubble-wheat,—-
Kept seven years in a drawer—-thy titles shame thee.

The breeze that used to blow thee
Between the hedgerow thorns, and take away
An odour up the lane to last all day,—-
If breathing now,—-unsweetened would forego thee.

The sun that used to smite thee,
And mix his glory in thy gorgeous urn,
Till beam appeared to bloom, and flower to burn,—-
If shining now,—-with not a hue would light thee.

The dew that used to wet thee,
And, white first, grow incarnadined, because
It lay upon thee where the crimson was,—-
If dropping now,—-would darken where it met thee.

The fly that lit upon thee,
To stretch the tendrils of its tiny feet,
Along thy leaf's pure edges, after heat,—-
If lighting now,—-would coldly overrun thee.

The bee that once did suck thee,
And build thy perfumed ambers up his hive,
And swoon in thee for joy, till scarce alive,—-
If passing now,—-would blindly overlook thee.

The heart doth recognise thee,
Alone, alone! The heart doth smell thee sweet,
Doth view thee fair, doth judge thee most complete,—-
Though seeing now those changes that disguise thee.

Yes, and the heart doth owe thee
More love, dead rose! than to such roses bold
As Julia wears at dances, smiling cold!—-
Lie still upon this heart—-which breaks below thee!

—Elizabeth Barrett Browning

SONNETS FROM THE PORTUGUESE
Sonnet 43, familiarly known as
"How do I love thee? Let me count the ways."

How do I love thee? Let me count the ways.
I love thee to the depth and breadth and height
My soul can reach, when feeling out of sight
For the ends of being and ideal grace.
I love thee to the level of every day's
Most quiet need, by sun and candle-light.
I love thee freely, as men strive for right.
I love thee purely, as they turn from praise.
I love thee with the passion put to use
In my old griefs, and with my childhood's faith.
I love thee with a love I seemed to lose
With my lost saints. I love thee with the breath,
Smiles, tears, of all my life; and, if God choose,
I shall but love thee better after death.

—Elizabeth Barrett Browning

ACKNOWLEDGEMENTS

My deepest appreciation to those who have helped with the birth of *Claire's Song.*

To my family and friends, thank you for your continued support and love.

My appreciation to Proofed to Perfection editors, Pamela Guerrieri and Kevin Cook, who continue to encourage me toward a greater depth of writing. (www.proofedtoperfection.com)

The cover for *Claire's Song* was designed by Donna Casey. Donna took my fantasy of the perfect cover and created a work of art. (www.digitaldonna.com)

Maureen Cutajar provided a professional and insightful touch through her formatting and talented interior design. (www.go published.com)

A very special thanks to Kerrie Lotsu, UK registered midwife, for guiding me on the birthing scenes in *Claire's Song.* Kerrie offered her expert advice and provided many links to aid in my research on childbirth. Kerrie has been involved in maternity care since 2005. In 2011, she founded the website www.ask-the-midwife.co.uk, which provides a question-and-answer facility on all aspects of pregnancy, birth, and the early days with a new baby.

My deepest gratitude to Barbara Dickson-Oatley, who has been designated my "better beta-reader." Barbara not only read my pre-editing draft of *Claire's Song,* but also never failed to offer her input, love, and encouragement.

About the Author

Sunny Alexander lives in Southern California, near the beaches and the Santa Monica Mountain hiking trails.

Semi-retired from her private practice as a psychotherapist, she devotes her time to writing novels dealing with social issues.

Her debut novel, *Flowers from Iraq: The Storyteller and the Healer* brought to light the plight of post-traumatic stress disorder in returning veterans, as well as the inequality of the military's "Don't ask, don't tell" policy.

Her second novel, *The Girls*, was inspired by her experience in working with victims of spousal abuse, as well as her passionate belief in marriage equality.

Sunny Alexander can be contacted through her website: www.sunnyalexander.com.

Made in the USA
San Bernardino, CA
29 October 2014